GHOSTS OF HALODWYTH

Ghosts of Halodwyth

M. WARREN ASKINS

Ghosts of Halodwyth
M. Warren Askins

ISBN: 978-1-7341200-9-7 (paperback)
ISBN: 979-8-9938670-0-7 (e-book)

Books by M. Warren Askins

Through the Thorns
Ian
The Dead Men are Dying Saga
Beyond the Spire of Navarene
Martyr for Cowards
Orphan's Rite
Ghosts of Halodwyth

In Loving Memory
Mary K. Crowley
Eric W. Flint

Author's Note

This book occurs five hundred years before the events described in *Beyond the Spire of Navarene.*

For those who have yet to read the works within the **Dead Men are Dying** Universe, here is a very short list to help make this book more accessible.

Laif — An elf, in the nearest traditional sense. You know, tall, slender immortals with pointy ears.

Divine Marks — Humans are sometimes born with a mark (typically adorning the side of the neck) that imbues the bearer with powerful abilities. For instance, a child born with the Warrior's mark will have heightened reflexes and extraordinary strength, as well as a myriad of other gifts pertaining to warfare.

~ 1 ~

THE EXECUTION

"At this juncture, the condemned may issue his final statement, if he so wishes," announced Vicar Turnbull of Celliwig to the assembled crowd. He stood atop a raised platform, several yards left of center, not wanting his robes to be tainted upon the executioner's swing.

"He does," interjected the shackled man, a bag over his head and his knees to the block. He turned toward the executioner. "When exactly was the last time you sharpened that axe?"

The executioner grinned widely and thumbed the blade. "She ain't seen a stone in some twenty or thirty collars, I'd imagine," he replied, showing the crowd that the blade had unsuccessfully nicked his skin. "Took the last chap only 'bout what?" He paused, looking to the vicar. "Maybe three good hacks to get the neck clean off? And I mean *good* hacks. He was a right plump individual, he was. Not like you, all skinny and muscley. Not a lick o' fat on ya, I'd wager."

"Is this supposed to be comforting?" asked the condemned.

The vicar and the executioner traded a look and burst into laughter.

"Don't you worry that scrawny little laif-neck of yours, chum," said the executioner, patting the condemned's head. "This'll all be over soon. That bein' said, I ain't never had the pleasure of loppin' off a laif's head before, so this'll be a learnin' experience for the lot of us." He gazed up at the balcony over the stage and nodded. "Might take my old gal here a few extra smacks to get ya proper dead, but who knows?"

"You really should sharpen your blade after every use," murmured the laif.

"What was that?" asked the executioner, leaning down with a hand cupping his ear.

"Faltzgrif!" a voice interjected from the balcony. "Take the burlap off for this one! I want to watch his face when it happens!"

The executioner removed his hand from behind his ear. "Not a problem, my Duke," he replied, straightening. "You really ticked him off good and proper, didn't ya?" he whispered to the prisoner. "He *never* wants to see the faces when they get the ol' chop chop."

With a terse pull, Faltzgrif removed the sack from the laif's head, revealing a handsome, cordial face.

"Must be nice having a steady workflow," the laif commented mildly, shaking his newly freed head. "My work ebbs and flows, it's never so constant as yours."

Faltzgrif curled his upper lip. "I'm proper busy most weekends, but the rest of the week is iffy, to be honest with ya."

"Well, I hear there's war on the horizon," said the laif.

"Very true."

The prisoner looked out to the crowd. "Not a bad turn out, I'd say?"

"Not at all," replied Faltzgrif, appraising the numbers. "More'n usual actually."

There was a sudden commotion in the Duke's box. "Turnbull! Faltzgrif!" The Duke shouted, sounding on the verge of hysterics. "Get on with it! This lout killed one of my sons!" An indiscernible feminine voice could be heard chiding the Duke. "One of *our* sons!" he amended.

Vicar Turnbull lifted his hands to the skies and all sound died away. The crowd stood still, rapt. The executioner hefted his axe upon his shoulder.

"My dear children of Celliwig," began the vicar, "you are no strangers to this ceremony. You have been gathered here to witness what befalls those who commit such treacherous, heinous acts that only through the shedding of life may then be redeemed." He paused while dramatically lowering his hands. "Today you shall find yourselves witnesses to one such offender. A scoundrel who deserves this sentence ten times over. Nay! One hundred times!"

A smattering of cheers went up throughout the quad. Commoners jostled one another and clapped. Those who had brought pitchforks, for whatever reason, raised them in agreement.

Turnbull waited for a new silence. "My children," he said, smiling at the crowd. The last few snickers died upon his words. "The condemned is Sprael of the Gentle March, a ranger, a laif, and one whom our glorious Duke entrusted with the life of his precious son, Gilbert Pemberton. It was a frivolous, simple excursion into the wilds that began as any other of the sort, light-hearted and carefree. Yet at some point the tone shifted. This party ended in tragedy. In betrayal. In murder." He glared at the onlookers as if they had taken part. "In treason," he concluded.

Sprael laughed.

"Silence!" Turnbull wheeled toward the condemned laif. "You've had your final say," he said with a sharp kick to the block. "Now," he began with false sincerity, "I must offer a final plea to our sovereign, the great Harold Pemberton, Duke of Celliwig." He turned to the balcony arrayed in the reds and whites of the land. "What say you, my Duke? Must this execution—"

"Yes!" shouted the Duke, dramatic effect abandoned.

Turnbull offered a sanctimonious frown. "So be it," he cried, sweeping an arm toward Faltzgrif. "Executioner, at your leisure."

Faltzgrif hoisted the axe off his shoulder. And whatever he may have done next never happened.

If not for the dark fletching suddenly sprouting from beneath the executioner's jawline, the arrow would have been imperceptible. The burly axe-man gaped and tugged at the arrow's shaft, clearly confused. Then blood came pouring out all at once from his nose and from his mouth. He gave Sprael an almost apologetic look as a second arrow took him in the temple, killing him.

The vicar fled the stage, leaving Sprael alone. The crowds broke.

"Somebody kill him!" howled the Duke. "Carry out the sentence!"

For a moment, it seemed as though no one had paid mind to the Duke's frenzied commands until a group of four leapt onto the stage.

"About time!" shouted the Duke. "Keep your heads down and make yourselves small targets! And use the dull side of the axe!"

And as fast as the men had arrived, the four—now five, including Sprael—discreetly exited the scene, leaving the Duke's chopping block bereft a neck, and his stage utterly deserted.

DOUBLE PUNISHED

"That went off without a hitch," whispered Marius, collapsing his spyglass. "Another job in the books." Vaskar did not reply. He remained prone upon the ledge, his hood still drawn.

That's the way of it with a job like this, thought Marius. You wait and wait, wading through the sticky pre-dawn hours, unmoving. Long before the block is set, before the crowds arrive, before the executioner and his dull axe. If an observer looks your way, concealed as you are, you won't alarm. You were there before him, and to him, you have always been. Just a huddled lump on a ledge.

"I think it's safe to move," whispered Marius, fearing the master archer had fallen asleep. Sweat was beginning to pool in Marius' chest plate as the midday sun tunneled down on him.

The index finger Vaskar had been resting upon his longbow casually lifted.

"I mean, there hasn't been—" Marius stopped abruptly.

A contingent of armoured figures in white and red livery appeared on the execution stage. Their commander, a dour-faced knight with freckles that could be seen from the mercenaries' perch, removed her helm and signaled for two soldiers to attend the executioner's body.

"Go after him!" the Duke could be heard shouting. "What are you waiting for?"

From his vantage point, Marius could not see the Duke, and had unwisely assumed the man had already taken his leave.

The commander squared her shoulders toward the Duke's balcony. "My lord Pemberton, we have dispatched riders to pursue. The prisoner will be caught and will see punishment."

"He must pay!" demanded the Duke. "I want his head! And the head of whoever is responsible for his escape!"

The knight commander nodded before turning her attention back toward the executioner's body.

"Double punished!" the Duke continued, punching the wooden balustrade before him.

The commander started. "Yes, my lord."

She tugged at her gorget, returning her focus to the soldiers. "Oi! Siefert! Hold a moment would you? Let me inspect those two arrows."

The soldiers obeyed, dropping the corpse at their commander's feet.

Marius shifted his eyes to the man beside him. "Look at me, I'm trembling," he said. "We're going to be *double* punished, eh? Wonder what that entails?"

"Unsure," replied Vaskar, harsh.

Back on the platform, the commander pushed the executioner's body with her boot, rolling the corpse onto its side. She eyed the arrow protruding from the neck before snapping the head from the shaft. Placing her thumb and forefinger to the fletchings, she withdrew the arrow. The commander walked past the shadows, bathing the peculiar arrow in sunlight. For several moments her gaze wandered the arrow's translucent shaft, then abruptly her attention shot upward, bounding and leaping from building to building, parapet to rooftop, flying from buttress to buttress.

Marius held his breath.

The commander methodically raised the arrow aloft, angling its broken tip in several directions, trying to deduce its place of origin.

Vaskar's leather gloves crackled as his grip tightened on his longbow.

"We should run," whispered Marius. "While they're still far out."

"She will not see us," assured Vaskar.

"She's looked our way like six times!"

"She may look, but she will not *see*."

Over the past four years Marius had learned to trust his mentor. The man had yet to be proven wrong. And in truth, they had been in plenty worse situations. Besides, Harold Pemberton, Duke of Celliwig, was a blowhard and a whoremonger, and whenever Marius thought of the man, fear and dread were not among the emotions produced.

He's certainly no Ban of Benwick, thought Marius. *May he rest in peace.*

Furthermore, the idea that the notorious mercenary, Vaskar of Rhionydd, would be brought to justice by the hands of a man like Harold Pemberton was laughable.

Marius quieted his next breath. *This storm will pass.*

They waited.

The sound of steel striking stone came abruptly. Marius recoiled and rubbed one eye. He had dozed off, but for how long? Vaskar had not moved an inch, but judging the passage of time based on his position was like chasing wind. That man could sit in one place for days, even weeks if the pay was good enough. Marius glanced down, the sweat in his chest plate had barely expanded. Minutes. Mere minutes had passed.

Vaskar tilted his head. "They've discovered our decoy," he said. "We must now take our leave." In one movement, he rolled left and leapt from the perch.

Unlike the master mercenary, Marius needed a moment to measure the drop. In this profession, heights were often an asset, occasionally an obstacle, but they were always a consideration. Especially when the time came to jump from them.

"Those pricks can't be far!" a nearby soldier shouted in frustration.

"This way!" another voiced.

After being played for fools, their search would double in ferocity.

It was now or never. Marius took the plunge, gracefully tucking himself into a roll upon hitting solid turf. Muscle memory thankfully took over that last bit. After all, he had made higher leaps onto less forgiving ground. Marius had been marked an Architect at birth, so it was only natural for him to make calculations, but he hoped to someday calculate such dimensions with the speed and efficiency of his mentor.

"Quickly," Vaskar commanded, wearing the raiment of a washer wench. His maroon bodice nearly climbed to his chin, cleverly concealing the curly forest of hair lurking beneath. "Don this." He held out a matching set.

"Oh, come on now!" groaned Marius, grasping the offered clothing. "We're doing trollops again?"

"Whatever it takes," replied Vaskar, not for the first time.

~ 3 ~

THE BIRD EXPERT

The horse Sprael's rescuers had provided him with had a real issue with listening.

Once they had hurtled out of the city's gates and into the waiting arms of Celliwig's open hillsides, he had made several attempts to break from the party. It was no use. No matter how many times he tried to steer his horse away, she continued to follow the others. As stubborn as she was regal, he wagered she was an Orkney breed. And judging by the fact that they had not wavered from their northward bearing, they were more than likely headed for her homeland.

While his mount's hard dash dwindled into a gallop, Sprael tried to tally the number of enemies he had amassed in Orkney. As a laif who had been alive for centuries, the math for things like this became increasingly difficult. For instance, a Baron he had angered two centuries ago bore a striking resemblance to a Viscount he spurned two weeks ago. Like checking off a balance sheet, he began to weed out those who must have expired by now. After that, he had to determine whether they were *actually* from Orkney. Humans had an unfortunate tendency to appear the same throughout the ages.

Moments later, Sprael grunted, giving up his tally. It had been a considerable amount of time since he had entertained business in Orkney, so prayerfully each and every ghost from grudges past had already seen themselves out.

Now that they were riding at a more leisurely pace, Sprael turned to the rider beside him. "You lot are from Orkney, I take it?" he asked, lifting his still-shackled wrists. "Who in Orkney did I manage to piss off more than Harry Pemberton?"

"No one that I'm aware of," replied the rider.

"Huh," Sprael said. "So why am I still in cuffs?"

The rider leaned back in his saddle and yawned. "We don't have a key."

Sprael waited several moments for the man to elaborate, but no such thing occurred. "Thank you for the rescue, by the way," the laif remarked. "Top notch work. Your archer is a real crack shot."

"Don't thank us," replied the rider. "Thank our employer."

Sprael cleared his throat. "Well then," he began, "please extend my gratitude to your employer."

The rider leaned down and gave his horse a solid pat. "Thank him yourself," he said. "You'll be meeting him shortly."

Unfortunately for Sprael, he was traveling with humans, which meant that they required sleep, mucking up his whole timetable. Resting the night at an inn was off the table, as Celliwig would certainly be scouring the lands for the recently sprung prisoner. But as luck would have it, his Orkney saviors had secured their lodgings beforehand. Sprael had to applaud this outfit; they seemed to have planned for everything.

Shortly arrived a day later. Ordinarily, the hop from capital to capital would have meant an all-night ride, concluding with an arrival at daybreak. But this journey landed them upon Orkney's welcome mat just after suppertime. Not bad timing for mortals, all things considered.

Quite honestly, Sprael could have attempted to depart their company at any moment, but he was far too keen to see how things played out. Now, striding through Locus Castle, flanked on all sides by the finest knights of Orkney, his intrigue reached its highest point.

Sprael turned to the knight behind him. "The Duke-Knight, huh?"

The knight appeared confused by this sudden exchange.

"You're taking me to the Duke-Knight, right?" continued Sprael slowly, gesturing his shackled wrists toward the approaching gateway. "That's who saved me from the chopping block?"

"Oh, of course," replied the knight, his confusion stumbling into awareness. "Apologies, I'm not accustomed to fielding questions."

"Understandable," said Sprael, smiling, glancing to the floor as he moved forward. "Well, I'll bother you no longer."

"No bother at all," said the knight.

"Oh, one more thing!" Sprael burst out, turning back to the startled knight. "Who is the current Duke-Knight? It's been some time since I've been welcomed into your lands. Orkney does still elect *Duke-Knights*, not simply *Dukes*, right?"

The knight peered behind him as though the question had been directed elsewhere. "Sir Demetrius from the line of Purefoy," he admitted, sounding almost hesitant. "And yes, he is our Duke-Knight."

"Ah! So Orkney continues to promote knights as Dukes. A Warrior-born leader is *fun.* Although, it does almost always end in tragedy. But the ride to that downfall is... well, yeah, usually pretty *fun.*"

"If you say so," said the knight, disconcerted.

"Purefoy, Purefoy, Purefoy," repeated Sprael, rubbing his chin. "Was his father named Gaston by any chance?"

"Nay," replied another knight at Sprael's back. The entourage had stopped before a set of heavy doors. "Gaston was his great-great grandfather."

"You see how far out of touch I've become?" Sprael said. "Thank you for catching me up."

Quietly and quickly, Sprael was funneled into a sanctum. A banquet table sat in the center of the space, supporting an expansive, meticulously crafted war diorama. Tiny flags insinuated objectives, wooden trees stood near tiny structures, and geometric shapes were sprawled all over its surface. Sprael, being very familiar with Fenrirfang Forest, recognized that this diorama represented the most recent scuffle at Fort Navarene. Last Sprael had heard, the King had prevailed.

Behind it all Sir Demetrius Purefoy, the Duke-Knight of Orkney, sat surrounded by advisors barraging him with their thoughts. His long silvery hair was drawn back into a loosely tied knot. The distinct angles of his jawline framed a tired face. A handful of Scholars nearby scribbled notes upon the table. Others crowded the room, huddled against the walls, their noses firmly pressed to scrolls with candles practically singeing their ear hairs.

"My lord," the leader of Sprael's knightly escort called out. Sir Demetrius looked up and greeted her arrival with a relieved smile. "The ranger has arrived." She stepped aside, allowing Sprael to come forward.

"That was fast," commented Sir Demetrius, readily extricating himself from his advisors. "He's much earlier than expected." A troubled look came and went across his weatherworn features. The counselor responsible for the poorly timed estimation shuddered and lowered his cap. "Your name, ranger?" Sir Demetrius stood before the laif, gauntleted hand extended in welcome.

"Sprael, my lord," he responded, politely lifting his hands to display his fetters.

"Why is he still in manacles?" demanded Sir Demetrius.

The knight commander shook her head and shrugged.

Sir Demetrius bowed a step backward and drew the dirk at his hip, flicking the blade in an upward arc between Sprael's hands. The trailing draft impressively scattered the laif's hair across his forehead.

"Gramercy," said Sprael, smoothing his locks into a fashionable slant with his newly freed hands.

"Think nothing of it." Sir Demetrius shrugged. "Cheap Celliwig steel. Doesn't take much." Every shoulder in the room shook with laughter. "Let's try those introductions again, shall we?" The Duke-Knight extended his hand. "I am Sir Demetrius Purefoy."

Sprael obliged, clasping the Duke-Knight's armoured forearm. As Sprael stepped away from the Duke-Knight, the advisors suddenly broke into frantic whispers, their eyes and hands wild and flailing. The term *archenlaif* was repeated several times, arriving at the beginning and punctuating the closure of several remarks.

"Yes!" Sir Demetrius shouted. "I am aware that time is of the essence!" He glanced at Sprael. "You eventually grow accustomed to the noise."

"Reminds me of an aviary set ablaze," remarked Sprael.

"Ha!" Sir Demetrius barked. "Minus the feathers and the grit upon the floors!"

The advisors shook their heads and muttered into their robes as the Duke-Knight returned to his seat. He retrieved a flagon that had been placed upon the north-eastern portion of Fenrirfang and drank with an almost ceremonial fervor.

"Speaking of birds," Sir Demetrius began, dabbing his moustache. "May I ask what you know of Kardowiffs?"

It was now Sprael's turn to laugh. "My lord," he sputtered, returning upright. "The *Nocnik*, as my people call it..." he trailed off, noticing the mood in the room had suddenly gone sour. The Duke-Knight was regarding the diorama as if it were a familial gravestone. A Scholar seated upon the floor furiously swiped at his face, vainly attempting to stem the surge of tears overtaking him.

Sprael soon discovered the only face that was not lost to despair belonged to the knight commander standing right beside him. When he caught her eye, she shifted her feet and coughed. He received this as the signal to continue.

"The Nocnik," he began again, nervously tugging his collar. "Or Kardowiff—as some may refer to it—is a bird that, well... If you will, recall a cockatrice in your minds. Alright? Well, the male cockatrice is proportionately larger than the female, and the female can grow eye to eye with your knight commander here." The laif stood taller than all within the room, save for the knight commander, who rivaled him by a journeyman's inch. "Now, picture a bird of that size in this room. I believe this man can." He pointed down to the Scholar who had been weeping ferociously moments ago.

"I can," agreed the Scholar brightly. "It's very big."

"An understatement, my friend," said Sprael. "But points for the offering. I was looking for *gargantuan*, or *excessively mammoth*, or—"

"It's really bleeding huge." The Duke-Knight cut the list short. "I have encountered cockatrices in the wild before, though I have never been up close to a living one. I have always waited for the archers to fell it before approaching."

"Wise, wise," said Sprael. "Close quarters with a cockatrice is ill-advised."

Sir Demetrius rubbed his forehead. "What do cockatrices have to do with Kardowiffs?" he asked.

"Size, Demetrius," replied Sprael. He rushed to the knight commander's side and rose onto his tiptoes. "A Kardowiff would need to spend considerable energy bending down, if he wanted to gaze into your knight commander's..." He leaned into her eyes. "Dreamy emeralds," he concluded, rounding away before receiving the gut punch he was overdue.

"You mean to tell us that a Kardowiff would brush his head upon a tavern ceiling?" scoffed the knight commander. "When simply walking upright?" Her face had flushed from Sprael's recent proximity. "That's preposterous!" she claimed as her features returned to their everyday hue.

"But no one has actually seen a Kardowiff before," pointed out the weepy Scholar. "Surely a bird of that stature and scope would have been spotted at some point."

"No one has actually seen a Kardowiff *and lived*," amended Sprael. "Humans, monsters, creatures, and yes, the occasional laif, that turn up petrified indiscriminately in Fenrirfang are simply chalked up to an encounter with a gorgon or a cockatrice."

"Or a basilisk," offered the weepy Scholar.

"Yes, a basilisk," agreed Sprael, steepling fingers to his bottom lip.

Another Scholar threw out an opinion. "Or possibly a lich?"

Sprael scowled. "Also, a good answer," he said with narrowed eyes. "As much fun as a night spent together going on about petrification sounds—"

The Scholar who had mentioned lichs lifted a scarf over her mouth in a clumsily seductive gesture.

"I meant, I meant..." Sprael sputtered, caught off-guard. "That wasn't an invitation." He turned to Sir Demetrius. "I appreciate our Duke-Knight here funding my rescue, but you can't have brought me here to simply discuss birds and fae tales?"

A reserved stillness fell throughout the room. Hopeful eyes began darting about, filled with the expectation that *somebody* else would be the next to speak. As if *somebody* else in the room was better qualified. The silence only deepened, until...

"Fae tales?" a voice crooned from deep within a wedge of shadows.

Sprael rounded on the speaker, clearly spooked. The voice had emanated from a shape bundled up to a desk, marooned to the farthest corner of the room. Her reading posture served as camouflage, and she had not stirred until the moment called for her to do so. She was surrounded on all sides by tall stacks of parchment, which only added to her obscurity.

She stood, shakily. "I expected better from someone with centuries of wild forest experience beneath his belt," she stated, finding her feet and entering the candlelight. "We were told that you, more so than any other ranger, were unafraid to tread within *any* boundary of the mighty Fenrirfang. It is the sole reason we saved you from the axeman's blade."

The woman appeared no older than nineteen winters, and her attire was not that of your garden variety intellectual. The workman's bodice she bore over her tunic was well-seasoned with thin scratches, and a number of lengthy tears had seen repair from thick out-of-color twine.

"That is what people say," agreed Sprael, turning to Sir Demetrius. "But to be fair, I've never made that claim myself."

Sir Demetrius ignored the laif, shifting his smile toward the young woman. "Allow me to present Calliandra Violetear of Tintagil. Her expertise on birds is unparalleled."

"Tell me true, Sprael," said Calliandra, foregoing further introductions. "What do you know of the karst in the lands beyond Lhaewyn's Fount?"

"It's cursed," replied Sprael off-handedly.

Calliandra nodded and smiled at him.

Realization dawned on Sprael in measured doses of horror. "You can't be serious," he balked. "How many knights do you have on hand?" Before anyone supplied the number, he continued. "Good, okay, keep that tally locked in your head, because that exact same number is the number of knights you are willing to lose, should you go there."

"Oh, we are not sending any knights," said Sir Demetrius.

"So, what legion of monster have you tamed and lined up to protect this expedition?"

"No legion of any shape or form, ranger. From all the information we have gathered, stealth is what we require."

Sprael folded his arms across his chest. "So, you have commissioned a wraith, I take it?"

"Better," replied Sir Demetrius. "Vaskar of Rhionydd."

Sprael gaped. "Vaskar of Rhionydd has agreed to this? *The* Vaskar of Rhionydd? The notorious mercenary Vaskar of Rhionydd has agreed to enter the cursed lands beyond Lhaewyn's Fount? You have his agreement in writing? Are you certain that you have not erred and wrongfully commissioned *Vasper of Garlot*, or *Vesknar of Lowthean*? Because you might want to double check that. Are you sure you have *the* Vaskar of Rhionydd on the hook for this?"

"One and the same," replied the Duke-Knight with stone cold surety. "The Vaskar of Rhionydd."

~ 4 ~

OF ALL PEOPLE

"No." Vaskar turned, making for his horse.

"Wait a moment!" Dafne, the mercenaries' broker, called after him. "You haven't heard the value of the purse!" She looked to Marius across the tavern's dining booth. "It's the largest sum I've ever seen."

"He doesn't seem interested," replied Marius, sipping the foam from his pint. "But good luck convincing him."

"It's enough to buy several estates in Ghore!"

"Who wants to buy land in Ghore?"

"A significant palatial parcel in Tintagil or Lowthean!"

"Ack!" Marius spluttered, ale spraying from his mouth. "What? That would be like..." His eyes rolled back as he counted. "Carry the two... You're talking around three hundred gold farthings!"

Dafne raised her eyebrows at the man. "Should've carried a dozen more twos, my friend. We're talking five hundred."

"What?!" Marius shot to his feet. "My father was lucky to make three farthings from a solid harvest! That much would be... that would be..." He stammered, clambering to his feet. "Even after divvying up the profits, that's more gold than I could spend in a laif's lifetime!"

"Precisely," said Dafne, but the young apprentice had already fled through the open door.

He found Vaskar still preparing his mount for the ride from Celliwig to wherever next. Home? Marius had never received an invite, and as far as he knew, no one ever had. As far as Marius knew, Vaskar had no friends, no family, nor any materialistic attachments. He went from job to job without much of a rest between. His personal life and his history were all great question marks. The mercenary was equally as mysterious as he was infamous.

"Vaskar!" Marius called. "This job for the Duke-Knight of Orkney is the biggest haul in Camelot's recorded history!"

The mercenary did not seem to be listening.

"It far overshadows the Widow of Laclan job. It's more than twice that amount! And unlike the Widow of Laclan, Sir Demetrius probably won't have us living with goblins for any length of time."

Vaskar's head shot up. Marius was startled by the hatred in his eyes. The mercenary was not one to show emotion often.

"I mean, the goblins werren't that bad," Marius backpedaled. "The accommodations were a bit cramped, and the food wasn't as gross as I thought it would be, which was a plus. I recall the only real trouble I had was that one who kept poking my—"

"Forget the goblins," said Vaskar, securing a strap with more force than was warranted.

"If not the goblins, perhaps Sir Demetrius?"

A slight tremor of anger coursed through Vaskar, one that those less familiar with the mercenary may not have noticed. "You and the Duke-Knight have a history, I take it?" asked Marius, treading cautiously.

"We have a history," muttered Vaskar.

This was the rarest of occasions, receiving even the tiniest glimpse into the mercenary's past. Marius longed for his pint. There was nothing better than a good tale and a pint.

"What sort of history could you have," began Marius, eyeing the pub's open door, "that five hundred farthings couldn't solve? Why don't we hustle back to Dafne and get some more details, eh? Let her explain things."

By this time Vaskar had completed his preparations. "No," he said. "I have business elsewhere."

"Wait, wait! We're talking five hundred gold farthings here! Did he shortchange you on a job or something? What could he have possibly done?"

Vaskar mounted his horse.

"Come on!" begged Marius.

"I will send a missive when next I require your aid," said Vaskar, making a farewell salute. He urged his horse into a casual trot.

"Five hundred farthings," mumbled Marius. "Five hundred farthings," he repeated, mustering his courage. "Five hundred glorious farthings!" he shouted. "What are you afraid of, Vaskar?!"

The mercenary's horse stopped abruptly.

Marius knew he had just struck a chord. A discordant, discourteous, sort of chord. A chord that wise musicians avoided completely. He could feel his bowels tighten as the mercenary turned his head.

"Hey!" said Dafne, suddenly from behind.

Marius looked at Dafne, then back to Vaskar, where he discovered empty ground.

Dafne handed Marius a fresh pint. "Where'd he go?" she asked. "I thought you of all people could convince him."

"What makes you say that?" Marius asked, taking a swig of the ale.

"Aren't you two friends?"

Marius nearly gagged. "Can you wait for me to swallow," he choked, "before saying any more ridiculous things?"

* * *

A short stack of archenlaif scrolls had been pilfered from the warfront and delivered to the Scholars of Orkney. Calliandra had spent the better part of the morning discussing the findings with Sprael in an open courtyard. The Kingdom was starving for intelligence, desperate for any sort of leg up. Calliandra had no doubt these scrolls would unlock something that could put an end to the archenlaif threat once and for all.

Thus far the Scholars had managed to decipher many of the scrolls that contained glimpses into archenlaif culture and commerce, which all proved useless in regard to warfare. They had, however, also discovered scrolls packed with descriptions of archenlaif magics and incantations. The only problem was that they were written in an ancient script that was beyond any Camelot Scholar's ability to translate.

"You mean to tell me," Sprael said, skeptical, "that you believe a feather from the Nocnik is capable of all that the fables claim?"

"Not *all*," replied Calliandra, "but we need our own secret weapon. Something that will give us an edge when all the light goes out. Our own *dagger in the dark*, if you will."

"You need a dragon, not a dagger," commented Sprael, taking a bite of egg from his fork. The two had been sparring wits all morning, ignoring the generous breakfast spread beneath them. The laif frowned, chewing slowly, finding the egg cold. "Or several dragons. Any of your stolen scrolls relay that sort of insight?"

Calliandra nibbled at a soggy corner of her over-buttered toast. "Regarding dragon commands?" She paused to scrape her tongue onto a napkin. It appeared that the soft foods had turned to slop, so she turned hopeful eyes toward the meat. "We need to be realistic here."

"Realistic?" he coughed. "You're telling me with a straight face that a Nocnik feather can decode any tongue?"

"That's what we believe."

"Based on what? An old legend that talks of a mystic, elusive bird that bestows 'the worthy' with a feather that grants them the ability to write sultry sonnets, or pen cunning battle strategies, or, or..."

"Decipher riddles in a foreign tongue," Calliandra concluded for the laif. "Which would perfectly suit our purposes."

Sprael rocked back in his seat and crossed his arms. "This food is inedible," he complained. "This whole quest makes no difference to me, honestly. If Sir Demetrius wants to pay me top gold to lead a flock of idiots to their deaths, that's all fine and dandy. Done it hundreds of times."

"So what has you so riled?"

Sprael's jaw muscles tensed. "The location," he admitted, unlocking his arms.

"The karst," Calliandra said. "And the Handsome Death Caverns."

"*Halodwyth* Caverns," amended the laif. "Though Halodwyth did cut a rather handsome figure, truth be told, which is why I graciously accept your people's misnomer. But, getting back to the expedition, I will openly admit," Sprael placed a hand to the side of his mouth, whispering the words, "it terrifies me beyond belief."

Calliandra nodded. "Yes," she muttered, trying to flag down a passing servant, "I have my reservations as well."

"Why would *you* hold reservations?" asked Sprael, cocking an eyebrow.

The scholar relaxed in satisfaction. "I caught his attention. He's coming over."

"Forget lunch," said Sprael impatiently. "I must admit that I've grown rather fond of you over the last several hours. So please, choose your words carefully for what I am about to ask." The laif was interrupted by the appearance of a rotund man wearing the grays of Orkney.

"What do you require of me?" asked the servant, his eyes tracing over the wasted food. "Might I alleviate this burden?"

"Yes, please," she replied. "May we have luncheon served, if you would be so kind?"

The servant bowed. "It would be my pleasure," he replied, setting off for the kitchens.

A ream of clouds scuttled over the sun, passing shadows, sending goosebumps across Calliandra's forearms. "I should have brought my mantle out with me," she said, shivering, "I'm always cold, no matter the season."

"I must pose my question—" began Sprael.

"The answer would be an unequivocal yes," said Calliandra. "I will be joining you and the mercenary on this expedition to serve as your key bird expert. The Duke-Knight has already commissioned my services—"

As if summoned by his title, Sir Demetrius swept furiously into the courtyard. The courtiers flanking his sides struggled to keep up, their eyes filled with regret. "Ranger!" he shouted, bringing the laif to his feet.

"My lord," Sprael replied with a nod.

"Tell me truly," said Sir Demetrius, "how perilous is the journey beyond Lhaewyn's Fount and into the catacombs?"

Sprael hesitated, exchanging a glance with Calliandra. Before he could answer, the Duke-Knight spoke again. "Never mind that. Would you be able to accomplish it without the aid of Vaskar of Rhionydd?"

"My lord," Sprael said warily. "With or without the mercenary, the entire journey is rife with perils, and the Halodwyth Caverns are cursed. It is said that vengeful wraiths haunt every corridor, every chamber. Not to mention, that it is also said—"

"*It is said!*" spat Sir Demetrius. "Tell me what you know for certain! We don't have time for speculation! War plagues our horizon! And my young spellcaster, trained in the ways of battle, must learn these spells! We must decipher the scrolls!" The courtiers' heads swung between one another, unsure how to handle Sir Demetrius in his current state.

"I understand this, my lord," said Sprael mildly. "Am I gathering that Vaskar of Rhionydd has declined your offer?"

Sir Demetrius scowled, crinkling the flesh unconcealed by his beard. "He has," the Duke-Knight admitted. "A newly arrived dispatch revealed as much, though I do not understand why. His broker relayed her condolences, claiming that once he discovered who was funding this excursion, he refused outright and would hear no more. She never even had the time to explain our purposes or how dire the situation has become!"

"Did you not pay for my rescue from the chopping block?" asked Sprael, confused.

"I did," replied Sir Demetrius, returning the look of confusion. "He must not have known that I was the benefactor. Your rescue did not require a meeting beforehand, as this new contract requires."

"Huh." Sprael rubbed his chin. "What did you do to him?"

Sir Demetrius' eyes rolled toward the sky. "That's just it!" he shouted. "I have never met this man! Your rescue was the first time I ever sought his employ."

Sprael turned to Calliandra. "Is there any other way? Perhaps we could attempt to capture an archenlaif? That may prove much less dangerous."

Calliandra shook her head. "It is highly doubtful that the average archenlaif is versed in such an ancient script," she said. "And from what we know of archenlaives, one would rather die than betray their own kind. Plus, capturing an archenlaif would take much, much more time. The trek to the Fount is what? Two, three days? And the

Caverns aren't much further. Making a trip into archenlaif territory could take weeks."

"And weeks are something we do not have," stated Sir Demetrius.

"Wait," Sprael interjected, lifting a finger in question. "Did you not say that Orkney possesses a battlemage?"

"Out of the question!" Sir Demetrius said. "Earon is yet in training and has been confined to the keep. He is far too valuable for this mission."

Sprael shook his head. "There really is no other way, is there?"

Calliandra handed the newly arrived servant a platter that was just beyond his reach. A few cubed potatoes spilled over as she made the transfer. "The elite Scholars of Camelot are all in agreement," she answered, swatting the fallen cubes off the table. "We should offer a final plea to the mercenary. Explain to him what hangs in the balance."

Sprael nodded. "If there is to be even a sliver of a chance of completing this mission, there is no one better."

"We waste time standing here," stated Sir Demetrius, turning to address his courtiers. "We will deploy a second bird to Vaskar's broker immediately. I will elaborate on certain details and pray that persuades him."

"I wonder why he despises you, Sir Demetrius?" Sprael mused.

"On my daughter's unmarked grave," swore the Duke-Knight of Orkney, signaling his attendants depart, "I know not."

~ 5 ~

THAT SADDER NOTE

If an ordinary carrier bird, such as your basic rock pigeon, set off in the early morning from Benwick and flew to the farthest corner of Tintagil, he would reach his destination a little after midday. Depending on the situation, a lord may select a heartier candidate from the aviary, like a raven or a harrier, keeping in mind that when using the larger bird, speed is forfeited for certainty. Needletails, on the other hand, can fly from Benwick to Tintagil in a mere fraction of the time, without the lord wasting concern on storms, war, or stray arrows. Aside from their unmatched speed and efficiency, the needletail is also extraordinarily intelligent. Like any other homing fowl, the bird can return to its keep after delivering the message, but it may also be trained to return to its keeper, wherever that keeper might be. One might wonder why every lord in Camelot would not keep several needletails in his aviary, as they are clearly the superior bird. The answer, of course, is that only the wealthiest of lords can afford to employ them; needletails are gratuitously expensive to purchase, and their maintenance costs are nearly as forbidding. For the vast majority of lords, the joy of receiving a lightning-fast response was not worth the steep cost. But not for Vaskar of Rhionydd.

The following morning one of Vaskar's needletails arrived, frantically tapping on Marius' bedroom window. The diminutive white-throated birds were known for their efficiency, not manners.

"Yes, yes," said Marius drowsily as he lumbered to the window. "I'm coming." Messages from Vaskar could arrive at any time, and this one had arrived an hour before sunup. The early hour of the message did not make Marius uneasy, but the frequency did: he had only parted with the mercenary yesterday.

Has the devil changed his mind?

It was more likely that some wealthy Baroness required aid silencing some blackmailers, or that a lordling wanted a jawbone off a rare beast. Sure, those contracts paid well, very well. Just not five hundred farthings well...

Upon the parchment had been written the phrase '*Fear is not a motivation*' in Vaskar's distinct scrawl. Never once had Marius received a message from Vaskar like this one. He had been expecting something that read '*the Blind Dog midday tomorrow*' or something similar. A location, a time, and a date. That was the way it went. Sometimes there were special instructions in the postscript. But other than that, there was never anything remotely personal included. Never a "*Remember last Tuesday when I used you as bait in that nest of Manticores? Yeah, sorry about that, mate. Buy you a pint?"*

"This isn't good," said Marius to the bird. He could not help recalling the last words he had spoken to Vaskar. Foolish words. "Now you've stepped in it," he said to himself. Meanwhile, the needletail continued to feast upon the plate of dried fruit that he kept by his bedside for such occasions. Despite his best and most meaningful efforts, Marius had seen each and every one of his most recent relationships crumble to dust. Such was the life of a mercenary, as had been explained to him countless times.

Over his twenty winters, he had amassed far more wealth than cheer. Contrary to common belief, he had discovered early on that the two did not often coincide. And now it seemed that he had crippled his last standing relationship. Vaskar.

A vicious series of knocks startled Marius to his feet. Glancing out the window, he noticed that the cap of the sun had only just crested the horizon. *Who could possibly be calling at this hour?*

"Marius!" Dafne stood upon the front stoop, seeming ill at ease. "May I come in?"

"Of course," Marius replied, stepping sideways to let the woman enter.

"Hope I didn't wake you," said Dafne, pressing a scroll to Marius' chest as she passed him. "Tea?" She spun in a circle in the kitchen. "Preferably a dark tea from dark leaves?"

"I have dark coffee from dark beans," offered Marius, placing the scroll upon the table before hurrying toward the hearth.

Dafne took a seat at the dining table. "Even better!" she said. "Listen, have you heard from Vaskar by any chance? I know we only just parted ways yesterday..."

After his third attempt, Marius managed to ignite the dried grasses resting inside the kindling. He blew on the embers until dark gray tendrils of smoke came forth. "Hand me that clay jug, please?" He pointed toward Dafne's bent elbow.

"Sure, yes," she said distractedly. "Did you hear me?"

"I did," replied Marius, tipping the jug into the hanging pot. "You wanted coffee, so I am making you coffee." He went to a cupboard and took a satchel from a lower shelf. "And yes, disturbingly enough, I received a message from our friend Vaskar before dawn. The bird is actually still in my chambers."

"And what exactly is the disturbing part?"

Marius carefully poured the satchel's contents into a waiting bowl. "How fine do you prefer your grinds?" he asked, working the beans with a stone pestle.

"Forget the coffee!" Dafne yelled. "That scroll over there is the second that I have received from Sir Demetrius. The *second*. A knight, particularly a Duke-Knight such as Sir Demetrius, does not ask twice."

Setting the pestle aside, Marius leaned against the counter and gave the broker his full attention. "I'm fully on board with Sir Demetrius' contract, though I don't know any of the details. That amount of coin would get me out of the blood-for-pay game. And then maybe I could find—"

"Find a wife," interrupted Dafne, "and father a dozen babies, and enjoy a life of peace, and yada yada." She paused, fixing him with a stare. "Here's the thing, if Vaskar does not take the contract, you won't have any of that. Your dreams of a peaceful life, free from day-to-day drudgery, will never be possible."

"What do you mean?"

Dafne pulled closer to the table and snatched the scroll. "If the archenlaives prevail," she began, crinkling the scroll and punching it into Marius' chest, "then none of that will be possible. What Sir Demetrius seeks—" she cut off, taking in a deep breath. "The fate of Camelot could hang in the balance. Go on. Read the scroll. The Scholars actually agreed on something for once, and it's all in the ink on that paper." Taking the pestle from Marius, Dafne quickly went to work preparing the coffee. By the time she had boiled water, poured it over the particles to steep, and served, Marius had read the scroll twice.

"First of all," began Marius, "that is way more *involved* than I could have imagined. The Handsome Caverns are off-limits to every soul living—laif and human and ogre and gremlin alike. Nobody goes there. Second," he carefully took a sip from his cup, wary of scorching his tongue, "a pinion from the bum of a Kardowiff? Come on, Dafne."

"Pinions are on the wings," corrected Dafne. "And yes, it's a long shot. But imagine the knowledge that you could help unlock. And just think, your hands would be metaphorically pressing upon the blade that finally severs the archenlaif head. At long last, humankind's fear of a return to slavery vanquished!"

Marius regarded Dafne with a flat stare. "Vaskar does not care for crown or kingdom. He'd accept archenlaif currency same as any other."

Dafne grimaced and shook her head into her hand. "What about the part involving Sir Demetrius' daughter?" she asked quietly. "Might that sway your mentor's aversion?" Marius' unchanging expression confirmed the frailty in her plea. "Well, we must try again," she stated. "This is of far more importance than I first realized."

"I'm still on board. If anyone can achieve something impossible like this, it would be Vaskar. Don't think he's seen anything more difficult though." Marius scraped a knuckle to his chin. "This may possibly be the pinnacle of insanity."

"Camelot grows desperate," added Dafne.

"Aye," Marius agreed with a shrug. "Vaskar's needletail is still here. It would be simple enough to send her back with a note requesting a chat."

Dafne lurched forward in her seat. "You think he'd oblige?" As fast as she had gone forward, she sat back. "Wait, what was the disturbing message he sent you this morning?"

"Uh…" Marius tried to conceal his hesitation with an abrupt slug of coffee. "It was just some advice. You know, mentor-apprentice stuff. Not a veiled threat of any sort."

"Why is your eyelid twitching like that?" Dafne asked, cocking her head. "I've known Vaskar long enough to know that he would never send one of his priceless needletails out just to say, *'keep that chin up, little turnip!'* Not to anyone. Not ever."

"It was an inside joke?"

"You're still his apprentice, aren't you?" she pressed. "His disturbing message was not a notice of dismissal, was it?"

Marius rose abruptly. "Let's find out, shall we?"

"The man is simply ruthless," Marius told Dafne as the two rode to meet Vaskar. "Every detail I know about him enforces the fact that he's ruthless. His efficiency, his pragmatism, his sense of time —"

"How many jobs does he take without you?" interrupted Dafne. She knew Vaskar well enough and did not require a refresher on his personality. She was also privy to the amount of work that he took.

Marius shrugged. "No idea," he replied. "It seems, nowadays, he only beckons me if his target is a monster that needs a distraction. Or if he needs a spotter when the target's range is well beyond your average longbow span."

"It seems the term 'apprentice' is used rather loosely," said Dafne. "Does he allow you to carry out any contracts on your own?"

"Does a blacksmith allow his apprentice to complete the most difficult, master-level blade unsupervised?" asked Marius, shaking his head. "No, I don't believe Vaskar is capable of relinquishing such control."

"There's always hope." Dafne murmured. "Do you think that you're ready for a trial run?" It was well within her power to slide a few contracts Marius' way.

Before Marius could answer, the pathway before him widened into a clearing with an ancient maple tree punctuating its center. The tree was so theatrically large that one might assume it had been transplanted all way from the depths of Fenrirfang. "Honestly, I've felt ready for a trial run since leaving the garrison," Marius replied, looking around for Vaskar.

Something feels off.

"A garrison, you say?" An unfamiliar voice wandered out from the clearing at the same time as a fury of white and red surcoats burst from behind the great maple.

"Celliwig," growled Marius as the soldiers encircled him. "What do you want?" Marius directed his question toward a sauntering knight whom he had determined held the position of command.

The knight lifted her visor to reveal a face wholly covered by freckles. "I just knew that whoever had orchestrated Sprael's rescue was no slouch." She placed a hand atop one of her soldier's spaulders, her sword remaining sheathed. "Out of curiosity, which land did your garrison serve?" the knight commander inquired.

"Rhionydd," replied Marius, not seeing any point in lying. He unfortunately did not see any way of escape either; the seven soldiers held their halberds in a way that mandated strict compliance.

"How long did you serve?" the knight commander asked.

"Two winters."

"That's a rather short stint."

"My services were called elsewhere."

Dafne surveyed the Celliwig weaponry, her aggravation growing. "What are we doing? Playing twenty questions?" she demanded. "Let's skip to the end, shall we?"

A corner of the knight commander's mouth lifted into a smirk. "I prefer to savor my victories."

"Don't come often, do they?" Dafne rebuffed. The anger in her tone caused her mount to stir. "Poke my horse," she said sharply, directing her attention to a soldier who had lunged toward her, "and I will see your entire family culled."

"Humor in the face of an impending demise," remarked the knight commander. "Admirable, but played out, in my opinion." She pointed toward Marius. "That bow you have," she said. "Where was it crafted? It's not native to Camelot."

"Good eyes," Marius replied. He remembered seeing her predatory gaze on the execution stage. "I had this longbow crafted in a canton deep in Fenrirfang, the name of the place escapes me... Tarbokleever? Tanbarkover?" He shook his head, giving up. "Anyhow, I'm afraid this weapon is custom fitted for my wingspan, and it would prove quite unwieldy for those of a greater stature." His eyes traced the knight commander upward from her sabatons to the crest of her helm.

"I don't wish to use your bow," scoffed the commander. "I mean to hock it for profit. I'm simply curious of its value. Authentic laif craft always spices up a negotiation." She raised her hand, palm facing outward. "Now, if you answer honestly, we *might* let you off with a warning. But the moment my hand drops, my soldiers will begin stabbing, until I raise it again." Somehow her mouth sneered and scowled all at once. "From dawn's breaking until this very moment, for reasons unknown to me—my hand, you see—my hand has been feeling abnormally heavy. And I do not know why."

Dafne rotated in her saddle to smile at Marius. "I think she's trying to be scary," she whispered loudly.

"I picked up on that," agreed Marius, trying to match the broker's coolness.

"Enough of this!" announced the commander. Dramatically, she turned her back, hand still upraised. "Tell me where Sprael, the murderer—"

Throughout the years, there were things that Marius believed he would grow accustomed to. In his four years as a mercenary apprentice, he had seen many kinds of deaths. Some people die slowly, piteously, their guts exposed. And some die quickly, gone before they even know it. But when a body bent in places where they are not designed to bend... that was something Marius was sure he would never grow accustomed to.

Soundlessly Vaskar's whipcord had launched from within the upper boughs of the maple, latched the commander about the waist, and snapped her backwards with such terrible violence that the back of her helm collided with her spurs. To his everlasting shame, Marius squealed loudly at the sight. Then in an instant, the knight commander was torn from the ground and disappeared into the maple's overwhelming canopy.

Over half the Celliwig soldiers were unaware of their leader's fate, and perhaps they were the lucky ones. Those who were privy to her demise not only met their end surprised, but they also died *terrified.* Engulfed in separate flashes of blue flame, each soldier was reduced to cinders, their ashes gently swept away by the passing breeze.

"Is that why you acted so confident?" Marius asked Dafne. "Because you knew Vaskar was up that tree the whole time?"

Dafne's features were haunted, terror-stricken. "I had no idea."

~ 6 ~

LETTING GO

Just how old was Vaskar of Rhionydd? Marius wondered.

At times Vaskar strode as wearily as a man who had survived a hundred winters without refuge. Other times, like now, he seemed younger than thirty, spryly dropping from a high perch.

"How did... how was..." sputtered Dafne as the mercenary approached. She turned to Marius. "How?"

"I stopped asking those kinds of questions long ago," Marius admitted. "Have you not been afield before?"

Dafne nodded. "Yes, I have," she replied, "but it wasn't like *this.*"

"Well met, Vaskar." Marius saluted his mentor. He turned back to Dafne. "Never is," he said

"You wished a word," said Vaskar, standing before them as if he had all the time in the world.

Marius dismounted and took a deep breath, extending the new Orkney contract toward Vaskar. "Sir Demetrius has elaborated on his proposal."

45

Vaskar's eyes flicked to the scroll. "Paraphrase it," he said.

Marius breathed a sigh of relief. He had feared that Vaskar would turn heel and vanish without hearing him out. "He's increased the payout by one hundred gold far-things. And he apologizes for any wrongdoings he may have committed toward you in the past."

"Wrongdoings?" Vaskar asked quietly, tilting his head. "Did he elaborate?"

"Well, he, uh..." Marius was unprepared for the question. The missive had not been explicit.

Luckily, Dafne was nearby. "Sir Demetrius didn't specify," she answered. "But, like Marius stated, he has generously increased the amount of the bounty." Seeing Vaskar's stony expression, she quickly added, "Might I point out that the job in Celliwig was contracted by Sir Demetrius, and you carried that one out."

Upon that statement Vaskar spun on his heel to leave, as Marius had feared. Perhaps Dafne's presence was not so lucky after all.

"Wait!" Marius rushed to catch up. "She has a point."

Without turning, Vaskar spoke. "If I had known for whom I worked, I would have spent my time elsewhere." His tone conveyed a warning, clear as a fenland cobra spreading its hood.

"The kingdom needs us!" blared Marius. "This quest, should we succeed, could see an end to the archenlaif threat!"

Vaskar continued striding toward the maple.

"It's six hundred gold farthings!" cried Marius, running up to him.

Vaskar summoned his horse.

"Why even show up?" Marius clasped Vaskar on the shoulder. "Teach me something!"

The mercenary halted. He gazed across the burnt Celliwig armour, then deliberately pinned those same eyes on the gigantic tree.

"I see," said Marius, pursing his lips. "You used our meeting as a means to put down our Celliwig pursuers. You never had any intention of hearing us out." Marius furrowed his brow. "But how did they know where..." With sudden awareness, his forehead smoothed. "You tipped them off, didn't you?"

"Never say that I don't teach you anything," stated Vaskar before turning away.

Marius grew desperate as he watched his mentor's laif-bred horse emerge from the thickets. Suddenly recalling the message he had received from Vaskar earlier that day, he spoke again. "If fear is not your motivation for shunning Demetrius' offer, what is it? What could possibly provoke Vaskar of Rhionydd to decline six hundred farthings?" While he spoke, eight riderless saddled horses wandered into the clearing.

Mounting his horse, Vaskar turned away from his apprentice.

"Did you hear me?" said Marius, needing to shout to be heard over the clattering horses.

"Ensure these Celliwig roans do not follow me," said Vaskar.

"Don't want them to end up like their riders, do we?" said Marius bitterly, placing a steadying hand to the nearest bridle. The Celliwig breed was not known for durability, but was renowned for their remarkable coloration. "They would fetch a fair bit of coin."

Vaskar gently tapped his horse's ear, and the horse replied with a snicker before lunging forward. "Best of luck with that," he called out.

Maybe it was out of desperation, or perhaps a hidden longing for a sudden death that drove Marius to leap atop the nearest Celliwig filly and give chase. "Sir Demetrius is a good man! However he harmed you, I'm sure it was a mistake! He didn't mean it!" Vaskar was not slowing, so Marius decided to shift tactics. "His wife tragically passed away twenty-five years ago! Some say from a broken heart after their only daughter died while courting a young baron some years back!" Unexpectedly, Marius found himself next to Vaskar.

"She died while courting some Tintagil baron," Marius continued hurriedly, shocked to suddenly have Vaskar's full attention. "She was around my age, twenty years or so, and well, I mean, maybe she didn't *die*. She was captured, held for ransom, and no one has heard or seen anything from her in decades, so it stands to reason that she has left this earth one way or another." Marius felt himself rambling, but was helpless against the tide of urgency. "Demetrius, fair and honorable as he is—and was—refused to pay the ransom. At that time, he was not given to displays of weakness. So throughout the years, he has been adding coin to his daughter's dowry."

Something dangerous flickered in Vaskar's eyes.

"You see," Marius continued, "the Duke-Knight believed that one day his dear Elodie would return home. And drawn from more habit than hope, the man has never stopped investing in her dowry."

"And now the proud Duke-Knight of Orkney has finally given up," Vaskar commented.

"That's the short of it," Marius assented ruefully. "Demetrius had no other children, and if she is gone, so is his legacy. With the archenlaives breathing down our necks, he believes it is finally time to let go."

At that moment Dafne appeared, navigating between the riderless horses that were busy eating the taller stalks of fescue that hemmed the pathway. Both rider and mount approached the men tentatively.

Vaskar smiled at his broker coldly. "See if he is willing to let go of one hundred more farthings."

* * *

Sprael strode to the window in his chamber.

Five days had passed since he had been rescued from the executioner's axe. Four days spent in Locus Castle, safely whiling away the hours with wine and games. The past three days ran together as one, and he only grew more restless.

His enthusiastic arguments with Calliandra had been the glowing highlights of his stay thus far. Each row began as rational but quickly devolved into absurdity. Sprael had noticed a bond creeping between them, which gave him pause. Though her friendship brought gusts of fresh air into his life, it also pained him. If Calliandra were to join the quest for Halodwyth Caverns, she would most assuredly die. Though, in truth, he was fairly certain that he would also perish. As someone who could count the number of his friends on one finger, he was most unwilling to see that solitary member meet her end.

A vision of Gilbert Pemberton convulsing in the forest graced his memory, the juvenile basilisk's venom taking effect nigh instantly. Sprael's dagger secured an ending for the lad's agony, but to provide that same act of mercy to Calliandra, would be... His mind traveled further into his past, to an old friend from the Gentle March, another whose end came long before it should have.

Dear Prija...

The laif turned away from the window, banishing the thoughts with a curse. A sudden knock upon his door lent a welcome and well-timed distraction. "Enter," Sprael called. The door opened slowly, the gap between oak and stone filled by a hesitant Orkney page. "At your leisure, my young friend."

"A-Apologies," stammered the page, clutching a wooden crate to his chest, and easing the door wider with his foot. "The last time I called upon this same door, there were *activities* at play that I wish mine eyes had not witnessed."

Sprael cocked an eyebrow. "Seeing as I am the only occupant of this room, such *activities* are unlikely to take place."

"The previous occupant was alone as well..."

"Alright." Sprael clapped his hands. "That is most unfortunate, but this world has never been safe." He shook his head, unsure where he was heading. "Anyways, what brings you here?"

The page stepped forward and extended a large crate. "Master Flaggart has fulfilled your order," answered the page. "And he wanted you to know that the whetstone has been sharpened, and it is full tang throughout the handle, as you requested."

Sprael accepted the crate. Tugging at the lid, he discovered nails sealed each corner. He instinctively reached for the dagger at his hip, but came up short, forgetting that his Celliwig captors had confiscated his weapons.

Without a word the page passed Sprael a flat-bladed turnscrew.

Sprael nodded gratefully.

Once each nail had been pried loose, Sprael freed the lid with a firm pull, revealing a hunter's dagger sheathed in a gray leather scabbard. A whetstone, mimicking the dagger's exact shape, had been laid beside the weapon, appearing as its stone-hewn twin.

"What do you think?" asked the page.

"Appears suitable," replied Sprael, undoing his belt. "Tell Master Flaggart that he has done very well by me." He slid the scabbard's carry loop onto the end of his belt and secured the weapon to his left hip.

"But you haven't even unsheathed the blade."

"True," said Sprael unconcerned. "I don't see any ghouls or hobs leaping about, do you?"

The page swiveled his head, confused. "I do not, sir, but this is the Locus Castle, and we don't have—"

"I only draw my dagger when I perceive a threat," interjected Sprael. His eyes lifted over the page to see Calliandra raising a fist to tap upon his still-open chamber door. Another figure trailed her shadow. "You may leave us." The laif placed a coin in the page's hand. "And please, give Flaggart my compliments."

Calliandra stepped aside to grant the page exit. She strode into the room, her eyes darting emphatically toward the young man beside her. "Allow me to introduce Earon."

The Scholar's mannerisms conveyed to Sprael that he should clearly recognize this *Earon*, but alas, he did not. "Oh, yes, it's... Earon... of course... It's Earon." Sprael extended a cordial hand in greeting.

Calliandra narrowed her eyes.

"I'm the mage apprentice Sir Demetrius loves boasting about," said Earon wryly, gripping Sprael about the wrist. "Pleased to meet you."

"Sir Demetrius did mention you the other day." Sprael tapped the side of his head. "Forgive my lapse of memory."

"There is nothing to forgive," Earon replied, straightening his mantle with a tug. "We are well met."

"Now that introductions are out of the way," Calliandra began, "I was wondering, well, *we* were wondering if you could detail a few of the more dangerous monsters that exist between the uppermost regions of Benwick and Lhaewyn's Fount."

Sprael groaned from the prospect of further labor. "I'd wager there's tomes in the Castle library that would prove more helpful."

"But you've been there," said Earon earnestly, his features pallid. "You know what to expect."

"Yes," added Calliandra, nodding. "What better source than a real one?"

Sprael strode to the bedside table and withdrew his whetstone from the smithy's crate. "Sir Demetrius is growing impatient, I take it?"

"What do you mean?" asked Earon. Visible beads of sweat had gathered upon his brow. "We're just curious."

"Not just impatient. Desperate," Sprael corrected himself, balancing the center of the whetstone upon his index finger. "Demetrius believes that the realm cannot tarry a day longer. The archenlaives have struck once, and it's only a matter of time before they strike again." When he rotated his wrist, the whetstone teetered sharply. "And now Sir Demetrius has hatched a plan that involves his precious apprentice. An apprentice he adamantly insisted would remain sheltered in the keep." The whetstone dropped and the laif, with unnatural speed, rescued the implement a moment before it could impact the cold stone. Crouched on the floor, he gazed up at Calliandra. "You should remain here among your scrolls and chronicles, dining on perfectly cooked eggs. Fenrirfang does not welcome pampered housecats."

As Sprael rose, his attention shifted to the apprentice. "This quest is a lost cause. Your liege's time would be better spent fortifying his outer walls. If the notion of facing down ogres makes you all soft in the kneecaps, then I recommend abandoning your caster's wand for a longbow-upon-the-ramparts." Sprael appraised Earon for a second time, weighing the young man's build. "Or perhaps a crossbow, if I were you."

As Earon wilted beneath the laif's words, Calliandra stepped forward. "You've impressed upon me, time and time again, that I am not suited for the wilds of Fenrirfang. I've heard your claims clear as a war bugle. You may be right, but we agree on one matter. Time grows short. The archenlaif threat dims Camelot's horizon."

"And Orkney cannot linger another day," added Earon. "We had hoped to bend your ear regarding what we may expect—"

"Expect?!" spat Sprael. "Expect demise!"

"It matters not," Earon stated calmly. "As we speak, Sir Demetrius is finalizing the members of a bold company—" The apprentice cut himself off as he found the remainder of his confidence suddenly moored by uncertainty.

"A bold company of what?" demanded Sprael, unable to conceal his contempt. "I assume Vaskar of Rhionydd has refused your liege once again?"

"Demetrius has not received a response in days," replied Calliandra.

"I ask once again," said Sprael, directing the question to Earon. "A bold company of what?"

"To a laif?" replied Earon. "A bold company of *dead men.*"

Sprael calmly placed his whetstone in its box. "In this situation, never has that old phrase rung truer."

~ 7 ~

FAREWELLS AND
NEEDLETAILS

There was no throne room in Locus Castle, for there was no throne. The lands of Orkney had been governed by knights since its inception.

Sprael followed the page through the corridors at a reluctant pace. Ordinarily such a trek would conclude in a grand throne room with a weak-wristed ruler awaiting their arrival. As Orkney was lacking such a space, the laif was unsure where Sir Demetrius' proclamation would occur.

Hours had passed since his rather poorly steered conversation with Calliandra and Earon. The Scholar had, unfortunately, departed his quarters with more resolve than when she had first entered. Sprael had discovered throughout the years that forbidding certain humans from doing something often acted as encouragement. In this case, he was left feeling as one who had unwittingly sparked such a reaction, and now only wished to stamp it out.

Perhaps my diction was the culprit? Sprael reflected as he passed beneath a threshold opening into a moderate-sized refectory. Sir Demetrius, seated at a round table that occupied much of the space, faintly smiled as Sprael entered. Only eight of the seats were occupied, and of the eight, Sprael immediately recognized the slightest of the frames among them. *Perhaps my next choice in words may yet keep Calliandra safe from the darkness of Halodwyth Caverns.*

"Ranger Sprael." The Duke-Knight's voice was edged in irritation. "Please take a seat."

As Sprael assumed the chair beside the knight commander, he could sense several sets of eyes warily observing him. Positioned directly across the table from him sat Calliandra and Earon, stacks of parchment obscuring his view of them.

"In the hopes that a few mercenaries might *discreetly* join our cause, I dispatched missives to a few trusted mercenary brokers a few days ago," Sir Demetrius began. "Do not be surprised if you are joined by aid at the onset of your journey." The Duke-Knight stiffened. "The hour grows late. We grow desperate. By this time, we had hoped that you would have already reached Lhaewyn's Fount." His spaulders rose and fell with a shrug. "Yet, here we are. Still planning. Still preparing. Still waffling over details." He pointed a steel-clad finger toward the parchment resting before Earon. "I understand that this is not a quest requiring an army, for we would have already set out if that were the case. Nay, this quest requires stealth, cunning, intellect..." Sir Demetrius trailed off, pinching the bridge of his nose. "I want all of you to know I did not come to this conclusion without great debate. In truth, there was a great amount of pleading involved as well.

"As you can see," continued Sir Demetrius, "my council is absent from this gathering. Their hopes have been dashed, believing that the gates to this quest have been barred shut. They believe that it's hopeless, even if we manage to reach the caverns tomorrow." Groaning, he sat forward, placing his armoured fist to his chin. "But they are not knights and have never witnessed what we have. They only know what is scribbled upon parchment, rarely venturing forth from the Castle. There is value in knowledge, for certain, but when it comes down to the shedding of blood, the bone and the brick and the steel..." Sir Demetrius petered off, appearing weary. "I do not know much," he said, his eyes meeting Sprael's, "but I do know that when it comes down to that, *that* is when a knight wakes his blade."

The knights struck the table as one, the resonance of their agreement bounding from every corner of the refectory. The noise drew Earon from his stupor, his expression looking much like a drowning man about to be overtaken by the tide.

Sir Demetrius looked at Sprael as though he sought the laif's approval.

Measure your words, Sprael told himself.

"I will lead your party to Halodwyth Caverns," he began. "The path is dangerous, and I won't go on about how impossible your quest is as I can tell you're loath of that discussion. But I will only 'wake my blade' upon one condition: the party must be comprised of Warrior-born only." Sprael had anticipated that his demand would garner outrage from Calliandra, but the Scholar simply quirked an unexpected smile.

Sir Demetrius angrily worked his jaw. "Given the vast amount of gold I am offering," he said, "you do not hold the right to foist any conditions upon me, laif. I have the final say in who comprises this company."

Sprael eased back in his chair. "Fine, then. Best of luck finding a laif willing to help you on such short notice." He dramatically lifted his arm and looked beneath it. "I don't see any."

Sir Demetrius leaned forward, scowling. "We haven't the time for this!" he seethed. "I see your point. But you neglect to understand what I have already said. We require cunning and knowledge, and a Warrior-born cannot even dream to match the acuity of a Scholar, nor that of a marked Mage." At the mention, Calliandra straightened. Earon wilted.

"My Duke-Knight of Orkney," began Sprael solemnly, "have you ever encountered a wraith before?"

The wrinkles on Sir Demetrius' forehead deepened. "I can't say that I have," he replied. "My foes have all been made of flesh."

Sprael grunted. "Lucky you," he said, averting his glance to Calliandra. "What have your scrawls and ledgers told you?"

"Regarding wraiths?" asked Calliandra. "They are spirits of unrest, created from a grave injustice or tragedy. It is often believed—"

"That they congregate inside one's body like raindrops in a puddle?" Sprael cut in. Calliandra adjusted in her seat, startled. "Dozens upon dozens can inhabit a single person's body without the body even knowing it." He leaned toward the knight commander beside him. "You could be a hive of these spirits without even being aware."

"What's the danger?" Earon interjected. "What's the danger of having wraiths inside you?"

Sprael cocked one eyebrow at the apprentice.

"Voices," replied Calliandra. "The possessed hear voices when no one is around. The effects are generally mild when compared to other monsters."

With a sigh, Earon's shoulders sank in relief. "That's not so bad," he said, reaching for his goblet.

"Voices." Sprael nudged the knight commander. "You hear what she said? Voices." The laif paused, glancing around the room. "This Scholar's information is accurate, I cannot disagree. She is speaking, however, about juvenile wraiths."

Earon's beverage froze midway to his mouth.

"You think those restless spirits inside the karst are juveniles?" Sprael asked Calliandra. "Allow me to answer for you as your expression betrays uncertainty. You see, the wraiths of Halodwyth Caverns date back to the age of the first laives when our Creator first called us 'Elves.' And as our clever Scholar here has informed us, wraiths are created from rather vile acts: murder, betrayal. The tale of the Caverns does not have a happy ending, and I'd wager that the passage of time has not been fun for these spirits. If one of these wraiths manages to get inside any of us..." Sprael casually looked away, as if distracted.

"What would happen?" stammered Earon, mouth agape.

"Oh." Sprael looked to the apprentice as if he had only just noticed him. "I'm not entirely sure, but I can assure you that *voices* would be a bottom tier affliction."

With a trembling hand, Earon brought his goblet the rest of the way to his mouth.

"How does one ward himself from a wraith?" one knight asked.

Before Sprael could answer, another knight cut in.

"So it stands to reason that these vengeful spirits have been within the Caverns for generations," she began, rubbing at her forehead. "Is there anything else that has been lying dormant for just as long?"

With that statement, a veritable floodgate of questions opened.

"Is the trek to the Caverns just as perilous as the Caverns, or is it more so?"

"Can a jaculus leap through three men standing in a row?"

"Does gnawing a flagstone brick nullify a gorgon's gaze?"

While the questions were flung about with growing desperation, Sir Demetrius had slowly risen from his chair.

"Enough," he stated calmly, seeming weary. "I will not entertain further discussion. War is upon us, and though I do not wish to send my finest knights far from home, I believe in this quest—" He stopped, sighing as Earon's whimpering undercut the fervor in his speech. "You may batter the ranger with as many questions as you like during your quest, for you depart in two hours."

The knights rose as one, and saluted Sir Demetrius. Like the knights, Calliandra appeared unsurprised by the slim timeframe. Earon, beside her, buried his head into his trembling hands.

You did the best you could, thought Sprael, standing to bow before taking his leave. *Two hours is plenty of time to gather supplies for a one-way trek.* He knew his odds of surviving the karst were not great, but he favored them over the Celliwig headman's stump. He chuckled as he departed the refectory, overhearing a scowling Sir Demetrius turn toward one knight in particular.

"A *flagstone brick*, honestly?"

* * *

Witnessing the good-byes and farewells of the Orkney knights was a somber, unsettling affair. Husbands, wives, children, sisters, brothers—all weeping and clasping at one another. *This may be the last time these people see one another,* Sprael thought. He had never fathered children himself. Not for lack of trying. Humans bred so easily, but it was a rarity for laives to experience successful conceptions. Humans, however, seemed as though one could fling a contorted eye at their spouse and have a spry babe by the next morning.

Sprael turned his gifted mount northward. He had seen enough. The sound of slowing hooves nearby caused him to shift his gaze to the right.

"This may be the final time these knights see their families," said Calliandra, echoing his thoughts. "And poor Earon..." The Scholar trailed off, furtively motioning behind her. The laif, pretending to yawn, rounded in his saddle and saw Earon riding a mare, hood drawn, eyes downcast. It seemed the apprentice did not have anyone to see him off or wish him well.

"The lad has no family?"

Calliandra shook her head, smiling sadly. "Oh, he does," she replied. "When the war horns sounded at Fort Navarene, his betrothed had no desire for widowhood, so she left him for his unmarked brother."

Sprael felt a pang of concern for the young man. "That caused a rift, I take it?"

"The family is now divided," admitted Calliandra. She leaned forward in her saddle to speak softly. "Earon has not informed them of this departure. As far as they know, he'll still be in the tower studying the fine arts of spell-casting."

It looked like the knights had concluded their good-byes, setting the last of their kin upon the ground. The window for departure was narrowing, and the ranger did not want to incur more of Sir Demetrius' anger. Gulping back the yawn that rose in his throat, Sprael dug his spurs into his mount and rode beside the knights.

"Might I have your names?" he asked.

The knight nearest the laif turned her face in his direction. "I am Sir Madelyn Luban," she replied with a courtly nod. "The hairy oaf beside me is Sir Brentin Napur. Despite appearances, he sometimes knows how to handle himself."

"Oh, har, har," said Sir Brentin.

Madelyn flung a thumb over her shoulder. "The skinny bloke just over there is Sir Clarence Kanat, and beside him is—"

"Sir Tyrol Burgot." The knight introduced himself. "We are much obliged to you, ranger." He brought a hand to his chest in salute.

Sprael returned the knight's gesture. "Wish I could say it's a pleasure," he said with a nod. "I fear this quest will be anything but."

"All the same," insisted Sir Tyrol.

"All the same," agreed Sprael. He exchanged a nod with Sir Madelyn and urged his mount to the front.

As Sprael joined his trot beside Calliandra, she glanced at him from the corner of her eyes. "You wish that I would stay behind," she began. "But you need me. How else will you be able to distinguish the Kardowiff from all the other birds?"

"Fair point, I suppose," Sprael replied. "But explain to me just how you'll be able to identify any sort of bird without any breath in your lungs?" He looked away, turning toward the knights joining from behind. "Where are the squires for these knights? And is Demetrius not seeing us off?"

The midday sun ignited the brilliant golden maille gracing Calliandra's arms. "We require stealth," she snipped. "Squires bumbling beneath the boughs would defeat our purpose."

"And sparkly gold armour won't garner notice..." mumbled Sprael.

Calliandra sneered, refocused her glower elsewhere. "And Sir Demetrius," she continued, "refused to be a part of our exit because he feared he would abandon his duties and join us." She paused, smiling suddenly. "I'll have you know that I've brought appropriate forest garb with me. I won't be a shiny emblem of Tintagil once we've crossed Fenrirfang's treeline."

"Glad to hear it." Sprael fought the urge to say *'It'll be the garb you'll be buried in'* but decided to lay that aside. His point had been made.

The journey continued in relative silence. Sir Kathryn Laemont, the knight commander of Orkney, rode vanguard, insisting upon it until their journey reached Fenrirfang.

"Have you given thought to your horses?" Sprael asked, turning to Sir Kathryn. "The karst is unforgiving terrain, and we'll have to abandon them before departing the Fount."

"I brought gold," replied Sir Kathryn.

"Ah." Sprael nodded. "You'll pay some poor forest laif to ferry your horses' return?"

"It's what has been done in the past."

"*The past* did not include archenlaives invading their lands."

"I suppose we may beg one of the villages to care for them until we return?" she asked, after much thought.

"Don't ask me, my lady," replied Sprael. "I'm not certain what we will find in Fenrirfang."

"Do you believe the forest villages will be desolate?"

Suddenly, a blurred object darted a course from the horizon, narrowly missing Sprael's head. "Creator's crotch!" Sprael cursed, ducking low.

Calliandra laughed loudly. "An ivory chested needletail!" she called, following the object with a pointed finger. "What a marvel!"

All Sprael saw when he looked back was a clear blue sky. The needletail had completely disappeared. "Is that what that was?" he asked.

"Would my lord care for a change of trousers?" offered Sir Kathryn, igniting laughter within the entire company.

Sprael joined in with the knights' laughter, laughed louder, and continued to laugh long after the rest had petered out. When a pair of mounted riders appeared over the crest of the roadway, however, his laughter abruptly ceased. He feared Calliandra's brilliant golden maille had drawn the attention of brigands.

As Sprael hesitated, Sir Kathryn spurred her mount, approaching the riders "Well met," she said, one arm raised in a friendly salute. "We are knights of Orkney on a mission for the Crown." Her mount halted, greeted by silence from the armoured strangers. One of the men appeared youthful and friendly, offering a smile in response. His companion, however, gazed back at the knight commander with humorless gray eyes. His drawn cowl and scarf revealed very little of the visage beneath.

The strangers, unmoving, seemed to be waiting for something. Sir Kathryn's mount fidgeted. Beneath his mantle, Sprael's hand eased over the hilt of his dagger.

Once the remainder of the Orkney knights drew to a stop, the youthful man spoke. "Tidings," he began in a jovial tone, his eyes locking onto Sprael. "Is this the excursion meant for Halodwyth Caverns?"

"Pray, who asks?" Sir Kathryn replied cautiously. "I fail to recognize the colors of your land."

"We hail from everywhere and nowhere," said the young man, his smile not wavering. "And our names are more important than our lands." He lifted a parchment of folded vellum, its front emblazoned with the stamp of Orkney. "Your Duke-Knight requested aid?"

Sir Kathryn cleared her throat, aggravated. "Sir Demetrius made mention of dispatches to mercenary brokers," she said. "Speak plain. Is your aim to join, or thwart?"

"Neither," he replied. "We aim to complete."

~ 8 ~

ODD ONE OUT

Sprael and Sir Kathryn did not see the harm in adding to their ranks. The strangers, dubbed by Sprael as Grins and Grunts, appeared capable enough. Certainly more than both Calliandra and Earon. At Sir Kathryn's behest, the strangers rode vanguard as she wished to maintain eyes upon them.

As the company crossed the road venturing toward Fenrirfang's archway entrance, Sprael noticed soldiers in Royal livery roving the ordinarily vacant battlements. Along the base of the structure workmen cleared invasive vines while behind them others busily applied mortar.

"Hey!" A scout shouted. "I hope you aren't looking to enter the Forest anytime soon!"

Sir Kathryn reined in her horse. "Why's that, friend?"

"Not five minutes ago the leaves along the hem were all shaking!" replied the scout. "Monsters passing by! And the Forest is none too happy!"

"You wager we should wait?" Sir Brentin, the knight riding beside Sir Kathryn, called out.

The scout fiddled with the visor of his helm. "I wager you should go back from where you came..." His eyes combed the company. "Orkney and Tintagil?" the man queried. "I don't know what your aims are, don't much care, but I recommend a drastic change of locale."

"Your candor is appreciated," said Sir Kathryn, "but we must enter." She urged her mount forward. "Creator keep your eyes sharp for the coming days."

"Likewise," replied the scout somberly. "And the same for your blades."

During the exchange between the knights and scouts, Grins and Grunts had continued onward apart from the company, and waited beneath the great stone archway at the mouth of Fenrirfang. The longbows that had been on their saddles were now strung and held ready, clasped in their fists.

"I can tell you boys don't mind riding vanguard," Sprael commented, "but I will take the lead from here on out."

"As you wish," replied Grunts with a nod.

Sprael shivered. This was the first time he had heard the man speak. *He sounds as though he's made of ice.*

"I'm not sure whether you heard or not." Sprael continued, "It seems that Fenrirfang is in a rather frantic state at the moment. Keep your blades and eyes at the ready." The squeak of Grunt's hand wraps impatiently strangling his longbow was ample assurance. "Perfect." Sprael nodded, turning his attention toward the opposite side of the archway where Earon and Calliandra had stopped to peer into the depths of the Forest. The knights of Orkney drew up beside them and looked expectantly at the ranger.

Sprael shrugged. "Shall we?"

***

It was Calliandra's first venture into Fenrirfang, and the first moments were exhilarating. The vivid descriptions she had read failed to give the Forest its proper due. The trees, on average, far exceeded the oldest ones in the gardens of the Sovereign Keep of Tintagil. And the oaks and elms and maples of those gardens were *centuries* old. Wherever she looked, fearless wildlife teemed among the vast carpets of vegetation. Unlike the skittish squirrels and hedgehogs that dwelt in the forests of the Realm, the Fenrirfang creatures appeared utterly unconcerned about the knights passing through.

"Oh! Is that a nockbogle?" Calliandra excitedly asked Sprael. The ranger's quick pace made fauna identification difficult. Her head swiveled back to see the short-statured creature scurry beneath a thick overhang of pillared fronds. Several more nockbogles tailed close behind. "It was, wasn't it? Oh my!"

"That or a gremlin," Sprael murmured distractedly.

"Gremlin appendages are brawnier and much less gangly," corrected Calliandra. "Though now that you mention it, the creatures do appear similar…"

The path they traversed was wide enough for a carriage to pass through, yet the company rode two riders abreast. The trees opposite one another reached across to create an awning of greens and browns. To her right, Calliandra could hear the eastward trickle of a tributary to the Patreka River. To her left, through the trees and beyond the Forest, the tamed lands of Camelot spanned. And further still, her home. Her mind drifted and she wondered what her mother and father were doing at that moment. Perhaps they knelt inside the family sepulcher, fervently offering prayers for their only daughter's safe return. Why they prayed there among the bones of her ancestors, Calliandra never knew, never dared ask.

Turning her face away from Tintagil, she looked far ahead, beneath the needles of persistent orange light that pierced the canopy of leaves. In the distance two unique shapes appeared, one struggling while the other seemingly provided aid.

"There's people!" said Calliandra, pointing straight ahead. "I see people on the path."

Sprael cleared his throat. "I'm aware," he said. "I've been able to both see and smell them for quite some time."

"Who are they?"

"They're a pair of victus," interjected Grins from behind them. Calliandra turned in time to see the man stowing a retractable spyglass. "One appears injured."

Sprael cocked his head. "Can you tell if they're armed?" he asked.

"Not unless you consider a make-shift crutch weaponry," replied Grins. "I'd bet my finest fletching that they're fleeing the impending war but were slowed by the injury."

Calliandra admired the man's use of alliteration. She also admired the way his plaited pigtails nestled beneath the cut of his heroic jaw line. "Finest fletching..." she mumbled, unaware of the concerned look this drew from Sprael.

It was a matter of moments before the party was close enough to hail the traveling victus. Sprael brought his mount to heel and raised an arm in salute. "Well met, friends," he called out. "How do you fare?"

"Not as well as we might have hoped," replied the victus who steadied his wounded friend.

Though Grins had identified them as victus, fur bearing monster-folk who looked like humans with the head of rats, Calliandra noted several contrasting features between the two creatures. Their furs were of different shades, the wounded victus a dark gray with traces of white dappling his exposed belly, but his companion's was shot all through with light silver. Also, the textural consistency of their fur was inconsistent, and their heads didn't... *match.*

"What has assailed you?" implored Sir Kathryn, bringing her horse to stand beside the ranger.

The silver victus lifted his long snout. "A Daeban was roused by the Forest."

Sir Kathryn's forehead wrinkled. "Daeban?" she questioned.

"A destructive spirit," clarified the wounded victus quickly. "We don't have time for lessons, my lady, so if you please, my companion and I must be on our way if we hope to join our clan by nightfall."

"Of course," said Sir Kathryn, abashed. "Sorry to trouble you."

The company parted, allowing the victus to pass through the center. As the pair came beside Grins, the young man leaned down to pass the silver victus a wineskin. The victus' face contorted into what Calliandra assumed was a smile. His companion was the first to drink, and after the silver victus threw back a slug, he moved to return the offering, but Grins refused with a shake of his head.

"Gramercy, my lord," said the silver victus, bowing with heartfelt gratitude. Gingerly he tucked the wineskin beneath his vest before shouldering his companion onward.

When the man swept his face back toward his companions, he caught Calliandra staring at him. He smiled at her and Calliandra's throat constricted with embarrassment. As the group continued on their way, she found herself, to her immense relief, riding beside Grunts. If she had ended up next to Grins, she feared that her babbling mouth would land her in a nest of awkwardness.

Sir Kathryn had assumed Calliandra's previous position beside Sprael, and behind them, Grins had joined Sir Madelyn. Behind the other knights, Earon rocked in his saddle, intermittently blowing his nose into a kerchief. The apprentice seemed to grow more distressed as they traveled.

"What's the matter with the lad?" Grins quietly asked Sir Madelyn. "He doesn't seem to enjoy our company."

"That is Earon Lockwhistle," replied Sir Madelyn. "Our born-Mage apprentice. For the longest time Sir Demetrius and his council forbade his joining, but something changed, and the poor lad was mandated to come along." She leaned toward Grins. "I do not think they arrived at this conclusion easily, but our Duke-Knight believes the fate of the Kingdom requires our success."

"What do you believe?"

"I believe that Demetrius was so thoroughly vexed by Vaskar's refusal that he decided to throw his best offerings into the Handsome Death Caverns," replied Sir Madelyn candidly. "And he can now only pray that we come back with that magical feather."

Grins shook his head. "That's pretty harsh, forcing the lad to be a part of this. But that's not what I meant. Do you believe the fate of the Kingdom truly rests on us?"

Sir Madelyn stared blankly for several moments. "I must believe such things," she replied at length. "If I do not, then my heart may flag when it must hold fast. So I must oblige you with a resounding *yes*."

A trumpeting nose blow issued from the rear of the column, concluding into a gurgling, damp whimper. Grins cast his eyes askance. "If it were up to me," he said, "I'd send the boy home. His mewling is likely to draw draconic attention."

"Halt! Halt!" Sprael barked suddenly, a fist upraised. "Dismount! Bring the horses to barricade!"

Maille scraped plate as the knights briskly alighted to the ground. They immediately guided their mounts into a ring formation around the company. The meaning of "horses to barricade" became quickly apparent to a momentarily confused Calliandra. She grabbed her mount by his bridle to steer him into position, but discovered that the octagonal barricade had already been completed.

"Bring that courser to ground!" demanded Sprael, his eyes wild. He had drawn his dagger and was sharpening it upon his whetstone.

Calliandra raised her arm so that the flat of her palm faced down. "Whoa, whoa," she repeated, motioning the horse to ease downward. Somehow her command registered, and the horse obediently lowered down onto his belly.

The knights, swords drawn, paced the area like it was a tower under siege. Grins and Grunts leaned their elbows upon the foremost horses, their eyes fixed to the road.

Sir Kathryn abruptly noticed Calliandra. "Sir Brentin," she called to the knight. "Protect the Scholar." Sir Brentin nodded his assent and hurried to Calliandra's side.

"What is it?!" Calliandra asked. "What's going on?"

"The ranger senses something," replied Sir Brentin. "More than likely a monster that had been tailing the rat men."

And we ambled right into it.

A hand gripped Calliandra's shoulder. "If my courser is slain, do you think I can go back to Orkney?" It was Earon.

"Fear does not suit a mage," Sir Brentin stated. "Why don't you ready a missile spell? We may have need of it."

"Of what element?" bleated Earon.

"Ice!" Sprael answered, pointing at the apprentice.

Earon bobbed his head, wiped the snot that had congealed over his lip. "I'll—I'll try!" The lad dropped to a knee and feverishly rifled through his satchel.

Calliandra turned to Sir Brentin. "Why ice?" she asked

"He aims to slow the monster's approach," replied Sir Brentin with surety. "Usually works pretty well."

No sooner had Sir Brentin offered his opinion, than one of the knights pointed upward. "Drake!" he shouted. "It's up that oak!"

Sure enough, between the branches and leaves, Calliandra saw a panther-sized lizard clutched to the trunk, slowly moving downward headfirst. If not for the severe weathering upon its scales, Calliandra would have believed it to be a juvenile wyvern. Pages of bestiary texts flipped through her mind, settling on a page she had reviewed not one day earlier.

"Jaculus!" she screamed, clutching Sir Brentin's vambrace. One very important fact regarding the jaculus burst in her mind, and she struggled to speak through the terror that gripped her.

A jaculus darted from underneath the horse opposite the oak, a step shy of where Grins stood. The knight who had been the first to raise the alarm straightened abruptly and released a tremulous shriek as the jaculus' head shot out from his abdomen. Calliandra clasped a hand over her mouth. The creature may have passed clean through the knight, had he not been wearing plate and maille. With terrific violence the jaculus writhed, tearing great hunks of flesh from the knight's back as it struggled to free itself. The knight's legs soon gave way and he dropped straight down to his knees, and Grins rushed forth and severed the jaculus' head from its body with a decisive chop.

"They hunt in groups!" Calliandra managed to shout, albeit too late.

The knights responded accordingly, casting glances to the ground. As one, they shifted their longswords, one hand to the hilt and the other halfway up the blade.

There was nothing to be done for the coughing, dying knight. The man, moaning in pain, was lying on his side, the jaculus' lodged corpse twitching its death throes. In an act of cold mercy, Grins knelt beside the quaking knight, and swiftly ended his suffering.

Another jaculus appeared. Wiser than the first, it opted to lash out from the ground. It managed to trip Sir Madelyn, drawing blood with its attack. She groaned. The jaculus feinted toward her again and hissed, lapping its tongue to the razor-edged tip of its nose horn.

"Mage!" shouted Sir Brentin, nudging Earon. "Pelt that beast with cold!"

In spite of the fear in his eyes, Earon rose. With hands bundled into fists, he took a step in the jaculus' direction, a greenish glow leaking between his fingers.

As if alerted by the sorcerous light, the jaculus raised its chest, appraising the lad. At that moment, a horse behind Calliandra screeched an otherworldly sound. Yet another jaculus had appeared, this one piercing clean through the flesh of the horse barricade. Earon whirled, opened his hand, and a pale bolt of light battered Sir Brentin's shoulder. The knight spun, brought a hand to his arm, and collapsed.

Sprael was the first to react to the second jaculus. He dodged the monster's initial leap and opened its belly with his dagger. The jaculus lay in a bed of entrails, claimed by death before the horse it had injured. The poor beast's tormented death shrieks caused the other horses to break and scatter, rendering the company fully exposed.

Meanwhile, Grins and Sir Kathryn had stilled a third jaculus. Sir Tyrol threatened yet another with a spear, and the one before Earon had not shifted its position. Calliandra counted five of the creatures: three dead, two yet breathing. The texts claimed that the jaculus lived in prides and their hunting packs consisted of no less than twelve. *Perhaps the archenlaif unrest had caused this pride's number to dwindle?*

She looked around the area, counting her companions as she had the monsters. While Sir Tyrol maintained a defensive stance, Sir Madelyn hobbled toward him. Sir Brentin, recently struck by Earon's spell, had yet to move. And Sir Clarence was still quite dead.

Where is Grunts? wondered Calliandra.

With an impassioned growl, Sir Tyrol recovered from a successful lunge. The jaculus momentarily writhed in pain, but recovered quickly and retreated. The knight had scored a wound on the beast's winged forelimb, preventing further flight. Guessing the jaculus' route, Sir Madelyn buried her blade into the beast's other forelimb as it tried to escape.

The monster's scream activated the last jaculus, and it gathered onto its haunches, aiming to leap for Sir Tyrol's back. Suddenly the beast uncoiled in a ragged slump, all life draining from its body. Across the way, the injured jaculus mimicked its kin's lifeless slump. It was as if a pair of invisible blades had sliced clean through them. Both jaculus heads slid from the base of their elongated necks, falling to the ground a moment before their bodies.

It was then that Calliandra noticed Grunts standing at the center of it all, both hands outstretched. *Is he a secret mage?!* she wondered in pure shock. From the beasts' severed heads, the grass parted in two separate courses toward Grunts, and she noticed the glint of steel wire returning beneath the man's vambraces. He had simultaneously severed the heads of the creatures using some sort of wrist-sprung steel chord.

"Creator keep us," intoned Sir Tyrol.

Beyond Grunt's back, a number of jaculus corpses littered the pathway, most having been torn asunder. The others had met their end by less obvious means, and right then Calliandra discovered the answer to what had become of the jaculus' pride.

He slew the rest, she thought, awestruck.

"Who—how?" Sir Madelyn squawked, noticing the jaculus corpses for the first time. The horse barrier had prevented sight of Grunts' activities. "That's impossible..."

"Precisely," remarked Sprael. "And the impossible is what you specialize in, am I right?" The laif cocked his head. "Vaskar of Rhionydd."

THE GREAT DEBATE

"I agree with Marius," began Calliandra, looking at the man formerly known to her as Grins. "It won't be long before all this fresh blood lures more monsters here. I believe it is in our best interest to move forward on foot." The notorious mercenary's reveal had been dampened by their dire reality, and this debate had carried on far longer than desired. It seemed—aside from monsters, wraiths, and archenlaives—time would ever be their foremost adversary.

Sir Tyrol's face looked like he had smelled something foul. "You mean to send our remaining horses back to the kingdom?" he scoffed. "Get serious."

"I agree with Tyrol," said Sir Kathryn. "We should—Creator forgive us—leave Clarence where he lies." She looked at Sir Madelyn who was seated out of earshot as Sprael wrapped her wounded ankle. "A jaculus scratch should be seen by a lampyr. If it should fester, she may lose the appendage, possibly her life. Not to mention the danger of draconic fever." She looked toward the knight propped against a tree adjacent to Madelyn. "And I fear brave Brentin may never wake from his slumber."

"What do you advise then?" asked Calliandra. Three of the horses in question unassumingly grazed upon summer vegetation. The others had yet to return, and in this forest, it seemed wise to assume the worst.

"I advise that Madelyn returns to the realm, placing Brentin across her saddle—"

"Nay!" interrupted Sir Tyrol. "We can't afford to lose a horse! I say we send Madelyn back on foot. We can fashion a limb for a crutch. If she sets out now, she'll meet aid before nightfall. Then we hide Brentin amongst the foliage as best we can and pray that he wakes before further harm befalls him." He batted away the glares he received from both Calliandra and his knight commander. "He knew the risks! And we need the horses if we're to finish what we started!"

Marius bounced a finger, tallying each unscathed member of the party. "So, that's three horses for seven people?" He blinked and worked his jaw. "If we continue onward, riding pillion, which is extremely ill-advised, how do we determine who walks?"

"Draw straws?" Sir Tyrol suggested, his eyebrows rising out of view within his helm. "Flip a farthing?"

"We could send the mage back with Madelyn?" offered Sir Kathryn.

Marius and Tyrol nodded agreement. Earon, who had been silent, twitched as if woken from sleep. "I'd like a chance to prove my worth," he said unexpectedly, looking over to Vaskar who was standing three paces distant, smoking his pipe and seeming entirely disinterested. The mercenary's arrival appeared to have bolstered the lad's resolve. "I don't mind walking."

"You've already proved your worth," said Sir Tyrol.

"But I think that—"

"The lad leaves." Sprael bit off Earon's protest. The laif had suddenly joined the group, steadying Sir Madelyn with his shoulder. "Along with the rest of you. There are three mounts, three provision allotments, and three riders."

"Whom do you mean by 'the rest of you'?" inquired Sir Kathryn.

"All save Vaskar, his apprentice, and me," replied Sprael resolutely. He rocked forward to rouse Sir Madelyn. The knight had dozed off while she stood. Her face was soaked in sweat and reflected a pallid gray, heralding the arrival of draconic fever. "It's simple math, my friends."

"You couldn't wait for this," Calliandra said scornfully, "you just couldn't wait for an excuse to send me back. You didn't need to wait long, for it came fifty steps into Fenrir-fang. Congratulations, laif!" The Scholar glared at Sprael. "You've known me for what, less than a week? My parents hardly brokered argument!"

Sprael gaped at her. "I just don't want you die," he whispered.

"I say we put it to a vote," declared Marius, lifting his hand. "All in favor of returning the dead and wounded on horseback, leaving the rest of us to hoof it, simply raise a hand."

Calliandra and Earon exchanged a look and raised their hands in unison.

The scowl on Sir Tyrol's face vanished once he realized Marius did not hold the majority. "All in favor of *our* sensible plan," he said, nudging Sir Kathryn, "raise your hand." The two knights of Orkney raised their hands, though Sir Kathryn raised hers with marked reluctance.

Sprael weighed the divide between the two quickly formed factions knowing his recommendation would receive no support. With more hesitation than Sir Kathryn had shown, he raised his hand and joined the knights.

Calliandra huffed, balling her hands into fists.

"That's three against three," stated Marius, eyes roaming to find Vaskar. "Vaskar, that makes you the deciding vote."

Boots shifted uncomfortably, awaiting the mercenary's determination.

In response, Vaskar pulled a draw from his pipe, withdrew the stem, and replaced it with a bronze whistle. The ensuing note seemed to permeate the boughs, the trunks, and the leaves. "If you're finished bickering," Vaskar said once the sound faded. "We must move. Now."

"What of the wounded?" asked Sir Tyrol. "What of the horses?"

"Strip them of provisions or mount them," replied Vaskar. "I care not."

"But, what of the wounded?"

"I already gave reply."

His statement applied to both, thought Calliandra. *He truly does not care.* The mercenary quickly gained ground and departed their company. A decision had to be made.

"Earon," began Calliandra, placing a hand to his shoulder, "take two of the horses. You can ride double with Madelyn while leading the other laden with Brentin and Clarence."

Earon slapped Calliandra's hand from his shoulder. "Why must it be me?" he said hotly. "Madelyn is fully able to make the trek on her own."

As if in reply, Sir Madelyn wretched, heaving dryly. Sprael had to support her full weight in order to prevent her collapse.

"We don't have the time for debate!" said Calliandra, watching Marius join Vaskar along the path ahead.

"It's a sound enough plan," agreed Sir Tyrol. "The vital provisions will be burdened upon the remaining mount."

Earon shook his head and crossed his arms.

"Come on lad," pleaded Sir Kathryn. "We are willingly entering a storm from which we may not return, and now that Vaskar of Rhionydd has joined, I daresay that even the greatest among us may no longer be necessary."

Earon glowered, watching Sir Tyrol moving supplies onto the back of a single courser. "Then why aren't you the one to ensure Madelyn and Brentin's return?" he argued.

"Because I swore an oath."

Her reply caused Earon to scowl. They all knew there was no point in trying to argue a knight from their vow. And as Calliandra started to worry that an ice missile was being readied for the knight commander's kneecaps, Vaskar spoke up from behind, his return having gone completely unnoticed.

"The mage leaves," he said. "We continue."

Earon broke into laughter as he moved toward the horses. He accepted the bridle from a bewildered Sir Tyrol while muttering under his breath. Whether he was enraged or enraptured was not initially clear, and Calliandra feared he was intoning incantations or conjuring a spiteful spell. Her fears abated when she finally managed to catch the words that he had been repeating over and over.

"Vaskar of Rhionydd called *me* a mage."

<h1 style="text-align:center">~ 10 ~</h1>

WHEN WALKS THE TREES

Even under threat of death, Sprael would be entirely unable to provide the name of the current Lord of Benwick. In truth, he could not even name five of the finest Royal Knights in Arthur's current employ. And if Arthur was not a fellow laif, he may even have struggled coming up with the King's first name. Humans and their quick-fleeting lives held little interest for the ranger. But there was one human's name that perked the laif's sharp ears if uttered, one name that never failed to capture his attention...

"Vaskar of Rhionydd," said the laif, formally addressing the mercenary striding next to him, unable to contain his excitement. "What sort of power does your little whistle have? Can it summon a kettle of wild gargoyles? Or perhaps it sends out a warning signal to the nearby monsters, advising they steer clear of your path?" He knew that the whistle must be something entirely beyond his comprehension.

"You may simply call me Vaskar," corrected the mercenary. "And all will be made apparent shortly."

"Oh, surprises!" said Sprael, unable to stop himself from speaking. "I do enjoy a good surprise."

After rounding a slight bend along the pathway, the laif could see the swishing of equine tails. "The Orkney horses!" exclaimed Sprael gleefully. He lunged behind Vaskar to punch Marius upon his shoulder. "Your mentor truly is a wonder!"

"He certainly has a way about him," Marius replied.

In the clearing, a large destrier roamed among the six surviving mounts. In the sunlight, the destrier's coat appeared a shade of olive but looked pale gray in the shadows. From his remarkably sinuous build, the shape of his muzzle, and how he twitched his ears, Sprael could tell that this beast was, without any doubt, laif-bred.

"I wondered if Salve would be making an appearance on this journey," remarked Marius, looking at the horse.

"Wonder no longer," said Vaskar humorlessly.

"That—that whistle you have!" sputtered Sprael. "That's a dragoon whistler! That stallion is a skin changer!" The laif pointed at the destrier.

"Steady now, friend," Marius said lightly "We have quite the trip ahead of us, and we can't have you swapping trousers every half hour."

Upon realizing that his finger was still aimed at Salve, the laif quickly lowered his arm. "It's just that—in all my years of ranging, I have come across merely two skin changers, well, three if you count Arthur's—"

"And you have lived quite a long time," commented Sir Tyrol as he shuffled past. "I count eight mounts for six riders." He stopped to adjust the cumbersome supply satchel upon his armoured shoulder. "I'd wager that great gray behemoth will serve as an excellent pack horse. And look, how perfect! He's not even wearing a saddle."

"Did you not hear what I said?" Sprael snapped at Sir Tyrol. "That beast is meant to slay dragons, not serve as our mule."

The knight had the good sense to nod, and stash his provisions across the back of a different horse.

Calliandra watched Vaskar offer an apple to Salve, her face aglow with awe. "I've read that the person who he imprinted on at birth is the only person he will permit to ride him! How many times has he transformed?" Calliandra asked Marius.

"Not sure," replied Marius. "I've never borne witness."

"It's said that they may only shift thrice, and upon the third —"

"Upon the third," Sprael interrupted, "doom hounds their remaining steps."

* * *

In much higher spirits, the newly mounted company continued onward, their clip determined by Salve, riding forefront with Sprael beside him. It was a rather fortunate arrangement, for if either detected any sort of monster, the company would be afforded plenty of time to react.

Calliandra turned to the knight riding beside her. "Sir Kathryn," she began, "your landsmen knight, Sir Clarence, he was a truly valiant man. He will be missed."

Sir Kathryn nodded. "I'd say he got his answer." The knight commander shifted in her saddle to grin at Sir Tyrol.

"To what question?" asked Calliandra.

"You attended our Duke-Knight's final summit," said Sir Kathryn as if that were answer enough.

Calliandra nodded, recalling the session. "But what question did he voice?"

"If a leaping jaculus could pierce clean through three men," Sir Tyrol replied. "Ironic, I'd call that." The Orkney knights shared a laugh that Calliandra felt was in poor taste.

"What do you think, Tyrol?" Sir Kathryn queried. "You wager that Clarence's jaculus may have gotten two more with that leap? Perhaps if the beasty hadn't gotten itself all tangled in his maille?"

"Clarence was a scrawny brute, so I'd say aye," replied Sir Tyrol, "if the next in line were two skinny squires. Maybe if that jaculus had gathered better footing, it coulda gotten two more average-sized blokes. Now, just think if that lizard had lined up on big boy Brentin..." He hooted and slapped his mount's neck. "If it managed to avoid getting knotted in that lug's guts, I'd wager it may have passed through one more regular-sized man."

Sir Kathryn and Sir Tyrol raised wineskins that, until that moment, had gone beneath Calliandra's notice.

"There's your answer, you dolt." Sir Kathryn said to the heavens before bringing the wineskin to her mouth and taking a drink.

"Aye! Your answer is two," added Sir Tyrol, swiping at the string of crimson dribbling down his chin, "barring an ill-timed wind."

Sir Kathryn, cognizant of the Scholar's growing displeasure, leaned forward in her saddle. "Have you never lost a loved one, girl?"

Honestly, Calliandra had only seen pets to their grave. Three cats, and a bird named Smolly. Never a friend or loved one. "No," she replied.

"You believe us cold and callous?"

Calliandra maintained her honesty, nodding at the knight.

"I'll let you in on a secret." Sir Kathryn took another deep pull from her wineskin before stowing it beneath her mantle. "I'd rather spend the day in mourning. Deep in my soul, I want to weep. I want to grieve for his children now abandoned forever from their father's protection, his wife who will never again feel her husband's touch." The knight gave a wry smile that puckered the scar on her cheek. "But we are rarely afforded the privilege of such a holiday."

Calliandra straightened in her saddle. "I'm sorry," she said.

"You are not required to be sorry," said Sir Kathryn. "Think nothing more of it."

Marius, riding ahead of Calliandra, turned to offer her a heartening smile. She returned the gesture, glad to have been born a Scholar.

"It's odd though," Sir Kathryn mused, and Calliandra was glad for the distraction. "A warhorse such as Salve should struggle upon this terrain."

"Salve is no ordinary warhorse," Calliandra reminded her.

"I understand that, yet it remains odd to me." Sir Kathryn returned the wineskin to her mouth.

"Is this your first encounter with a creature like this?"

Sir Kathryn swallowed and shook her head. "Nay, I've ranged with laif breeds in days past, but none such as this."

"Well, this is Vaskar of Rhionydd you're now riding with," said Calliandra quietly. "I expect there to be many wonders in store for us."

Sir Kathryn smirked. "Wonders!" she barked, much louder than Calliandra felt was warranted. "Not sixty paces behind us I espied the last remnants of jaculus offal. 'Wonders' would be a term I'd allocate for a great many things, but what we have witnessed thus far? Horrors, girl! I believe, the word you are searching for is *horrors!*"

"Perhaps I misspoke."

"You suppose I should take comfort in knowing we travel with Vaskar of Rhionydd?" Sir Kathryn bunched her hands into fists, one tightly gripping her reins and the other her wineskin. "We travel with dishonorable sell-swords who cull, cut, and kill..." she paused, her mouth contorting with unexpected rage, "for coin," she spat.

Calliandra was stunned. She had been certain that all in the company had been gladdened by the mercenary's presence. She looked rearward to gleam Sir Tyrol's reaction. He met her eyes and lifted a hand, gesturing in a way that conveyed *she's had a bit too much wine.* Evidently he did not share his knight commander's sentiments.

Dissension such as this oft bodes ill, thought Calliandra. *Perhaps she is simply lashing out from the loss of her fellow knights?*

"Cravens, cut-throats, killers," Sir Kathryn went on as if listing her least favorite things. "Cowards, caitiffs from their heads down to the worms." She waved toward the riders before her. "Not an ounce of duty to split betwixt the pair." It seemed the last mouthful of wine had dulled the knight's manners. Calliandra was surprised, as ordinarily the effects of alcohol were fleeting within marked Warriors.

"Kathryn..." Sir Tyrol began, He was cut off by a great rumbling in the not-too-far distance that stalled every horse.

"What is that?" asked Sir Kathryn. "Is that thunder?"

Sir Tyrol shook his head. "Thunder has never set my horse shaking like this."

After several tense moments, the rumble lessened and dissipated. Every head in the company swiveled, scouring the landscape for the slightest movement. Seeing nothing, Calliandra breathed a sigh of relief before the rumble renewed.

Sprael wheeled toward the group. "Set them to spur!" he shouted. "The forest is in turmoil! We make for the Royal Clearing!" The laif sprang forward. "Stop for nothing!"

Calliandra surged forward with the others, questioning whether it was wise to ride straight toward the terrible reverberation. But the ranger had lived through several centuries of peril. *I must trust that he knows what he is doing,* she thought, as her horse maintained an impressive clip beside Sir Kathryn. Calliandra leaned forward in the saddle and squinted into the sharp breeze. *Laives believe Fenrirfang is a living entity with emotions, reactions, and a... heartbeat!*

"Drevnigosts!" screamed Calliandra, her voice snatched by the wind. But Sir Kathryn had heard her cry and turned toward her with a puzzled look. "The sound!" the Scholar yelled. "They are the heartbeats of the forest! Drevnigosts! And they are stirring!"

The confusion only etched itself deeper into Sir Kathryn's stare.

"Ancient Guests!" clarified Calliandra as the sound continued to wax and wane. "We have nothing to fear from them! They won't harm us!" Calliandra smiled toward Sprael in admiration. The laif had clearly recognized the sound and had immediately known that the fallout from their upheaval would be unpredictable.

Hastening for the Royal Clearing was the perfect call!

Briefly closing her eyes, Calliandra envisioned a coal-drawn depiction of a Drevnigost. *Never in my life did I believe that I would witness such a creature in the flesh... or... bark.* Many Scholars from long ago had also ventured into the wilds and had famously lost their lives for their work. In fact, a number of Camelot's most revered texts had been exhumed from the skeletons of such brave Scholars. Calliandra wondered whether she was of a similar caliber, and if the passage of her life would end violently in the pursuit of learning.

Further ahead, a veritable junk drawer of four-legged creatures spilled across the roadway, interrupting Calliandra's morbid thoughts. Raccoon, badger, opossum, deer, all travelling together as if family. The youngest among their ranks moved with their ears flush to their skulls.

To Calliandra's tremendous worry, Salve and Sprael did not ease their pace. Sprael nearly clipped the backside of a badger that had lunged to its belly. Beside him, Vaskar stormed over a clutch of juvenile mink, somehow without casualty. And to Calliandra's immense surprise, Vaskar slowed his mount and allowed the stragglers to cross un-scathed.

Although the slowdown had been momentary, it had garnered Sprael's notice. Craning his head backward, the laif glared at the group. "Stop for nothing!" he shouted.

Their furious ride for the Clearing continued without further incident. When they reached their destination a few hours before dusk, Calliandra immediately looked for the tributary she knew was in the northeastern portion of the Clearing. As she led her horse toward the babble of fresh water, she heard the unearthly sound of Drevnigosts dragging their feet far off to the west.

Maybe some other day I'll see an Ancient Guest in the wild, she mused, experiencing a touch of despondency. A dramatic snapping in the taller tree boughs stopped her short. Looking upward, she caught the white underbelly of a griffin mid-flight, a juvenile soaring uneasily behind. Long after the monsters had fled her sight, Calliandra remained spellbound, staring beyond the trees.

Marius passed by, leading his horse to the water. "You sure you're ready for this?" he asked. "Whenever you see any monsters, your eyes fill with such delight, there's hardly any room for malice."

Calliandra blinked rapidly at him. "Why must I hold malice in my eyes?"

"There will come a time when it's either you or the monster," Marius replied gravely, looking in the direction of the griffin's flight. "And while you're busy swooning over the regal beauty of a griffin's plumage, the beast has already finished plucking the chords of your grave song."

"That hardly seems plausible," Calliandra scoffed, though her fingers traced her throat seemingly of their own accord. "If that time comes, then I will rely on my wits." She glanced at the dagger secured to Marius' chest. "And what is near at hand."

Marius withdrew the dagger. "*When* the time comes," he said, offering the handle to the Scholar.

"My thanks," she said. "But I was not implying..."

"You needn't imply," insisted Marius. "You should have been equipped from the start. And besides, I have plenty to spare."

Calliandra accepted the weapon, noting the simplistic design. There was not one fleck of ornamentation to be seen, not even a discernible maker's mark upon the rounded pommel. *This is not a tool meant for display.* She momentarily wondered about the number of monsters and men this blade had pierced. Then she thought of poor Sir Clarence, and with a shudder, realized this was the very same dagger that had seen his end.

"When this quest has ended, I shall return it to you, Sir Marius," Calliandra promised before turning to her horse.

~ 11 ~

OF LAMPYRS AND
WEREWOLVES

Dusk fell upon the Royal Clearing, and Calliandra and Marius hurried to arrange a fire while the two remaining Orkney knights prepared the evening's meal.

"Are they a support garrison, you think?" Marius asked Sir Kathryn, gazing off toward an encampment just beyond the northern outskirts of the Clearing. The tents had gone beneath their notice until Sprael had pointed them out.

The knight commander paused her stirring to shrug. Though she openly disfavored the mercenaries, she could not deny the utility of a cutthroat by her side when darkness gathered in the wilds.

"They do not fly pennants to signify their allegiance," commented Sir Tyrol, seated upon the ground. Casually he dropped a whole carrot into the pot. "I'll say the laif is certainly taking his time with his greetings."

"Aye," agreed Marius. "Wonder what's taking him so long?"

Sir Tyrol folded the kerchief he had been dicing ingredients upon and tipped the crumbs into the stew. "I haven't heard any screams," he said, "so I'd say the meeting has yet to turn hostile."

"What makes you believe it could turn hostile?" asked Calliandra, brushing particles of dried sphagnum from her fingers after applying tinder to the base of the tented logs. "Not everything results in conflict."

Sir Tyrol folded his arms and leaned against the stump at his back. "True," he said, working his jaw. "But I've found it's often best to expect the worst."

"Especially when the strangers have not made their loyalties apparent," added Sir Kathryn pointedly. There was no mistaking the target of her jab.

Marius gasped, good-naturedly. "Sir Kathryn, you wound me!" he said, clutching his chest. "I'll have you know my loyalties are many."

"Name one," said Sir Kathryn. "And don't say coin or I'll upend this pot on your head." She chuckled, concluding with an abrupt snort. "Speak true, sellsword."

Marius grimaced in a way that conveyed he had definitely been about to say *"coin,"* but fortunately for him, Sprael returned.

"Surely our friend Marius is loyal to his mentor," the laif commented. Marius briefly grimaced as if about to refute the claim before his mouth genially shifted into a smile. "Speaking of which," continued Sprael, gazing out into the gloom that gathered beneath the tree line, "where is the intrepid Vaskar? I have news to share."

"Pertaining to yonder encampment, I assume?" said Sir Kathryn.

With both arms behind his back, Sprael nodded. "That it does, milady." Though he gave reply to the knight, his eyes were locked on Calliandra. "Does anyone here have any wounds that they wish treated?"

Sir Tyrol murmured about an ache behind his shoulder while Sir Kathryn and Marius shrugged. Aside from travel soreness, Calliandra had no ailments worth mentioning. The emptiness of her stomach seemed a more pressing concern than anything else.

"Oh, perfect," said Sprael, his attention suddenly shifting somewhere above Calliandra's head. "Vaskar! Welcome."

The firelight brought the mercenary's eyes toward a softer shade of gray. Though his nose and mouth were concealed beneath his scarf, he had withdrawn his cowl, revealing long plaited hair that flowed over the front of his right shoulder. Calliandra could not help but stare as she wondered about the man's age and under which Mark he had been born.

Sprael looked away from the mercenary and clapped his hands. "I have just come upon a tidbit of fortunate news," he announced, rolling upward onto the balls of his feet. "The tents just beyond the Clearing are inhabited by a lampyr and four born Healers making their way to

Lhaewyn's Fount. Seeing as they travel in our same direction, I proposed that we join parties. What say you?"

Sir Kathryn was the first to respond. "Do you know this lampyr?"

"I know *of* this lampyr," replied Sprael, his smile unwavering. "Her name is Laekar." He spoke the name as if it would garner a reaction. He received a few reluctant coughs instead. "Come now, none of you have heard of Laekar, the lampyr that refused the post of Arthur's First Healer?" Sprael's smile wavered. "It wasn't *that* long ago..."

"We've never heard of the lass," expressed Sir Tyrol. "But we understand that she's infamous in certain circles."

Sprael snapped his attention away from the knight with a shake of his head. "Anyhow," he said, turning to Vaskar, "it's undeniable that traveling with a lampyr has many benefits."

"I'm fine with it," Sir Kathryn said. She sniffed the spoon she had lifted from the stew. "Needs more saffron..."

"Any objections," said Sprael quickly, suddenly seeming impatient. The laif was likely remembering the group's last attempt at a consensus. Thankfully, no one voiced further concern, so he set off for the encampment to relay the party's decision. As he left, Calliandra noticed Marius glance suspiciously at his mentor, but the elder mercenary did not seem to take notice.

The sun made its final descent, and Sir Kathryn added several more ingredients to the stew before Sprael returned to the fire with three figures in tow.

"Smells wonderful!" exclaimed a deep feminine voice. The figures were beyond the fire's influence, and Calliandra could only make out vague shapes. She imagined the voice belonged to the more brick-shaped of the three; stocky, sturdy, a woman liable to laugh off a sucker punch to the jaw. When the woman spoke again, her features were highlighted, clearly visible. "I hope there's enough for all of us."

With a start, Calliandra realized that her assumption had been way off for the deep female voice belonged to a comely human woman, no older than thirty winters. Not a single blemish marred her lovely visage. *I can't seem to find a wrinkle,* thought Calliandra. *It seems this lady's face has never once met a scowl!*

"There's plenty," replied Sir Kathryn. "I oft struggle with portion sizes. It's a weakness of mine."

"It's not a weakness tonight, friend," commented a female laif in tarnished armour, mainly comprised of green leather. "Allow me to introduce myself and my companions." She formally placed one palm to her chest. "My name is Laekar and this is Primula and Toskus. The others, Bryant and Tari, are seeing to our horses and our camp."

"Sprael told us that you're journeying to Lhaewyn's Fount," Sir Kathryn said as she filled a wooden bowl and passed it to Laekar. "Are all of your companions looking to become lampyrs?"

Laekar smiled, her fangs visible. "All of them, yes," she replied, handing the bowl to Toskus, the stocky man, who accepted it with relish and immediately began eating. "If base humans are transforming into werewolves for the realm, then why not born Healers? Lampyrs are tremendously useful during such times."

"Arguably more so than werewolves," added Marius with a smirk.

"Werewolves serve a purpose," said Laekar dryly. She seemed to size up both the mercenary and his words. "But yes, I do believe that an army of lampyrs would be a tremendous force." She went on to explain further the benefits and drawbacks of such an army.

Afterward they conversed on several subjects while Sir Kathryn readily doled more portions of her stew, overjoyed at the reception her cooking received. It was not long before the remaining Healers—Bryant and Tari—joined the fire and happily accepted bowls of their own. Everyone, at this point, had requested second helpings, save for Laekar, who had yet to dip her spoon.

"I can't help but notice that you're all humans," said Sir Kathryn, her eyes hardening on Laekar. "This does not concern you?"

Primula released a throaty laugh. "Not at all," she answered. "Each one of us is prepared to lay down our lives for Camelot."

Seeming of one mind, the Healers nodded. "For Camelot," they said in unison.

"The odds of a human surviving the conversion is rather slim," pressed Sir Kathryn. "Born Healers are given an inarguable leg-up, but the fact remains; none of you may survive."

"Or half may survive," said Laekar. "Or none. Or all."

"Answer truthfully." Sir Kathryn straightened her posture. "Each of you is here by your own cognizance? There is nothing forcing you to sacrifice yourselves?" While she spoke, Sir Tyrol surreptitiously reached for his arming sword. "No entity holds an unseemly weight over your heads?" she concluded, securing her full attention onto Laekar.

The following moment may have stretched for an eternity.

Then Primula rasped another laugh.

If only her voice matched the grace of her appearance...

"I assure you good knight, though your intentions are well-met," began Primula, "we have all made this decision of our own accord. No one has placed a blade to my throat, and there is no coercion at play." She shook her head with an intensity reserved for zealots. "Neither have any one of us accepted coin for what we endeavor. Not even our esteemed guide."

Calliandra found Primula's intensity rather off-putting.

"How admirable," Marius spoke with adoration. Apparently *he* did not find her demeanor unpleasant. "If you survive the slaying of your shadow, what are your plans afterward?" He absentmindedly spun the tip of his dagger into his forefinger, a habit Calliandra had noticed when he had asked her more personal questions.

"I'll be accepting service in Garlot," replied Toskus, much to Marius' disinterest. "The good Duke has assured me that I will find immediate employ amongst the foremost of his ranks. The entire realm knows that the knights of Garlot will be in the thick of the scrum, once battle is met. I even have it on good authority that Sir Seyfried herself once mentioned me by name."

"How neat." Marius turned his gaze back toward Primula, keen on hearing her plans.

"My uncle is a knight of Ghore," said Bryant, the same moment Primula opened her mouth.

"Is he now?" Marius sighed, pressing his lips thin.

Bryant nodded, oblivious of Marius' disdain. "That he is, sir. And he has promised me a place at Sir Ladane's table upon my return. And that should be what?" He looked toward Laekar. "Less than a week's time?"

Laekar smiled her approval, though her eyes betrayed a hint of sadness. Then Tari began to give account of her plans, should she survive, and that was more than Marius seemed able to handle.

"How fanciful."

Marius rose abruptly and brushed his hands upon his trousers. He met Primula's eyes and tilted his head sharply to the side.

While Tari continued her story, Calliandra keyed in on the hushed conversation that transpired between Marius and Primula.

"May we speak in private?"

From the corner of her vision Calliandra watched Primula's deep-seated grin spreading wider. *"Nothing would please me more."*

Soon the pair was lost to Calliandra's sight, lost to the darkness.

Sprael recognized the symptoms of jealousy at play upon Calliandra's face as the Scholar watched the handsome mercenary and the pretty Healer traipse off together into the night.

"Calliandra," said the laif. He received a glum look in return. "Would you like more stew?"

She cast her eyes downward and nodded.

Sprael looked to Kathryn, but the knight shook her head, displayed an empty serving ladle. "Sorry, that's all I prepared."

"The girl can have mine," offered Laekar, passing her bowl to Toskus. The Healer gave the meaty gravy a wanton smile and passed it along with a sigh.

"Was the stew not to your liking?" Sir Kathryn asked Laekar.

Laekar appeared slightly abashed by the remark. "It smelled exquisite," she confessed. "But I fear the meal contained onion and leek."

Understanding crept into the knight commander's eyes. "Foods related to garlic may kill a lampyr," she recalled aloud. "That means that all around this fire are immune to your healing arts!"

"For the span of a day," said Laekar in a placating tone. "Let us pray for mere sprains, cuts, blisters—"

"And not venom, dismemberment, and toxic boils," concluded Sprael with a laugh.

Laekar gave a dry chuckle. "This may be the last time the flavor of onion gathers on their tongues," she said.

Toskus heaved a ragged sigh, and flung a longing glance toward Calliandra's bowl. Instead of dipping her spoon, the Scholar dipped her chin, stretched the bowl toward the Healer. "Here," she said. "I should be preparing my cot anyhow, and it will be a joy to be free of this maille." She stood and smiled faintly into the flames. "Until the morning."

As the group returned her farewell, Toskus handed his newly gifted bowl to Sir Kathryn.

"It's cold," he said plainly. "Would you pour it back in your pot and grant it a bit of warmth?"

"My pleasure," replied Sir Kathryn. "I'm glad you enjoyed it so."

"It's wonderful."

It was then Sprael detected a foul scent in the air. Immediately he looked to Laekar, and from her expression, he knew she was aware. Both the ranger and lampyr shot to a stand.

"That stench," growled Laekar.

Sir Kathryn had only begun stirring the stew and looked blankly into the pot.

"I said my stew was cold," said Toskus frowning. "Not spoiled."

"She's not remarking on the condition of your vittles," said Sprael distractedly, noticing that Vaskar had departed their company at some point."

"The stink is gone," said Laekar.

With worried faces the Healers looked around the fire for further explanation. The knights sent their hands to sword.

"Greetings," a voice combed the gloom.

"And there it is again," said Sprael, nose wrinkled.

A mere ten steps shy the fire, four prismatic orbs hung, suspended in the darkness. Then two of the glowing elements split from the others, drew closer. "May we share your fire?" asked the same voice, the orbs becoming eyes. Then the fire's influence drenched the figure in light, revealed a rail of a woman garbed exclusively in the soiled tunic of a Royal knight. No other raiment clung to her earth-stained skin.

"State your purpose," demanded Sir Kathryn, sword in hand, stepping before the Healers. Her blade roiled orange in the firelight.

The second pair of glowing orbs stepped closer, revealed the eyes of another woman. "We are Royal knights of Camelot," she answered calmly. She was of a more muscular build and donned the same travelling garb as her companion. And like her companion, her exposed flesh was marbled in grime.

Both Sir Kathryn and Sir Tyrol refused to lower their swords.

"And what else..." began Sprael. His tone coaxed a grin from Laekar.

The leaner Royal knight abruptly turned her head, as if tracking something. "Our scent found us out, didn't it?" she drawled, focused her attention on her companion. "We'll need to score a more potent soap once we return to civilization."

"There isn't a stringent cleanser that can obscure the musk of lycanthrope," stated Laekar. One of the Healers inhaled a sharp breath, and the lampyr continued. "Now, as my companion has already politely asked, what is your purpose?"

With a face that reflected revelation, Sir Tyrol lowered his blade. "Hold a moment," he began. "Are you from the original Benwick pack? The pack that joined the battle at Fort Navarene?"

The more muscular Royal knight scratched the back of her head. "We are," she admitted casually. "I'm Sir Tawny and my friend here is Sir Sepia. Our alpha granted us leave, and we are on our way home to watch a tournament."

"We saw your fire," added Sir Sepia. "We thought we could share."

"So it's true what the missives claimed," said Sir Tyrol, sheathing his sword, and smiling at Sir Kathryn. "Arthur did indeed knight the lot of them for their valor at Fort Navarene." He gestured toward the stump he had been seated upon. "Please, please, come and warm yourselves. It would be an honor to share our fire with you."

The Royal knights selected stumps opposite one another. Sir Sepia extended her hands and rubbed them together, collecting warmth, meanwhile Sir Tawny displayed keen interest in Sir Kathryn's sword.

"I hope to have a blade of my own someday," said Sir Tawny, eyes fastened to the Orkney blade. She gestured for Sir Kathryn to pass her the weapon. "May I?"

"Sir Tawny," began Sir Kathryn hesitantly, "as a knight, should you not have been gifted a sword of your own?" With the blade at rest in her palms, Sir Kathryn offered her weapon to the werewolf knight.

Sir Tyrol scratched the underside of his chin. "Odd," he stated with his brow furrowed. "Certainly Arthur would have seen to that."

"Forgive me, I misspoke," amended Sir Tawny, lazily drawing her thumb across the blade's edge. "Truthfully, Arthur bestowed us swords along with our belts." She straightened her back. "I only meant that I hope to one day sport a *worthy blade*, such as—"

Toskus emitted a groan of satisfaction, presently supping his stew to its conclusion.

"This one," concluded Sir Tawny, grimly beholding the Healer.

"We owe you a debt of thanks," said Toskus, leaning back and patting his belly. The murderous gleam in Sir Tawny's eye had gone beneath the Healer's notice. "For it was your kind that we have drawn our inspiration from."

Tawny leaned forward as her features softened. "We're flattered," she said, flicking a glance at Sepia. "But, what has *my kind* inspired?" Her left eyebrow climbed midway up her forehead. "I'm most curious."

"Why, your tale of course," Toskus clarified, then suddenly appeared quite embarrassed. "Not the appendage at the end of your rump, of course! Forgive me! Rather your *story*, I mean to say. You know, a band of unmarked miscreants who endeavored to change their status." He adjusted his seat, burped into his fist. "My, my, that stew was excellent, anyhow... how should I phrase it?" After momentarily looking to his companions, the words sprung to his mind. "Your spirited initiative! Yes! In the face of an invading horde of archenlaives, you did not sit upon your hands. You drank a decoction that could have ended your lives! You risked everything to change your bodies in order to protect the realm—"

Sir Sepia released a yawn that brought the Healer short.

"It's truly remarkable," Toskus hurriedly concluded.

Sir Tawny returned Sir Kathryn's sword and folded her hands, tilted her head to the side, and thoughtfully appraised the Healer. "How kind of you," she remarked at length. "Now what is it that we have inspired in you, in particular?"

Toskus turned his neck toward Sir Tawny. "We are Healers," he replied, indicating his Mark.

"Making our way to Lhaewyn's Fount," added Bryant. "We are to become lampyrs."

Tari leaned forward and held her palms to the flames. "If we survive the process."

"That's the trick," said Sir Sepia, rising, admiring her fingernails.

"What is?" asked Toskus.

Before Sir Sepia clarified, Sir Tawny attacked.

YOURS BY BIRTHRIGHT

*G*lurk!

The noise awoke Calliandra from the beginnings of a pleasant dream. She bolted upright upon her bedroll.

The sounds of fast shifting feet and deep-throated grunts came from the fire. Before the flames, figures danced as shadows.

Toskus fell backward from his stump, clutching at his throat, where dark liquid poured freely.

An attack!

Terror flooded her veins, the same terror that froze her in place when that first jaculus had leapt.

Claws scraped upon steel plate. Sir Tyrol cursed. The firelight went out for a moment, before flaring back to life, after two shapes rolled through its center. One of the shapes looked to be Sprael, or perhaps it was Laekar, Calliandra couldn't tell. The other, doubtless, was a werewolf.

"This one is not a Healer," rasped a voice from behind her bedroll.

With her hands concealed beneath her travel pillow, Calliandra's fingers constricted the haft of her dagger.

"How can you tell?" said another voice.

Calliandra rolled up onto an elbow and peered into the darkness.

"She smells *different,* you know?"

"My nose isn't as good as yours," said the second voice, suddenly lurching into the meager light. Calliandra flinched backward, kicked free of her blanket. On all fours, a dark colored werewolf slowly stalked toward her. Where his fur began and the night sky ended was impossible to tell. "You're right." Thick foamy saliva dripped from the corners of his mouth as he spoke. "She doesn't smell quite right."

"Do you think she'll taste the way she smells?" wondered the other werewolf, sidling into view.

More werewolves! thought Calliandra. Though she was out in the open, Calliandra knew she was cornered. She did not have the time to stand, and even if she were to rise, she certainly didn't have the time to run.

"I certainly hope so," said the dark werewolf, as if entranced. He was now over Calliandra's knees, staring down into her eyes. He flicked his tongue at the slaver dribbling from left side of his snout. "Like braised mushrooms…"

Calliandra and the werewolf were equally startled by the speed with which the Scholar buried her dagger into the upper portion of the werewolf's ribcage. Wailing, the werewolf swatted the dagger from Calliandra's grip, but not before she cranked it a solid half-turn. Fearing the beast's retaliation, she curled onto her side and shielded her face. But in place of wrath, the werewolf appeared deeply troubled. He rose on unsteady feet, held both hands to the wound, and staggered off into the night.

After several moments Calliandra reluctantly uncoiled her body. She had expected to be set upon by the dark werewolf's companion, but no such event took place. Then she heard the familiar scraping of dagger upon whetstone, and she knew exactly where the raspy werewolf had gone off to.

***

Sprael squared his shoulders. It was the tallest werewolf he had ever seen. Moments before, he had watched this werewolf's companion wander off to die elsewhere, nursing a mortal wound. The laif had aimed to rescue Calliandra, but it seemed this Scholar had teeth. Teeth comprised of *silver*, it seemed.

Tawny, Sepia, and these two, counted Sprael. *Four werewolves.* He shook his head. *I hope there aren't more on the outskirts.*

"Why do you defend them, laif?" rasped the tall werewolf, hunching his shoulders. "Why not side with the victors?"

Sprael settled his feet, arched an eyebrow. "And that would be?"

"Us, of course," replied the werewolf, gradually unbending his torso, rising to his full towering height. "The archenlaives, the true rulers. Humans are chattel. They always have been. Always will be." He glared down at Sprael, expecting a reply, but instead received a smile and further scraping of dagger to whetstone. "You are a laif. This world is yours by birthright."

The fight near the fire, at Sprael's back, continued to rage. He could hear Sir Kathryn breathing hard, defending the Healers, still at odds with Sepia. Faint moans upon the ground relayed the existence of survivors, none of which were lycan.

But what became of Laekar's fight with Tawny?

"A laif?" said Sprael. "That much is true. Though I'm a tad unsteady about this whole *'the world belongs to me'* racket. Feels to me more like—" Then the absence of a scent, and the renewal of another, carried by the night's breeze suddenly revealed a pressing detail. By the creases of worry spreading across the werewolf's face, it seemed that he too had detected the same scent.

The werewolf feinted a backward step, signaling retreat. But Sprael was not fooled, and as he sprang forward, he dropped his weight to his right, narrowly avoided the werewolf's sweeping hand. Though his dagger was not made up of silver, it was exceedingly sharp, and after he buried it above the werewolf's left hip, the beast faltered, fell to the ground. The laif concluded his sprint a dozen steps beyond, turned, and flipped his whetstone into his sword hand.

"I admire your courage," confessed Sprael. "If I were you, I would have fled, knowing what was coming for me."

"And that is why you will lose," seethed the werewolf, rolling onto his side to watch the laif approach. "In the end, you will always lose."

"I don't know what that means," said Sprael. As he was about to ask the plot behind their attack, Marius neared them with a hand buried in a fibrous sac.

The werewolf settled his head upon the grass. "When we first made our way from Navarene, there were six of us," he explained to no one in particular. "Six strong. I fear that I am the last."

Marius knelt, withdrew his fist from the sac. Glittery particles cascaded from the heel of his hand. "You are," he replied. "Have you anything to say for yourself?"

The werewolf gagged as if his throat had already been slit. "Last words?" he coughed, arched his back, and raised his chest to gather a proper breath. "The archenlaives' arrival is upon you, so if you aim to accomplish something, I suggest you do it... soon."

Sprael gestured for Marius to draw back. "How soon? When will the archenlaives march?"

"They've already been marching," replied the werewolf, his laugh scraping its way free. "You fools."

Sprael and Marius exchanged looks.

Maintaining his hand as far as he could from the werewolf, Marius spared the beast for a few moments more. A lethal dose of silver powder already coursed through the werewolf, and the end would arrive within a few breaths.

"I was born poor, unmarked, and struggled to exist," rasped the wolf. "Then I changed all that, became a werewolf, a knight..." He began to fade, and Sprael nudged him. "Then I was immediately *ordered* to stay at Navarene..." Another nudge was administered and the lights flooded into the werewolf's eyes as if he would live another hundred years. "A place," he finally answered, then offered his last words, "a place to call our own."

~ 13 ~

WHERE (OR WHEN)
DETERMINATION GETS YOU

Moments after death claimed the last of the werewolves, Calliandra, along with Sprael and Marius,
joined the aftermath of the fireside massacre. Toskus and
Tari had been slain, Primula was still gone, and they found
Laekar and Bryant alive, standing an arm's distance from
Sir Kathryn, who was in a most pitiable state, seated upon
the ground, rocking back and forth, cradling Sir Tyrol's
upper torso.

"She struck him from behind! Where's the honor in
that?!" lamented Sir Kathryn. For all the gore, the knights'
armour could hardly reflect the firelight. "She claimed
to be a Royal knight!" Spittle intermixed with tears flew
from her mouth. Suddenly her eyes snapped to Laekar as
if she had just noticed the laif. "Heal him!" Sir Kathryn
heaved Sir Tyrol upward. "By the Creator's gentle hands,
please heal him! He breathes!"

Laekar drew back, eyes downcast. "I cannot," she
replied.

"Of course," said Sir Kathryn, suddenly wilting. Her state of delirium dissipated, leaving behind a stern face glossed by sorrow. "He ate of my stew, and his wounds came from a werewolf."

"Both true," agreed Laekar. She clasped Sir Kathryn about the wrist and gave a gentle tug. "Come on, sir knight, to your feet. Your friend is already gazing upon the shores of Avalon. There is nothing more we can do for him."

Marius moved to aid the knight from her other side but found his kindness harshly rebuffed.

"I'll have none of your help, sellsword," snapped Sir Kathryn. The moment her heels assumed her full weight, she faltered and cursed. Calliandra, out of her element, rushed to the knight's side, and aided Laekar in guiding her to the nearest stump.

"You say there is nothing more we can do?" Sir Kathryn spoke to Laekar. The laif nodded as she unlaced the knight's left greave. "I disagree," she continued. "We can give him a proper burial."

Calliandra caught the sullen look that passed from Marius to Sprael.

"We cannot, milady." Sprael cleared his throat, glanced to Marius. "We haven't the luxury of time."

"As these bodies grow cold, the archenlaives march," added Marius as he gestured to the dead werewolves and Healers sprawled a few feet shy of his ankles. "A werewolf revealed as much, upon his dying breath."

Sir Kathryn growled. "How unfortunate." The pain in her voice was bolstered from the direct pressure Laekar applied to her wound. "Then I will dig it myself." The knight rose abruptly, and immediately regretted that impulse.

"You won't be digging anything," advised Laekar, guiding the knight back down to the stump. "That's a vicious werewolf slash you endured, and without treatment, you're liable to lose the entire limb."

"Or your life, for that matter," added Calliandra, then turning to Bryant, the sole surviving Healer of the fireside. "You should seek out Primula and gather your belongings and prepare to set off. Daybreak will be arriving shortly."

"Good idea," replied Bryant, before hesitating. "How do I know she's alive?"

Marius tapped Bryant's elbow, gesturing for him to follow. "She's alive," he assured the Healer, "I'll take you to her and lend you a hand."

Sprael caught the sneer Calliandra directed toward Marius' departure. "Shameful," she muttered, shaking her head.

Sprael glanced in Marius' direction and nodded.

Calliandra noticed. "I meant the manner in which these werewolves disguised themselves as Arthur's Royal knights," she said, feeling her face go crimson. "It's shameful, the way they did that." She wished she had better control of herself.

"They were not disguised. They were true Royal knights," corrected Sprael. "Knights who had abandoned their oaths." He then gestured for the Scholar to aid him in ferrying the dead Healers from the fire. Calliandra obliged, agreeing that Tari and Toskus deserved consideration.

"If only we had the time for a proper burial," remarked Calliandra as they returned to the fire.

Sprael nodded. "We haven't time for digging graves, but we have the time for compassion," he said.

By the time they returned to the fire, Laekar had already bared Sir Kathryn's leg for treatment, the wound now plain to see. "Do you believe it wise," the lampyr began, pointing a glance toward Sprael while she sifted through her healer's satchel, "to trust the word of a false werewolf?"

"Makes no difference to me either way," replied Sprael, peering at the gaping wound, then kindly directing a reassuring smile toward Sir Kathryn. "Whether his final act in this world was to spin a tale, or reveal a truth, makes little difference."

Calliandra narrowed her eyes. "How so?"

"The archenlaives are coming, of this I have no doubt." Sprael sat down, withdrew his dagger and whetstone, and began to scrape one to the other. "If the timetable is squeezed tighter, that means we must move faster."

"There is logic in your words," said Sir Kathryn. "But what hope have we that we will succeed? We have hardly cleared an inch on our map and most of our party has either been slain or sent home."

"Or are gravely wounded," remarked Laekar distractedly. Whatever she searched for seemed to elude her. She lifted her eyes to meet Sir Kathryn's. "You plan to continue this journey?"

Up until that point Sir Kathryn's lower lip had been inert. "I can ride with a wounded leg," she explained. She sighed, suddenly on the verge of tears. "I've ridden under worse conditions."

"Oh you'll be riding alright," said Laekar as she renewed her search. "Riding back to Orkney, if my vial of shadesgill honey doesn't make its appearance known soon."

Sir Kathryn glowered, her face a lesson in fell determination. There would be no way to dissuade her, even if she lost both legs, the knight would crawl to the Caverns. *But if there was another way...*

"Sprael," said Calliandra, interrupting the laif's endless scraping. "You and Laekar do not require sleep. Well, not much sleep." The sound of her name drew Laekar's curiosity. "Anyhow," Calliandra continued, "what's stopping you two from carrying on without us? You could make it to the karst and back in half the time!" A band of doubt appeared across Sprael's forehead, and Calliandra quickly followed her statement with, "I could even sketch a few ideas of what I believe the Kardowiff may look like!"

"Kardowiff?" murmured Laekar, seeming offended. But before Calliandra could address the lampyr, Sprael's eyed widened with concern.

"That won't do."

Calliandra whirled toward the gravel baritone of Vaskar. The bloodstained mercenary materialized beside Sir Kathryn, between his thumb and forefinger he offered a small vial with a pipette clinging to its stopper. The tincture inside somehow held its shape after Laekar took it into her hands.

"What is the honey mixed with?" asked Laekar, as her eyes betrayed awe. "Basilisk antivenin?"

While Vaskar nodded, Salve approached from behind, forlornly lowering his muzzle down toward Sir Tyrol's stilled body.

"How did you manage to procure basilisk..." The lampyr allowed her question to fade. She knew better than to expect this mercenary to reveal his sources. "Thank you, Vaskar," she said simply, "you have saved this knight's leg."

Then with unexpected strength, Vaskar heaved the corpse of Sir Tyrol, armour and all, up over Salve's flank. From her angle upon the stump, Sir Kathryn could not see what Vaskar had done, she merely heard the scraping of maille. Furiously she spun toward the sound, and immediately discovered that Sir Tyrol was no longer where she had last seen him. Had it not been for the grievousness of her wound, the knight would have bolted to her feet and confronted the mercenary.

"What are you doing?!" Sir Kathryn shouted at Vaskar.

The mercenary administered a shove to Sir Tyrol's rump, balancing his dead weight. Based upon previous disputes with Vaskar, it did not seem as though a reply would be forthcoming. The man owed her nothing. Try as she might, Calliandra could not find fault with his attitude. And honestly, she had yet to see him prove less than his reputation claimed.

"I won't have scum like you desecrate his body!" Sir Kathryn roiled with rage while Laekar drew back to protect the delicate healing vial. But before the knight attempted to rise, Vaskar was before her, a hand to her shoulder.

"The knight deserves proper burial."

Upon those simple words, the wrath drained from Sir Kathryn. "My," the knight muttered, her tongue rendered docile. "My thanks," she finally managed. It seemed her immense gratitude outshone her humiliation.

Vaskar turned away.

"Hold a moment!" Sprael shot to his feet, sheathed his dagger.

Vaskar dropped his chin, and reluctantly turned to face the laif.

"Once Kathryn's wounds are treated, we will be setting off," explained Sprael. "We haven't the time for digging holes."

"We only require one," said Vaskar. "And it has already been dug."

"One more thing! About what you said before!" Calliandra, not wishing to halt the mercenary again, spoke quickly. "Why won't the laives succeed, if they should leave without us?"

The corners of Vaskar's eyes wrinkled as if he were smiling beneath his scarf. Sparing a moment for each human and laif, he seemed to weigh their very existences. "Not enough bodies."

Laekar grunted in agreement, returned to the treatment of Sir Kathryn's leg.

"No!" Calliandra fought against her better instincts and pressed further. "That's not a good enough reason," she said, then turned to Sprael. "I mean, if time is what's important, then what better combination could one employ than a *ranger* and a *lampyr*..." She looked back to where Vaskar had been. "And he's already gone."

OF HEXES AND SHADOW

Finally, enough sunlight had filtered through the trees, granting the brightness Calliandra required to secure her mount. The laives had a better time of it, what with their night eyes and all. Both Sprael and Laekar had proven most helpful to everyone all throughout the night, save for the mercenaries who had refused their assistance. Without making a fuss about it, Calliandra had dismissed the laives when it came to the care of certain *items* that she wished to handle on her own. Though she trusted Sprael, which came as a shock to her upon the realization, her trust had boundaries.

"Just what is our ranger up to?" asked Bryant as he leaned in his saddle and peered toward the river. "And what are those figures at his feet? I can just barely make them out."

Save for Sprael, the entire party had eagerly congregated at the mouth of the heavily trafficked pathway that flowed toward the village of Lepaskalica. By a small thread of good fortune, the course to Halodwyth Caverns brushed against the Healer's route, and the decision to conjoin the parties made so much sense that it nearly went without saying.

"He is brokering a deal with certain residents," replied Laekar. She had only just returned from sending the spare horses back to Camelot. It seemed Sir Tyrol's mount had proven a most stubborn courser, dutifully plodding behind the lampyr, refusing to leave. "We have learned that the werewolves have discovered a means to mask their scent from greater distances," the laif explained with a tight smirk, drawing beside Calliandra. "And Sprael received the notion that employing scouts would be our best option to avoid further lycan incidents."

"Scouts?" questioned Calliandra.

Laekar chuckled into her collar before replying. "Goblins and gremlins."

Calliandra knew the ranger to be clever, but employing *goblins* for anything beyond pillaging an anthill seemed a far cry from reason.

"He claims to have put them to use in the past," explained Laekar, easily interpreting the uncertainty scrawled on Calliandra's face. "With positive results."

Despite her vast doubt, Calliandra shrugged.

"Mayhaps he has a pact with their clan?" offered Marius, joining the conversation uninvited. "But gremlins? I've never heard of their kind volunteering any similar help." He smiled at Calliandra despite the less than favorable expression she directed his way. "Sprael told me that you put my dagger to good use last night. Well done."

"I did," replied Calliandra reluctantly. "I had no idea that it contained silver."

"Lucky for you," said Marius, "most of my weapons are tinged in the stuff. Though it's a bit slower acting than the pure forged." He gazed off toward the pile of werewolf carcasses they had amassed overnight. "Still does the job." Then he reined his mount closer to Calliandra and lowered his voice. "I was hoping I could speak to you—"

"Everything is in order!" announced Sprael from a distance. "We ride hard for the first ward before the Downfall!" By the time he finished his statement, he had already mounted and spurred.

The company drove forward in a favorable rush. *Favorable*, for it made ignoring Marius effortless.

Less than a month prior, the armies of the realm had marched this same path they now rode. Nearly every duke, liege, and lord of Camelot had roused their forces to face the archenlaif threat and rescue Benwick's outnumbered force. The sheer number of supply wagons had created rivets that formed trails which were easy for the eyes to follow. Any sort of invading tree limb had been shorn; every sprouting sapling had been tossed aside, which had proven rather luxurious for the eight riders accustomed to ducking branches and side-stepping obstacles. Not only had the trees and brambles been cut down, the time it would take to reach the ward had also been severely hewn.

Thus far, the party had stopped to refresh their horses once, as their sense of urgency pressed them forward, limiting the time for idle chatter. Calliandra favored this more focused ride, finding the silence granted her the space to peer deeper into the scrolls of her mind. In truth, her time would have been better spent piecing together a better portrait of what a Kardowiff, or Nocnik, may resemble in the real world. But, intermittently, and without her permission, the figment of two young lovers sharing a midnight kiss would emerge along the outer margins of the parchment.

Then, to Calliandra's present aggravation, Sprael lifted his hand to signal the party's second rest. This interruption forced her to set aside her images. The two compelling birds of note were a blue-breasted thrush and a grouse with gold banding about the neck. Much of her research pointed toward a familial thread between the Kardowiff and those two breeds in particular. But she felt as though she were missing something...

"We can't be outpacing our scouts now, can we?" said Sprael as he strode past Calliandra. The Scholar's disapproval must have been more obvious than she intended.

The laif went on. "With their tiny little legs, we need to give the little fellows some room."

They had stopped along a rather severe bend in the road, which cut closer to the river than the previous path.

It seemed an intentional formation, granting a shorter walk for those seeking the water's refreshment.

From the moment Calliandra dropped from her mount, she knew Marius' eyes would be trained on her. So, with the furtive speed of an aged man suffering from weak bowel control, she assumed her horse's bridle and sped for the river. She heard Marius call out to her, but she ignored it, pressing on all the faster. He called again, a bit more frantic, and Calliandra continued onward. Then, a few steps later, her horse shied, pulling the reins from her hand.

Calliandra, now standing alone in a silent forest, feared to shuffle a fallen leaf. *What is happening?!* she thought as a sense of dread suddenly overwhelmed her. *What new danger will unearth itself now?* Her nerves hummed as she slowly craned her neck toward the sound of snapping twigs.

"Have you seen my mother?"

The voice nearly caused Calliandra's spine to launch from her body. She screamed in fright, bundled both hands to the dagger at her hip, finding neither hand adept for the task. In the distance she heard Marius and Sprael scream her name.

"She was at the river with everybody else."

Then to Calliandra's intense relief, she discovered the voice merely belonged to a victus child. It seemed the diminutive creature had been separated from her family, and while the Scholar pieced this together, the child revealed more of her tale. "I saw a really big frog and so I chased it, and when I turned around, my mother wasn't there anymore."

Lowering down, Calliandra took hold of the child's hand that was not busy swiping tears. "What's your name?"

After a few shudders, the child replied, "Flevekka, my lady."

"Nice to meet you, Flevekka. My name is Calliandra."

Faintly she heard Sprael shout her name, sounding even further than before, as if a great distance had been slowly spreading.

Flevekka bobbed her head. "Cally..." she murmured.

"That's right," said Calliandra, rising to gain better view of her surroundings. "Now from which direction did you come from?"

Suddenly, Laekar had Calliandra by the wrist. "You must not stray from us!" She sounded more frightened than angry.

Calliandra reclaimed her arm, stunned. But Flevekka had disappeared.

"Where—where?"

"I found her!" Laekar shouted.

"There was—there was a lost little victus girl," stammered Calliandra. "Where did she..." She wondered aloud, straying from the laif.

"The only lost little girl in these woods is you!" exclaimed Laekar, lunging and clasping the Scholar's wrist.

Running footsteps approached, ushering the arrival of Marius, Sprael, and Sir Kathryn. The way they sighed and sheathed their weapons all at the same time made it seem as though they had practiced it beforehand.

"Where was she?" Sprael sounded agitated. Several locks of loose hair were plastered across his forehead. "Never mind!" He must have realized how stupid his question sounded. "Let's return to the horses, we'll water them at a different bend."

"But, she was here only a moment ago," said Calliandra.

"Who was?" Marius asked.

"Flevekka," replied Calliandra. The child's face stayed in her mind. "She was lost and was looking for her mother."

"Calliandra," began Marius, "there is nobody here."

Sprael grew more impatient. "It's a byproduct of the Daeban!" he huffed, exasperated. "Their magic creates channels, or paths, for daemons and spirits! Humans must remain near a laif in the forest, otherwise they'll fall prey to these curses!"

"She seemed so sad and lonely..."

"The magic affects everybody differently," explained Laekar, now gently taking the Scholar's hand. "But this *Flevekka*? She was a daemon of some nature, make no mistake, for if she were real, she would not have disappeared upon my appearance."

As she followed Sprael back to the pathway, Laekar treading close behind, Calliandra cursed herself for not being up to date on such things.

Over the past several weeks she had been more focused on aviary lore and had admittedly allowed her knowledge of forest magics to fall by the wayside. Years ago, she had been advised to regard Fenrirfang as if it were alive, as if it were an entity that would react to threats.

"Do you need help getting into your stirrups?" inquired Marius, once they had returned.

Calliandra shook her head, feeling the magic still clouding her headspace, as if a few tendrils from the dae-mon's dream had yet to dissipate. As she rose into the saddle, her body felt out of synch with her thoughts, as though her soul lingered a moment behind her move-ments.

She recognized this as a symptom of a curse. *But which one?* she thought. *A twilight internment?* Calliandra shook her head at that, discovering that she found being cursed to be most unsettling. *I wonder if this is this what it feels like to be envenomed by a serpent?*

She wanted to shout, call for aid, but her jaw muscles felt as though they had been rendered into paste. Then beginning at the nape of her neck, spreading upward, an eldritch hand enveloped her head. Once the chitinous nails of the invisible limb grazed her forehead, her hear-ing became hampered. And right after that, the filtered daylight was slowly devoured, and faded to black.

***

Sprael rounded his courser to give the company one final look-see before setting off. The map ingrained in his mind told him that the next bend in the path was not far, a mere half league distant.

Everyone appears ready, he thought, smiling at Calliandra. *The further we are from this cursed area, the better.* The Scholar did not return his smile. Sprael found this only a little bit rude, but totally forgivable. *In truth, it has only been a few minutes since the lass communed with a daemon. That's enough to ruffle even the staunchest of feathers.* He reasoned this out as he rotated forward, raised a fist, signaled progress. *We should ride at an easier clip. The bend is not far, and this will also give the goblins more time—"*

"The girl is cursed," said Vaskar. The mercenary had yet to round his horse forward. "Some manner of binder's hex."

This chilled the laif's veins. Now that Vaskar mentioned it, he had felt as though there was something *off* with the Scholar.

"It may not reveal itself for days or weeks," said Sprael, refusing to look back at Calliandra. Unlike Vaskar, he did not wish to tip the daemon off. "We can deal with it later, after we discover just what it is exactly." The mercenary did not seem to be listening, and this irked the laif severely. Curses and hexes were delicate matters that required discernment and proper planning. Judging by what he had seen of Vaskar's work, the mercenary was not one for agonizing over scrolls. Calliandra had been in danger the moment she set foot inside Fenrirfang, but right now she was practically fumbling at the knocker that rested upon death's front gate. "Just shrug and circle your mount. Pretend like you were following a strafing bird or something."

"These daemons are restless—" And that was all Vaskar managed to say before he was proven true. What appeared as a dark mist rising from the Scholar's back quickly formed a shadow replica of its host. The moment it snapped its torso to full height, the shadow solidified, became an onyx, faceless doppel of Calliandra. In upright slumber, the real Calliandra remained seated upon her horse, a look of pure tranquility on her face, her mind gone.

A wave of panic struck the horses. The doppel whirled, hunched, preparing to leap. And before anyone had time for reaction, it pounced upon the nearest rider. In a flash of onyx and rage, the doppel's arms enwrapped Laekar, messily clearing the lampyr from her saddle. Upon the ground, Laekar rebounded to her feet, coming out of her roll with the doppel clinging to her ankles. At some point along her fall, a curved dagger had appeared in the lampyr's hand.

"Harm the daemon and the same harm will befall the girl!" cautioned Vaskar. "Contain it if you can!"

Accurate, thought Sprael. Restraint would be the best course of action. Perhaps the mercenary was not quite as impetuous as he seemed.

"Marius!" Vaskar garnered his apprentice's attention. "See the girl to Salve!"

Marius immediately bounded from his mount, sprinting for Calliandra's mount. Meanwhile, Laekar attempted to maintain the doppel's attention as Sir Kathryn hemmed the Healers, edged them further from the daemon.

Laekar feinted lunges and shouted base-level insults that may or may not have hit home. The doppel had no discernible face, which made determining such things impossible. Either way, it had worked, for Calliandra had been spirited safely away, and the Healers had been planted well beyond its striking distance.

Laekar feinted another stab, but by this time the doppel had grown accustomed to the lampyr's routine, and the latest feint did not elicit any sort of reaction.

The same moment the doppel set its feet and stood upright, Marius, having approached unnoticed from behind, encased the daemon in a fervent embrace. It became viscerally apparent that the doppel could not tolerate restraint, as it began writhing and shaking with terrible force.

"Grab its legs!" shouted Marius to the lampyr.

The doppel's skull then posited its third hardened jab to Marius' chin, causing his knees to finally give way. The doppel freed itself, surging toward Laekar, who darted back in a blur of controlled motion, instinctually riposting, and launching her dagger.

Sprael screamed.

The doppel did not even stagger as it accepted the lampyr's blade. Its hands snatched the hilt buried above its hip, tossed it aside. Blood did not flow, and the dagger fell to the ground unstained.

A second dagger, flung by Laekar, found its way to the daemon. This one aimed above its leading knee. Issuing from somewhere behind the lampyr, and less than a beat afterward, an arrow struck the daemon's left shoulder. These attacks, in rapid succession, caused Calliandra's doppel to falter at last.

Sprael arrived to see the doppel ensnared upon the ground, writhing against its bonds, a third arrow protruding.

Vaskar's whipcord, thought Sprael, defeated. *If only he had been faster.* Any desire to stand had been stripped by the sight of those horrid fletchings.

Marius offered a hand to the fallen Sprael. "On your feet," he said, grossly aware of the blood dribbling freely from his cracked lip. "The archer claims to know you, and he expresses his condolences." Then he tried his best to spin things into a more positive light. "And the lampyr claims that she can heal Calliandra's wounds before they claim her."

"Impossible," growled Sprael, now on his feet. "She ate of Kathryn's stew."

The verity in the statement trapped the breath in Marius' throat.

Then Sprael located the archer standing with Laekar. "Elshur," he growled, inclining his neck toward the ground.

"Yes, that's the name he used," stated Marius, then indicated the pathway over his shoulder. "Vaskar has beckoned Salve, and he should be returning anytime now."

"And where was he?" asked Sprael, unable to prevent the tremble coursing his lower lip. "Digging yet another grave?"

~ 15 ~

A BLOW FOR REDEMPTION

Salve carried the gravely wounded Scholar to the next bend, where the Healers had gone ahead to arrange a fire. They brought a kettle to boil. Laekar wagered midnight was the soonest her healing magics would work, so their sole task until then was to keep Calliandra alive.

After securing the doppel, Laekar had wisely advised they leave the daggers and arrows buried in its body. This turned out to be most fortuitous, for had they acted otherwise, the Scholar may have expired from sheer blood loss.

Kneeling over the unconscious Calliandra, with their backs to the fire, Vaskar and Laekar continued to work in silent synchronicity. Aside from the lampyr's foresight, the mercenary's cache of potions had proven to be a saving grace. In truth, without one or the other, there would have been no hope for the Scholar.

Bryant and Primula dutifully tended the fire while fetching Laekar or Vaskar's requests. Sir Kathryn and Elshur—the laif who had felled the doppel, had gone off to water the horses. Amidst it all, Sprael and Marius had been unable to move.

This is exactly what I feared, thought Sprael. *I wish I would have been a better persuader! And now here I am, helpless.*

A gentle tug drew his attention toward Marius. The mercenary jostled an upheld flask, inviting the laif to join. Sprael nodded and followed him a few strides from the fire.

"Poor patch of luck, eh?" said Marius sadly. He whispered, as though speaking louder would incite further harm.

"Aye," agreed Sprael, accepting the flask and bringing it to his mouth. Slowly he tilted his head back, allowed the liquid to run its own course. Throughout the centuries, at occasions such as these, he strove to appear a seasoned drinker. "I care for the lass a great deal." He coughed and croaked, punching his chest at the vicious syrup wasting his entrails.

Marius raised an eyebrow at the laif presently doubled over. "You don't say?"

"This is some good swill," muttered Sprael before returning upright.

Marius appeared gladdened by this diversion. "It's of my own make," he revealed, speaking louder. "A recipe that I've been tinkering with, going on three years now."

Sprael returned the flask to the mercenary. "It's perfect."

"Kind of you to say," said Marius before pulling a measured sip, careful to avoid the gash on his bottom lip. "What do you think of this daemon?" he asked, unfazed by the swill. "Should we bring it along? Perhaps some wise old sage at Lepaskalica may know how to expel it?"

Sprael scowled, looked off toward the doppel latched to a nearby elm. "Would we have any other choice?" Then, from the doppel, he raised his eyes to the sun directly overhead. "Midnight will not arrive soon." He sighed. "If she survives, and that's quite an *if*, how would we transport it? We can't carry it there, like we carried it earlier. The journey is too far."

"Easy," said Elshur, insinuating himself uninvited. The laif had happened by while guiding a horse to the river. "The same way you transport any sort of prisoner you intend to preserve en route."

"And that would be?" asked Sprael.

"Strapped to a litter dragged behind a horse."

Marius opened his mouth to reply but Sprael was quicker. "Out of the question," he said. "That would only place Calliandra in further peril."

Elshur shrugged, then continued his trek.

"Lots of help that one is," said Sprael darkly.

A grating coughing fit erupted close to the fire, near Calliandra.

Marius and Sprael glanced one to the other and darted for the sound. This was the first noise the Scholar had made in hours, and though ribbed and harsh, it was a sign of life. By the time they reached her, she was seated, leaned forward, her face toward the ground. Laekar patted and rubbed the girl's back, oscillating between the two actions. Vaskar aided the lampyr in steadying the girl, his eyes their usual grim, conveying nothing of Calliandra's present condition.

"What happened?" asked Marius. "Is she recovering?"

"She's burning molten, and I can feel her heart racing through her back," Laekar spoke to Vaskar, her voice edged with grief. "I've seen this from arrow wounds before."

"Her blood's been tainted," Vaskar noted. With one arm upon Calliandra, he scoured his satchel with the other.

Another coughing fit overtook the girl, and by the end, sounded more like muffled sobs. Her constitution was unprepared to fight against the trauma she had sustained.

Sprael's sorrow began to give way to hatred. "You're saying the arrows brought on this fever?"

Laekar spared a moment to look up and nod. She seemed as though she wanted to articulate further, but then Calliandra began to shudder and wretch, and whatever she had wanted to say was quickly abandoned.

Against the edge of a jutting stone, Vaskar began to pound the element he had withdrawn from his satchel with startling ferocity. The mercenary's sudden violence activated something within the laif, every reasonable thought in his head evacuated, and before he knew it he was halfway to the river.

Elshur was knee deep, a hand resting upon an Orkney mare that greedily slurped at the passing waters, when he noticed Sprael's approach. "I can hear the lass' cough from here," he said. "I was only telling Sir Kathryn here that if I— "

But that was all the laif could say before all the wind was taken from his lungs. He doubled over, his voice stolen as well. Sprael refused to remove his fist from the cavity just beneath Elshur's sternum.

"Your arrows poisoned her blood." Sprael finally drew a step back, allowing Elshur to collapse. The current nearly toppled the rest of him. "She's dying right now because of you."

Elshur raised a hand in surrender, and would have spoken, had he the wherewithal. By the time his lungs could take on a full breath, Sprael had long since departed.

Sprael met Marius along his return trek to Calliandra, his anger abated for the moment. The young mercenary looked beyond Sprael, toward the river, and easily calculated what had transpired.

"Did you kill him?" asked Marius.

"No," replied Sprael, "but there may still be time later."

"About that," began Marius, and tried to arrest Sprael's march with a hand to his wrist. The laif, unwilling to stop, only relented after the mercenary refused to relinquish his hold. "Vaskar claims that he has done all he can for her fever."

"Yes, and?" Sprael was wholly uninterested in hearing more predictions of doom.

Marius took a great breath, his shoulders rising and falling. "Just prepare yourself, is all."

Sprael may have appreciated Marius' honesty were he not ready to throttle the next person who looked at him the way the mercenary was. If only the sun would neglect its vanity and expedite its descent...

His mind flashed to another time, similar circumstances, the reason he favored the company of goblins over that of laives. Or humans. The reason for which he preferred solitude. Sure, he was an affable sort when business called for it, but beneath it all, he greatly preferred the folds of a shadowy alley to a well-lit promenade.

Prija. In Sprael's mind, the name dispersed as quickly as it had arrived. But it had stayed long enough for him to recall the face of his old friend. *Dear Prija.*

"Sprael."

The laif returned to the present, a present where another friend may soon be passing to the shores of Avalon.

"If you want to say your good-byes," Marius continued. "Now would be the time."

"Is there nothing more that can be done?"

Marius shook his head.

"I see."

Sprael abandoned the mercenary. Though the moment seemed ripe for a comforting embrace, he was not yet at the point of abandon. There would always be time for mourning. It was that brief window of rescue that never lasted.

Upon his return to the fire, Sprael found Laekar seated against the trunk of a maple, the Scholar's fever-stricken head at rest in her lap, her lower body entirely encased in blankets. In his absence, Calliandra's pallor had not changed, although her countenance appeared more at peace.

As someone who has accepted their fate.

"You were right," murmured Calliandra feebly.

At first Sprael was unsure as to whom she addressed for her eyes were focused elsewhere.

"Is there nothing more we can do?"

Calliandra mumbled feverishly, "Certain demise..."

Laekar, not one to sugarcoat, shook her head. "The blood poisoning will claim her within the hour."

Sprael looked to the sun and cursed.

"Can you not bite her yet?" Sprael found that he was on his knees. "Perhaps the leeks have seen their way out of her body?"

Once again Laekar shook her head.

"Why not?" pleaded Sprael.

"Instead of one dead traveler, you would have two." Marius spoke from behind Sprael. "You know this."

"Surely Vaskar of Rhionydd has some sort of trick for this," said Sprael. "Thus far he has slain a pride of jaculus and faced werewolves in the pitch of night."

"You have my mentor all wrong," explained Marius. "Vaskar is skilled in the *taking* of life. Curing a condition such as this is his opposite. Though these are the greatest lengths I've seen him take in the preservation of life."

"If not for that horrid soup!" spat Sprael. He gathered soil into his hands and squeezed. "If I had the—"

Calliandra stirred, her eyes finding focus. "Sprael." She reached for the laif. "I fear we may have been wrong."

Taking her hand into his, Sprael found it weak, almost lifeless.

"Wrong about what?"

"The Nocnik." Calliandra tried to sit up but failed. "The Nocnik may not even be avian." She seemed to wilt. The source of energy she had drawn from now depleted. "Do not expect..."

Sprael looked to Laekar. "Has she gone?!" he somehow managed to ask through a rather severe lump in his throat. "Has she..."

"She breathes," replied Laekar. "Albeit faintly. When she is cognizant, she has been in a haze."

"Is there something we can do to ease her passing?" asked Bryant. He and Primula had been quietly observing nearby, their tasks at an end.

Laekar smiled courteously, as if the lad had simply offered a cup of water. "She confided to me that she wishes to pass naturally." With that said, no one else dared speak. In truth, they could do ought else, save sit, and wait.

At length Calliandra's breathing became sparse, and Laekar softly noted aloud that the Scholar's heartbeat had faded.

Then a riot of color brushed passed Sprael. At his back, he heard Sir Kathryn shouting a desperate plea. Brusquely, Elshur had arrived beside Laekar, and plucked the Scholar from her shroud. Laekar had not the time for dissuasion, as the invader pressed the dead Scholar to the tree, her feet dangling several inches, and interred his fangs into the slope of her neck.

Sprael arrived to his feet. "Elshur!" he screamed. Elshur's response was that of puckered suction. It appeared he was much too busy to respond. The party could only watch in stunned silence.

While the lampyr drank of the Scholar's blood, what began as several intermittent convulsions, had now become uncontrollable spasms.

"That's enough!" shouted Laekar. She too had risen and stood just beyond arm's reach.

Fearing that further harm should befall Calliandra, Sprael and Laekar worked in hurried conjunction to free her. Once Elshur's mouth had been removed from Calliandra's neck, Marius swiftly clasped the lampyr about the chest, and dragged him from the tree. The lampyr continued his frightful shudders after he was laid upon the ground.

While Laekar eased Calliandra down, two rivulets of blood steadily trickled from her neck.

"She breathes!" shouted Marius, spraying an arc of crimson. At some point during the upheaval his bottom lip had been split anew. "And her color has returned!"

Laekar lifted her ear from the girl's chest and blinked at the mercenary in sheer disbelief. "Her heart races," she said, then placed her wrist to Calliandra's forehead. "She is now tepid... her fever has broken... never have I witnessed such a... such a..." she trailed off, levelling somber eyes toward Elshur.

"A rectification," supplied Sir Kathryn, and all heads turned her way. "'I shall rectify, I shall rectify'—that's what he claimed over and over as he ran up that hill." Her face passed to Sprael and she cleared her throat. "After your prompting."

"I had forgotten he was a lampyr," admitted Sprael. "I wanted him dead for what he had done." He cast his eyes in Elshur's direction, beheld the manner in which his tremors had lessened. Then he turned to Calliandra, and at that same moment, she opened her eyes, and he saw that all the vibrancy she had lost had now been restored. "He has indeed rectified."

OF BURDENS AND BASILISKS

Elshur lived. His essence clung by mere threads. Laekar believed that if a treatment for Elshur existed anywhere in this world, it would exist in Lepaskalica. So without sparing a thought for daylight, the party set off. The first ward was not far, and after its crossing, the remaining stretch to the village was free of any other magical barriers.

Calliandra was hale and ahorse before the others, and acted as though she had never been poisoned, nor possessed. In an unexpected turn, Vaskar had volunteered to share his saddle with the doppel, and no one had argued.

Sprael had never witnessed the effects of garlic on a lampyr. It had been expressed to him that it was extraordinarily unpleasant and would ultimately result in death. In stories regaled, the lampyrs had either crumbled to dust or exploded into fits of agony. Elshur seemed more the latter. It had been the better part of an hour since he had assumed Calliandra's poisons and his symptoms were not abating.

Several yards shy of the first ward, Sprael leapt from his mount. When he glanced back, the expression on Calliandra's face was easy to interpret. *Hurry please!*

For Elshur's selfless heroism, the Scholar wanted nothing more than to see him survive. But a laif's blood barter at the wards was not an event to rush. One misstep threatened a painful death for all.

With dagger drawn, he stood facing the invisible boundary line. From behind he heard a horse whicker, tread the earth impatiently. Now that he had begun the rite, he dared not look back, but presumed it was Calliandra's mount mimicking its rider's restlessness. Purposefully, morosely, Sprael took one step before the other, as if balanced upon a tight rope. Then one step shy the line, the laif traced his dagger across his palm, and squeezed. The blood flowed healthily, trickling down onto the earth, and satisfying the ancient magics that guarded this region of Fenrirfang.

After sparing a moment to ensure that the earth remained unchanged, and hobs were not pouring upward like an angry nest of hornets, Sprael whirled for his horse.

Laekar, still mounted, called out to Sprael. "Would you like your wound treated?"

"No time!" came the hurried reply. "Perhaps once we reach Lepaskalica!" Now in the saddle, the ranger turned to Calliandra. "We ride?"

Calliandra nodded ardently, her mouth an uncharacteristic solid line. "We ride," she replied.

At the base of the bluff that overlooked Irphen's Down-fall, the tracks left by Camelot's armies hooked a hard right. The heavy traffic had worn ruts where puddles of rainwater resided, even though not a drop of meaningful precipitation had fallen in days. In contrast to the erosion on the right of the crossroad, untouched patches of clover sprung from the leftward route. Nary a broken twig, nor a bent blade of grass could be seen upon the narrow path-way that eventually passed Lepaskalica.

From the crossroads, the trek was too arduous for horses, save for Salve. The company abandoned their mounts and quickly divvied the supplies accordingly. If they had the luxury of time, the good-byes would have been more heartfelt and meaningful. In truth, the mounts deserved better. On the day they had set off, Sir Kathryn had revealed to Sprael that all but one of the Orkney coursers had made this trek before, and would assuredly make it back home, when the time came. The laif found her words reassuring as he observed the horses disappear around a bend, treading their return home.

This final leg of their journey was difficult enough without the burdens they had accumulated: a lampyr on the brink of death and a doppel piggy-backed to Marius. The mercenaries had tossed a coin to determine who would wear the daemon as an accessory. Marius had lost.

The travelers shrugged their various satchels and sacks, preparing to renew the journey on foot. And not two steps from seeing the horses free, Sprael came to a halt, threading his gaze upward through the bluff's steep gradient. It seemed that whatever had drawn his focus had also drawn Vaskar's.

"Is something the matter?" inquired Calliandra after a few beats of silence had gone by.

Vaskar lowered his chin, looked at Sprael from the tops of his eyes. "Is there ever peace in your Forest?" he asked.

Sprael faced the company. "Follow behind me single file," he directed, his words dangled above a whisper. "Do not make any sudden movements, move casually, and keep your breathing steady." He then sent a look toward Marius that conveyed, *"Best of luck with that, mate."*

Marius grimaced, gave the load strap across his chest a firm tug, sealing the flailing doppel tight to his back. Thankfully the doppel did not own a voice, and its motion was all that Marius needed to mind.

The Healers attempted to whisper inconspicuously to one another but were brought silent by a pair of stern sideways glances from Laekar and Sir Kathryn. It seemed that the mercenaries and Sprael were the only members keyed in on what the new danger was that they faced.

With Elshur secured to his back, Salve trudged silently between Sprael and the others. Calliandra picked up a hurried gait, bypassed Salve and drew beside Sprael. This drew a hard disapproving look from the ranger.

"What is it?" she mouthed.

Frowning, Sprael pantomimed a slithering motion with his hand.

Calliandra blanched as understanding dawned on her—*basilisk!*

"Stay calm," Sprael silently over-pronounced. *"Behind us now."* He thumbed over his shoulder and shook his head. *"Not safe."*

Calliandra nodded slowly. Choosing her footsteps in careful increments, the Scholar took up behind Sprael, hunched forward.

Sprael cast an eye back, dipped it to Salve, then returned it to fore. The basilisk had been curled about the base of an elm and had showed no sign of their detection. But Sprael knew better than to relax—the moment you think you have gotten the better of a basilisk is the moment you are turned to stone.

For nearly a mile they maintained relative silence. And once Sprael sensed the danger had passed, he looked to Vaskar for assurance. The mercenary's eyes displayed neither agreement nor quarrel, which was, quite honestly, the best council Sprael could ask for.

The ranger called for a halt. "I believe we are safe to move with a faster clip," he advised. "And for the sake of Elshur, I propose we urge Salve to run ahead..." Sprael held for a moment, awaiting Vaskar's permission, and once a nod confirmed the mercenary's agreement, the laif went on. "I suggest we shed our contingency supplies, make ourselves as light as possible. If we press hard until nightfall, we should arrive at the village before midday tomorrow."

Before the laif had finished his explanation, the company had already begun alleviating their burdens. Vaskar approached Salve and whispered into his elongated ears, recognition simmered behind the beast's eyes. Then after a sharp nod and whinny, Salve departed.

"I would like to have gone with him," said Calliandra to Vaskar. "Ride pillion to ensure his safe travel and explain his predicament to the physicians."

Sprael assumed her statement would go unanswered.

"Neither are necessary," replied Vaskar, to Sprael's surprise.

"They aren't?" pressed Calliandra. Somehow she had achieved Vaskar's undivided attention.

"No."

"Because I am slight and frail?" The Scholar stepped toward the mercenary. "Because I am not a hardened soldier, or a trained knight?"

"Salve does not require any help ensuring the laif's course," explained Vaskar. "And the physicians will know exactly what they are up against."

Calliandra did not appear satisfied. "Is that all?"

Vaskar scratched his scarf at the chin. "I am loathe to grant distance between yourself and your doppel." He gestured toward his apprentice, the doppel still secured to his back. "I do not believe it wise, for your sake."

Sprael caught the brief look of concern that graced Marius' face. Fleeting as it was, the laif caught it all the same. *Later,* thought Sprael. *I'll have to ask about that flash of worry later. Once we have a spare moment.*

"And what do you fear?" said Calliandra persistently. "That the doppel should sprout wings, or grow horns and tusks?"

"I am not the Scholar here," said Vaskar, turning away. "You tell me."

"You fear the expansion of our tether will cause a rupture," Calliandra spoke to Vaskar's back, but suddenly her voice sounded as if she were speaking to herself alone. "A rupture that could lead to a disconnect, and if that should occur..."

If Vaskar held a consideration for pride and proving points, he would have glanced at Calliandra to offer a condescending wink. But he was not that sort of man.

Sprael briskly walked the column. The Healers were standing impatiently, waiting for the journey to commence anew. Their packs had been the lightest, and everything within had presumably been deemed necessary.

"Have you given thought to where you shall go after your trial at the Fount?" Sprael asked Primula, deciding a quick chat would see the wait diminish.

The Healer smirked. "I am unsure," she replied, swaying impassively. "Should Lhaewyn deem me worthy of the mantle, I will go wherever my King commands."

Sprael hazarded a smile. "Your King, eh?"

Primula's eyes were now pinned to the soil at her feet. "Yes," she replied. "Service to the Crown and Camelot is all that I desire. Should I lose my life in service to King Arthur, then I would consider my purpose complete."

Sprael could not detect a hint of deceit in the Healer's claim. And just as his interest in the conversation waxed, the company finished their disposals. Amongst the members in wait, Sir Kathryn stood out the most, her powerful frame now enclosed by her simple arming tunic. The knight had deemed it necessary to relinquish nearly all of her armour, save for her pauldrons and greaves. Even her helm had been abandoned.

Bold choice, thought Sprael, admiringly.

"I believe this to be the best course of action," explained Sir Kathryn as Sprael passed her on his way to the front of the column.

"Suit yourself," said Sprael, spinning around, walking backward to further address the knight. "Or, un-suit yourself. Whichever you prefer."

***

Calliandra now strode beside Sprael. She had caught up with him when the party had slowed to navigate a series of trees that had fallen across the path. With Salve no longer in the party, Sprael appeared to be on higher alert than before. While they clambered over the centuries-old trees, which was no simple feat, Sprael had dashed ahead to ensure that the trees were not a mechanism for a larger trap. Calliandra deduced, by the amount of degradation upon the bark and the heady smooth cap growth, that the trees had fallen years before Sir Demetrius had even con-ceived this errand.

"We'll go harder once we cross the next bend," relayed Sprael. "We should have renewed the jog after we crossed over those logs, but I think the Healers will appreciate this stroll for the time being."

Calliandra smiled. "How thoughtful of you," she said, her eyes falling on his cloth-wrapped hand. The crimson stain had only spread. "Speaking of *healing*, how is that wound faring? You needed to make such a deep cut to pro-duce so much blood, I take it?"

"I've diced my palms at so many wards that it's hardly a thought at all anymore."

"All the same," continued Calliandra. "Maybe Laekar can resolve it when we stop for the night." She scanned what she could perceive of the horizon through the vast polyphony of branches scraping one another overhead. "Which shouldn't be long."

"Aye, milady," Marius interjected from behind. "The sooner I am rid of your dark sister here, the better." Sweat had soaked the cloth beneath the mercenary's armour into an entirely different shade.

Of everyone, Marius held the best claim for complaint, though his recent admission had been his first. If Callian-dra were asked if she enjoyed the mercenary's torment just a little bit, she would assuredly lie with a resounding *no*. And every time Primula attempted to approach Mar-ius, and the doppel would suddenly go berserk, she would also be lying if she stated that this did not bring a pang of glee. Truthfully, the ire that Calliandra had built up against Marius had diminished. Perhaps being rendered lifeless for several moments may have worked to counteract the effects of her jealousy.

"Yes," she said, sparing a fleeting glance at Marius. "That would be a boon." Before the mercenary had a chance to respond, the Scholar returned her attention to Sprael. "There is something I wished to ask you." When she had been waist deep in the waters of death, she could not recall much, but she did recall a name that Sprael had intoned while clasping her hand.

"Go on," encouraged Sprael. "But best be quick about it. That bend will be arriving shortly."

Calliandra noticed Sprael's eyes had begun their furious sweeping patterns, which meant his focus would be divided. Maybe it would be best to trunk her query for a later time.

"Never mind," said Calliandra. "It'll keep for another time."

Sprael snorted, preoccupied. "Works for me."

~ 17 ~

A MIDNIGHT SCRAPE

"Are you certain?" said Sprael to the goblin scout. "You'd tell me if you were joking?" The creature had been bobbing her head, but with that question, the goblin slowed for just the fraction of a moment.

"We would never play jokes on you," replied the goblin while the beads of her eyes twinkled. "You're far too clever for fishy goblin games."

Sprael reached into his satchel for the goblin's second payment. "The basilisks are far behind, and we should be clear to reach Lepaskalica by midday tomorrow?" He dangled the bundle of besalto-beeswax candles just beyond the goblin's reach. "There will be more candles waiting for you at the village when that leg is complete." He relented to the goblin's grabbing fingers, dropped the candlesticks onto her outstretched arms.

"Thank you Sprael of the Gentle March," cooed the goblin. Her eyes flicked upward. "Thank you so, so much, but there is one more thing." Her eyes narrowed.

For a few moments the goblin did nothing but quail and tremble, and Sprael was unsure as to whether her conclusion would be forthcoming. "Go on," he encouraged. "I'm listening."

In a hurried flourish, the goblin clutched her candles tight to her chest, and wrestled the hood of her mantle over her pointed ears. "Be rid of that daemon," she squeaked. "The Forest is watching." She then scampered away, her tiny frame lost to the encroaching twilight.

What an odd thing to say, thought Sprael, rising to a stand and brushing pine needles from the base of his tunic. Through the veil of trees he could make out the orange-yellow spectrum of the party's fire. *When is the Forest not watching?*

The Healers had been the first onto their bedrolls, and Sprael could hear their steady breaths before he had entered the clearing. Marius, Sir Kathryn, and Laekar sat by the fire, their conversation apparently stalled. By the look on Sir Kathryn's face, Sprael's arrival had struck at a most awkward time.

"Don't mind me," said Sprael, folding his hands behind his back. "We're all friends here."

Discreetly from the side of her eyes, Laekar regarded Sprael. "The apprentice here was regaling us of a few concerns." She flipped the branchlet she had been toying with into the fire. "I'm for a walk." She rose and bid Marius and Sir Kathryn goodnight then strode in the direction of the pathway.

"What sort of concerns?" asked Sprael.

Marius' eyes lingered somewhere over the flames, deep in thought.

"If Laekar is for a walk," said Sir Kathryn, brushing her fingers as she stood. "Then I am for sleep." She turned to the mercenary. "You have given us quite *something* to mull over, but if you ever mean to reveal your thoughts again—and I mean no offense—I'd rather be elsewhere."

Sprael watched the knight depart toward the sleeping Healers, and it occurred to him that he did not know where Calliandra had decided to spend the night, nor Vaskar for that matter. Although the comings and goings of Vaskar were not something that Sprael would waste any time monitoring.

As he took up Sir Kathryn's vacated stump, he noticed Calliandra curled several feet from the fire.

"Not like it matters much," began Sprael, "and I only ask out of sheer curiosity, but would you know where your mentor has taken up for the night?"

Blinking as if coming out of a dream, Marius turned his face from the fire. "Near the doppel," he replied at length. "I have never seen him act the way he has been..." The mercenary spoke softly.

Perhaps this may have something to do with that look of worry I saw on his face earlier. "How so?" asked Sprael, striving to sound more concerned than intrigued.

"Well," began Marius, scratching at the side of his chin. "First off, in the past, the moment that doppel sprung, he would have put it down immediately. Consequences to anyone else would have been completely ignored. When he is on the hunt, he never spares time on anything. Like when he dug Tyrol's grave?" Marius sounded affronted. "What was that?" He paused, awaiting a response.

"I know, right? What was that?" said Sprael, shaking his head, echoing the offense in the mercenary's voice.

"Right." Marius nodded gravely, then restrained his tone to a whisper. "And Calliandra? She has questioned him on more than one occasion, and he has responded! He's never doused an ounce of concern on anyone like that before!" He lowered his head dejectedly. "I don't know what to make of it all!"

Sprael inched closer to the front edge of his stump. "So what is it that you're getting at exactly?"

"Perhaps I am overtired, overtaxed," lamented Marius. "Carrying that awful daemon on my back has taken its toll, I fear. I just can't help but feel skeptical."

"You're more than welcome to view things that way," said Sprael. "But all I see is Vaskar working to keep us alive."

"But it's more than that," groaned Marius. "When we first set off, Kathryn *hated* us—Vaskar and I—but now, she favors us as friends. Not because of anything that she did, not by any action of mine, but because of Vaskar. Throughout this journey he has gone out of his way to prove to everyone that he can be trusted."

"Digging Tyrol's grave," muttered Sprael. "Healing Kathryn's werewolf wound..."

"And that's the thing!" Marius pointed at the laif's chest, then glanced toward Calliandra in repose. "Vaskar is like a force of nature, one that acts with a solitary purpose."

Sprael nodded. "And exists without the care of others."

"And nature is a great many things, and should be respected, but upon the same token..." Marius trailed off as the flames re-drew his focus. He seemed beyond the point of exhaustion. "It simply cannot be trusted," he concluded, his head in his hands.

It was then that Sprael understood Sir Kathryn's reason for departing before the discussion had re-opened. As Orkney's paid ranger, he had taken Vaskar as nothing more than an asset, his actions not really worth a moment's worry. Come the morrow, they would see their journey's end—the Halodwyth Caverns—and he had Vaskar to thank for their expedience. But in all honesty, Marius knew his mentor better than anyone else in the company, perhaps better than anyone else alive.

"What do you propose then?" Sprael asked.

The mercenary turned bleary eyes toward the laif, his jaw slackened by fatigue. "I have no idea," came the reply.

"You should seek the comfort of a bedroll, my friend."

Marius clenched his fists, pressed them to his knees. "Don't call me that," he growled. "Haven't you understood my point? I'm not your friend." Rising unsteadily, Marius surveyed the moonlit grounds. "I'd slit your throat for coin."

"I don't believe that for a moment," Sprael asserted.

"Matters not," said Marius, swaying his steps toward a free patch of ground. "It matters not what you believe." Having foregone his bedroll, Marius stretched out on the grass and fell asleep with his mouth agape, his yawn never reaching its end.

As Sir Kathryn had aptly stated, Marius' words certainly gave the laif much to mull over. He sat alone by the fire contemplating the many things in this world worth fearing. Even sparing a thought for the Halodwyth Caverns was enough to freeze the blood in his veins. *No one returns from that place.*

Whether Vaskar of Rhionydd's drastic change in character was something to fear, Sprael knew not. Aside from his claims, Marius' demeanor alone was akin to the ringing of a village invasion bell. All of this only battered more questions against the top of the laif's mind.

Then his eyes shifted to the blanket-shrouded lump upon the ground. He could not deny his love for Calliandra. A protective love. More powerful than romance, so much more than a passing fancy. It was similar to the feeling a father holds for a daughter, or a brother for a sister. For the centuries that had passed before his eyes, he had only experienced this feeling with one other.

Prija...

The elders had a name for this bond, but try as he might in that moment, Sprael could not conjure the word. Then his thoughts swam to Prija.

Poor Prija. Sprael had first made his acquaintance upon one of the laif's rare return treks to the Gentle March. The lad was the only son of a Jatel, an honored human friend. As fate often intervenes, the Jatel fell ill and eventually passed away. Upon his deathbed the Jatel had expressed to Sprael, of all laives, that he wished for the laif to aid the boy's mother in raising their son. While Sprael had been shocked by the request, as time passed Sprael grew quite protective of Prija. He spent many hours with the boy, teaching him how to survive the wilds of Fenrirfang. As Prija was human, straying far from the Gentle March alone was strictly forbidden for his kind. Each morning, Sprael would hear the gentle rapping on his front door, well before the birds began their songs.

"Sprael, is that a nockbogle?"

"Sprael, how many eggs does a griffin lay?"

"Sprael, show me how you unstring that bow so fast!"

"Sprael, wait up!"

"Sprael, show me the world outside the Forest!"

The lad's voice reverberated, tormenting the laif.

"Sprael! Where are they taking me?!"

The tears arrived unbidden.

"Sprael! Help me! Why won't you help me?!"

"I can't," whispered Sprael, alone by the fire's dying embers. "I could not. I have failed both you and your father." He choked back tears. "If only I could make things right, my dear Prija." As he had sat by helplessly while Calliandra perished, he had sat by as Prija met his pitiful end. Calliandra's treachery lay within her own body, her very life essence acting as the executioner. For Prija, the treason occurred beyond his mortal body, and the laives responsible were then, and still now, powerful lords, beyond the reach of arrows and steel.

"That was so long ago, Prija," muttered Sprael. "Doubtful the cowards even recall your name."

A harsh rustle in the thicket at Sprael's back stirred the dead of night back to life. Then he heard a muffled shout constricted into a groan of anguish. Sprael was on his feet before he realized it, his dagger already scraping whetstone. Swift as he had ever moved, perhaps swifter, Sprael hurtled toward the sounds.

Two forms lay upon the ground, locked in struggle, the one atop the other landed a barrage of potent blows. The defender appeared unwilling to participate in the violence, covering his face with his arms, absorbing the clouts. The moment Sprael realized what he was a witness to, he slowed to a halt, relinquished his dagger and whetstone to the ground.

"Vaskar!" he shouted in disbelief.

The mercenary rolled his head toward the laif. "There is no way to subdue without harm!"

The doppel brought its hands together into a hammer fist and, with all its weight, slammed it down upon the side of Vaskar's head. The mercenary's head rebounded from the soil as he stoically accepted the blow.

"I fear further trauma to the Scholar!" shouted Vaskar.

Sprael scoured the area for a means to bind the doppel. "I fear further trauma to your cranium!" he declared, then an idea rose to his mind. "Use your whipcords!"

As the mercenary was readying a response, he was interrupted by another strike to his head. "Proximity!" he asserted, his eyes tightening as he winced into the pain. "The daemon is far too close!" Successfully he deflected the doppel's second wielded hammer fist, and suggested, "Draw its attention elsewhere!"

"But if we lose it!" protested Sprael. "We may not find it again!"

"It won't stray far from its tether!"

"Are you certain?"

"What else can we do? It's much too wild for containment!"

He has the truth of it, thought Sprael, *attempting to capture the doppel in its frantic state may break a few bones.* Out of options, and out of time, Sprael launched forward, lowered his shoulder, and removed the doppel from its perch. In a fevered entanglement of its own limbs, the doppel scrambled upon the ground then sprang to its feet.

For reasons unknown, the doppel merely stood calm before the laif, a dark spectre that held the perfect outline of Calliandra. Sprael feinted a lunge. "Run!" he shouted. "Get out of here!"

The doppel craned its faceless head, much like a confused hound.

"Get going!" Sprael feinted again. For a moment the doppel's attention shifted toward Vaskar's rise and appeared about to renew its attack. "No!" Sprael intercepted its course, and upon the laif's shout, the doppel seemed to shrink. Then, unexpectedly cowed, the doppel stumbled off, dithering into the darkened creases of the forest.

"That daemon will be a shadow that we must monitor," stated Vaskar, straightening a spaulder. "Better that it's loose, than dead."

Even as he strained his night eyes as best he could, Sprael somehow lost track of the doppel. Then he looked to the tree that had been the doppel's tether. "How did it manage to free itself?" he asked, observing the restraints scattered asunder.

Vaskar shrugged. "It appears to have been aided," he said, admiring the rending points upon the cord. "I was awoken by the pummeling, not the freeing."

"But who would want to free the doppel?"

"That is one matter to ponder," stated Vaskar as he gathered the bonds, repurposed them as a trip wire should the doppel make a return. "The other is the debt that I have now accrued."

Sprael peered up from the filaments of tree bark he had been closely inspecting. "What debt?"

"I do not live by many codes," explained Vaskar. "But there is one that I adhere to, and only once before has someone achieved what you have done this night. You have rescued me, and I now owe you a favor." The ever so slight tilt of the mercenary's head conveyed an over-abundance of sincerity. "Any favor."

"And whom, may I ask, was the first person to have called in your first favor?" Sprael was curious as to the lengths Vaskar was willing to leap.

"Marius' father," replied Vaskar, now reclined upon his bedroll. The doppel's onslaught had, for the most part, been bestowed upon his armour, but the few solid strikes to the mercenary's head seemed to have been forgotten. "Pay your request proper heed, then we shall talk."

Sprael nodded. "We shall," he said, suddenly feeling as an intruder. He turned away and retrieved his dagger and whetstone. It seemed that Vaskar's *favors* were not re-stricted to murder alone. There were a number of secrets that Sprael wished Vaskar to reveal. Who were his par-ents? Was he actually from Rhionydd? Had he ever kissed a girl? Or perhaps he would call upon him to provide help with a few mundane chores. How funny would it be to re-quest *the* Vaskar of Rhionydd repair the wobble of a table, or whitewash a picket fence, or serve ale at a tavern. Hilar-ious as those options may have seemed in the moment, as Sprael plunked a log onto the fire, his thoughts returned to Prija.

Nay, he thought, warming his hands at the renewed flames. *My favor shall be of a more serious nature.*

After relaying the tale of the doppel's freedom to Laekar, Sprael remained on high alert throughout the night. Two sets of laif eyes were certainly better than one, but still, a daemon of this caliber was not one to grant too much leisure.

Dawn arrived and the doppel had yet to make an appearance. Sprael felt certain the dark-tinted daemon would launch another attack. *Where are you? And who released you?*

Morning came, and the party broke camp and limbered up, stretching reluctant muscles. Primula and Bryant were the first to begin their exercises and were the last to conclude. Breakfast would be eaten along the road. After Sprael explained what had transpired overnight, not one person wished to remain in the clearing long. At first Marius appeared relieved by the announcement, then he seemed troubled. No longer would he lug the daemon on his back like a confined ape, but now fix a cautious eye to the trees. And with Salve no longer among them, their daemon detection would be limited to their less-gifted senses.

As they made for the pathway to begin the final leg of their journey, a gentle hand upon Sprael's arm requested him to stall for a moment.

"It's as I feared," Calliandra began quietly, watching the others traverse beyond earshot. "I was afflicted by a binding hex." She paused to allow Sprael a moment to breathe, but continued before he could speak. "And with the conjurer being the Forest, this means the caster can't be slain to end the curse."

"From whence it came, so also it ends," Sprael recited the old adage under his breath.

Calliandra nodded agreement. "Exactly." Then covertly glanced over her shoulder. "On the brighter side, my connection with my dark sister only grows."

"So you know its whereabouts?"

"I do," replied Calliandra, scratching the side of her nose. "But that also means that *she* knows our whereabouts."

"That's not so bad."

"But there's another problem," Calliandra went on, "I fear for Primula."

Deep down Sprael understood. And though the Scholar seemed ready to explain herself further, time was of the essence. "I'll make sure the Healer is hemmed within our formation." Sprael reassured her by squeezing her shoulder, gently guiding her toward the main path. "Give us ample warning, should your sister decide to go for that pretty Healer's throat."

The goblin had spoken true. The way to Lepaskalica held only a few miniscule obstacles, easily managed by the ranger. The crooning of a chanticleer in search of its mate, and a small batch of hobs sunning themselves upon a rock formation held the most potential danger.

"Oh, thank the Creator," said Bryant as the half-moon gateway marking the Lepaskalica's entry point vaulted into view. "As refreshing as the river has been, I can't wait for a proper bath!"

"We haven't time for baths," said Laekar curtly. "We will make for the Fount, and should you survive, afterward you may spend your time however you please."

"Thus concluding your services," stated Primula.

With their pace dampening ahead of the gate, Primula strode close beside Marius. Sprael could see a future between them, though he would never voice such thoughts aloud, especially with Calliandra so near. He could not deny that a pairing between a mercenary and a lampyr held such interesting potential. In the future, should there be one, Sprael would not mind employing their services for his more arduous forays. That is, if they indeed formed a union. But it looked as though Sprael was getting ahead of himself.

After striding through the gateway, he was met by a small gathering of elder laives. Two males and two females, their status within the village indicated by the length of their sword pommels. In various shades of green, their ornate gowns sprouted up from the flagstone into the armour at their shoulders. Lepaskalica was not known to be a hostile seat in the laif kingdom, but they were not ruled by fools. While archenlaives prowled your backyard, you furnished steel.

"Your arrival was foretold, Sprael of the Gentle March." The taller female elder opened her arms in welcome. The length of her pommel was second to that of the taller male laif beside her. Though she recognized Sprael, he knew her not. "Your party is welcome," she continued, "but we request that your human companions keep to the common thoroughfare." A lilt cocooned her pronunciation of the word *human,* and Sprael feared what she would say next. "That is, the *humans* that have gone unmarked by the Daeban, are welcome."

No need to waste time counting the cursed humans, thought Sprael with a labored sigh.

There was only just the one.

~ **18** ~

WHERE ONE JOURNEY ENDS,
ANOTHER BEGINS

Calliandra noted that Vaskar now carried his longbow in his hand, unstrung. Ordinarily, the mercenary kept the weapon secured to his back.

This bodes ill.

From within the village proper, Salve had rejoined their side of the now-separated party, which gave the Scholar a measure of security. Marius, torn between journeying around the village and staying with Primula, had been encouraged by his mentor to remain with the Healers and Laekar. When the apprentice brokered argument, Calliandra had stepped in and agreed with Vaskar, to which Marius assured they would reunite at the postern nearest the karst. After Calliandra and Sir Kathryn smiled farewell to Laekar, the Scholar caught a strange exchange between Vaskar and Bryant. Judging by the grin wrinkling Bryant's features when he turned away, whatever had transpired seemed to have favored the Healer immensely.

Presently, the divided party made the trek around the village, which, according to Sprael, tacked on an extra five miles. If time were not of such essence, then perhaps this news would not have been so upsetting. By the contempt on Sprael's face, when facing the laif elders, Calliandra could tell that he wanted to spar, but knew better. He did not have the time, and no doubt the laives of Lepaskalica would notice the doppel's eventual entry and slay her without hesitation.

"By your swords you know that the archenlaives are on the march," Sprael muttered to himself, venting some frustration. He had been going on like this for the better part of the hour. "And *she* is our best shot at defeating them! Can you not rid her of the Daeban's curse? Your Healers or physicians must have some sort of a solution!"

Calliandra turned her attention further ahead and worked her fists, still swollen from the doppel's late night pummeling of Vaskar. Then a sharp lash across her shin startled her, and once again, she sustained another scratch courtesy of her careless counterpart. The Scholar was clumsy enough as it was, and certainly did not require the doppel's assistance. It did give her comfort, though, knowing that for each branchlet that sliced her cheek or every burrow that twerked her ankle, the doppel registered the same unheralded discomfort.

"Odd," stated Sir Kathryn as she joined Calliandra's side.

Believing she was commenting on Sprael, Calliandra replied in his defense. "It's not unusual for people to talk to themselves. Some of my favorite teachers were mutterers. And they created benchmarks in their respective fields of study. Even I am known to mutter on—"

"I am not talking about our ranger's behavior," explained Sir Kathryn. "We have trod several miles, and I have not seen one sign of village patrols."

"Is that so odd?" Calliandra wondered. "Perhaps they brought their details into the village to bolster their numbers in case of invasion?"

"Exactly," said Sir Kathryn. "Laives make the finest scouts, and with war at their porch, one would think they would be gathering as much information as possible."

It dawned on Calliandra what the knight was getting at. "All of their scouts have returned."

"The archenlaives are close, or they have already passed."

"Sprael!"

The laif was mid-mumble when he turned.

"We should double our—" Calliandra bit herself off, wary of her volume.

Then Salve suddenly grew restless and went to ground, Vaskar darted behind a tree. In a hurry, Sir Kathryn urged Calliandra lower herself into a thick cluster of bracken, while the knight opted for a tree adjacent. After molting her armor, Sir Kathryn had become quite shockingly nimble.

Confused, startled, and up to her chin in ferns, Calliandra strained her ears to listen through the quiet. *Just what manner of danger had Salve sensed?*

Brushing along the toe of the slope, perhaps one hundred feet distant, the answer arrived by the sound of maille on steel. Calliandra glimpsed tall knights in jet black armor routing through the trees. *Archenlaives!*

Luckily, the legion proceeded upon a pathway that's bisection occurred a good distance from where the party had taken up hiding. The slope also provided aid in obscuring their silhouettes. Under these circumstances, Calliandra speculated that detection would have been made easier from a higher perspective. Or upon a flatter plane.

Soundlessly, Sir Kathryn had bared her longsword, held upright so if the steel glimmered it would not catch notice. Her jaw was set tight and beads of perspiration cascaded her forehead. From Calliandra's perspective, she could not see Sprael or Salve. She could, however, espy Vaskar casually leaning his chest against a hickory, arms folded, appearing greatly unconcerned.

Physical descriptions of archenlaives had been recorded, but their histories never held great interest for Calliandra. In song school, with the other young Scholars, she had learned of their great banishment, but beyond all that, from a research standpoint, she had never cared to delve much deeper. That was, until the war arrived. Every parcel, every parchment within reach felt as precious as sapphire. Understanding their ancient scripts held the key to unlocking the magical potential imbued within the ink scraped upon their scrolls rendered long ago. Now the Scholar gazed upon the archenlaives, their ranks passing beneath her, and the descriptions failed to note the aura of despair that emanated from these knights.

Perhaps that is why they do not brandish banners? thought Calliandra. *The menace in their bearing alone is enough for identification.*

It felt rather curt to Calliandra the manner in which the legion's numbers concluded. The entire contingent, she wagered near two hundred strong, had not varied in the least at its end or beginning. In the past she had witnessed mounted knights and soldiers headed for battles to parts unknown, and their ranks held diversity of not only position, but of character. Particular knights could be distinguished by the color of their armour or the style of their helm. Squires riding behind their knights wore armour and pageantry respective of the land they hailed. Depending upon the kingdom, commanders and Marshalls were identified by some sort of indicator. In Tintagil, the field commanders enwrapped a scarf symbolizing their Duke-Knight, Sir Baern, around the crown of their helms, and a heavy crimson smear was administered to their right pauldron. Any further details were up to the commanders' discretion. In contrast, these emblems of individuality were utterly absent from the archenlaives. Though the onyx knights varied in height and build, their armour did not denote rank—nor hearth, nor allegiance. Bannerless, the warriors marched. Time, for Calliandra, seemed to slow to a grind, but in all reality, the legion had come and gone in a matter of minutes.

Calliandra began to doubt whether the forces of Camelot could withstand an entire army of such dignified, disciplined knights. Never had the success of this quest felt so dire. *Only a great force of magic could see an end to this conflict!*

Then without willing it, an image of Earon flashed into her mind.

Oh, Earon, I pray that you find the strength if we should fail. In her mind she saw the spellcaster huddled in terror upon a rain-soaked parapet. Just where, she knew not, but before she could comprehend his locale, suddenly the phantom dispelled.

"Calliandra." It was Sir Kathryn, her face a diagram of urgency. "We must be swift!"

Not ever had Calliandra agreed so ardently with a statement. It felt as though a crack had been discovered in the hourglass and time had been secretly draining at a double rate.

In a rare act of humanity, Vaskar pressed his forehead to Salve's muzzle. In the following moments, once the mercenary stepped back, Salve's neck dwindled into his shoulders, his powerful legs transformed into the clawed feet of a crag lion, and his head became that of a great maned feline. Spired bones trailed his spinal column, protruding the flesh like spikes, as the fearsome draconics are renowned to sport. In darkened patches around his hinge joints, Calliandra noticed the fur interlaced as maille. But before she had the chance to gain further inspection, Salve, no longer equine, pelted ahead.

Calliandra knew that laif bred skin-changers held finite transformations. Most were limited to three, and upon the third, the destrier would remain in its feline form indefinitely. There were other breeds that were also limited to a specific number of transitions, but upon their final change, would experience a decrease in their lifespan. Sometimes the decrease was so severe that it would only be a matter of hours, sometimes minutes. These particular breeds maintained a fearsome, disagreeable temperament until death, and she presumed this had more to do with the manner in which they were employed—dragon slaying.

Sprael called their first rest near a decrepit chapel, aged and forgotten by all but time it seemed. Calliandra strode the stone path leading to the front doorway, withdrew her canteen, tossed her head back, and gulped several mouthfuls. The respite was welcome, but the burning in her legs failed to eclipse her desire to continue on.

"For how long do you believe Camelot can hold out against them?" Calliandra voiced her question to no one, staring into the gloom of the chapel. On its face, the building yet bore a proud air, though it was centuries behind on maintenance.

From further behind than she believed the party to be, Sir Kathryn responded, "Long enough." She spoke with surety, but sounded like her attention lay elsewhere. "Why have you not attempted capture again?"

By its volume and direction, Calliandra knew the question had not been directed toward her. She then rounded from the chapel, curious to see what her companions spoke of.

"I fear further harm may befall the Scholar," replied Vaskar. By the time he concluded his statement, Calliandra had positioned herself directly beside him. Noticing her from one corner of his eye, the mercenary concluded, "Her body has suffered enough."

Where the remnants of a stone perimeter formed a shattered hedgerow that encircled the chapel, the party gazed off toward a shared focal point. The trees in this parcel of forest were spaced generously apart, the majority of which were evergreen.

"What are you looking at?" asked Calliandra, already knowing what they were talking about. She sensed a presence ahead of her.

"Your doppel," replied Sprael. "The further we travel, the more brazen it becomes." It took a moment for Calliandra's eyes to settle upon the figure peering cautiously at her from behind a tree. "It's a most curious daemon," continued Sprael. "It hasn't launched further attacks and seems blissfully content to follow."

"As long as it remains on the fringes," said Sir Kathryn, stowing her canteen. "And does not hinder us, then I care not for what it does." She looked to Calliandra and smiled, uncertainty framing the corners. "The Crown and Cloth will hold, but we do not have the time for repelling evil spirits. The amount of time we will tarry in the Caverns is unforeseeable."

"Let's pray the Nocnik makes itself known to us quickly," said Calliandra.

At just beyond a pebble's throw, Salve re-appeared, his muzzle and mane flecked in crimson.

"Our scout assures a safe course ahead?" Sir Kathryn asked Vaskar.

The mercenary nodded.

"Seems he wrangled a snack," said Sprael, standing.

Beneath her breath, Calliandra murmured, "Good kitty."

Sprael laughed, and broke into a run.

* * *

Atop a hand-piled embankment, on the outskirts of the Forest, Sprael waited for his companions. Beneath a covey of roiling storm clouds, the sunken landscape of the karst spanned nigh forever. Three crumbling, sunken towers littered an otherwise vacant expanse. They appeared in the semblance of a row, as though at one time they had been connected by a parapet walkway.

Where one journey ends, another begins.

"The gates to the Halodwyth Caverns are just beyond that first tower," Sprael explained to Calliandra as she joined his vantage. Though her breathing came rapidly, her movements were anything but sluggish. "Would you like to take a break for a spell? Don't be fooled by the open terrain, many lives have been consumed upon this final leg. It requires a heedless sprint. From here forward, the ground is cursed."

Calliandra swiped at her nose. "Then it seems the karst and I share at least one quality."

"Common ground," muttered Sprael.

Calliandra coughed. "That was rather low hanging, even for you."

"Couldn't help myself."

As Sprael stretched, he noticed that Sir Kathryn and Vaskar had taken up the neighboring embankment. Not quite ten steps afore the embankment, Salve lingered alone. Sprael held little doubt that this place set the beast's senses to a fevered pitch, but Salve merely flicked his tail as though he were only mildly annoyed.

"I wonder if this is his final transfiguration?" said Calliandra, somehow reading the laif's thoughts.

"I hope not." Sprael's reply came as reflex. "I sincerely hope not."

Upon his speaking, a heavy raindrop struck the laif above his sword wrist.

Not only must we contend with eldritch wraiths and ancient curses...

A wall of rain fanned from overhead, and within an instant the parched earth became a bog. Luckily the final grasping boughs of Fenrirfang had created a canopy, preventing all but Salve from instant saturation.

As Sprael looked from face to face, preparing his call for their final sprint, he hesitated. A prevailing *evil* permeated this storm.

This feels fabricated, conjured.

By Salve's sudden defensive posture, backing toward the Forest, the skin changer must have felt the same. And if both laif and dragoon destrier sensed this presence simultaneous, then that meant...

"Spellcaster!" shouted Sprael. The ranger retreated back, gestured for all to do likewise. "To cover!"

The embankments quickly became barriers of defense for all, save for Vaskar, who remained atop, stalwart, spyglass to eye, peering through the storm. Salve joined the others around the backside, dripping, soaked to the skin, eyes hidden somewhere behind his soggy mop of a mane.

Calliandra glanced between knight and ranger. "What can be done?"

Sir Kathryn appeared both mortified and perplexed all at once. "If Earon—if Earon had not gone back..." she trailed off.

Recognizing the logic in her stammer, Sprael nodded. "The best way to snuff a sorcerer is to employ another."

"Of opposing elements," added Calliandra, as if she had just recalled an important passage of text. "If we face a water caster, then we must somehow conjure flame."

"Not necessarily," corrected Sprael. "But fire would make quicker work of it."

Calliandra's nose wrinkled. "Yes," she nodded. "You're correct."

"But whom among us can wield magics of any sort?" asked Sir Kathryn. "Without Earon we are lost to this conjurer."

"We have come too far to turn around now," stated Calliandra, her voice imbued with forged steel. "The lives of those lost along the way will be for naught!"

Sir Kathryn recoiled as though she had been cuffed. "I'm not summoning retreat, my lady!" Then she seemed to withdraw a bit into herself. "I am merely calling out what I see."

Then Vaskar was among them. "We need not slay the caster to prevail."

"Speak plain, Vaskar," demanded Calliandra.

"A caster is limited by sight," Vaskar pointed out. "We must avoid her line of vision."

Calliandra nodded. "And we'll be safe from her spells within the Cavern."

"I never, ever thought I would seek *safety within* the Halodwyth Caverns." Sprael spoke from a place rooted in disbelief. "If any of you would have told me such a thing before we set out, I would have laughed every step of the way..."

The Scholar and ranger appeared mollified by Vaskar's counsel, but the deep scowl that beset Sir Kathryn demonstrated nothing but concern. "How?" she began. "How will we avoid the caster's gaze? How will we manage to get inside so swiftly?" She turned to the laif. "You informed us that the gates to the Handsome Death Caverns have been sealed for centuries."

Sprael gulped, tugged the collar of his mantle.

The riddle! He had forgotten all about the riddle! It is *how* the gates had been sealed in the first place!

"Well, I believed that we would approach the gates under much different circumstances," Sprael explained, feeling Calliandra's hard eyes come to rest upon him. In truth, he did not know the answer to the riddle, and had plum forgotten it existed. In his defense, many things had happened since his rescue from the chopping block at Celliwig.

"Sealed? How so?" asked Calliandra. "This is the first I'm hearing of this."

"By a riddle, or a puzzle," replied Sprael, shaking his head. "A rather dreary one at that, at least from what I can recall. Now, how does it go? I can never recall the closing bit..." The laif crimped the bridge of his nose between his thumb and forefinger. "By willingness or naught," he recited, "through throat or by the heart, one or the other, then after a turn..." He paused, bit his lip. "See, and that's where I—"

"A final breath panted," supplied Vaskar. "Thy entry be granted."

~ 19 ~

FOR CAMELOT

Vaskar revealed his plan as though he were describing the contents of his picnic basket. "Smoke screens and distractions," he said simply.

Sir Kathryn wondered how much time these diversionary tactics would allot them, and Vaskar merely inclined his head as a response.

"Right," said Sir Kathryn, nodding. "Dumb question."

Beyond the embankment the rainfall only intensified. The temperature dipped, flowing shivers down to Calliandra's fingertips.

Vaskar removed a nugget-sized cloth-wrapped bundle from a pouch at his hip and affixed it to a blunt-tipped arrow. "Once the fog rises, make for the gates," he instructed.

His longbow, now strung, connected by an ethereal silken material, appeared to Calliandra as an instrument of music. The simple elegance of the longbow's heavenward curve drew her thoughts toward the lever harp residing in her family's drawing room. Then a sudden longing for home came and went, dissipated like mist upon the breeze.

"Creator guide you," began Sir Kathryn. By her expression, she wanted to say more. If the mercenary had not whirled toward the storm, overtaking the mound in several leaps, maybe the knight would have revealed what was on her heart.

Vaskar stood atop the crest of the embankment as Salve crouched beside him. Calliandra wagered that his spyglass was useless against the thick blanket of rain, so he relied upon memory alone for retracing his target. When Vaskar drew back his longbow, the lion's muscles that had been at play beneath his skin suddenly grew taut.

"This land has not seen such a deluge in many seasons," warned Sprael. "Be careful of sinkholes!"

The soft twang of Vaskar's release was immediately complemented by what sounded as stone rending the earth. Startled by the noise, Calliandra's eyes widened at the sight of a spear constructed of ice thrusting upward mere inches from where Vaskar had stood the moment before. Leading up to this moment, Calliandra had taken the mercenary's courage for granted.

Somehow Vaskar had reacted in time to avoid impalement. While he darted left, Salve tucked right, the upright spear impaling their last locale.

Sprael extended a hand toward Calliandra. "Now or never, milady," he said, teeth gritted. Calliandra accepted the laif's hand and was immediately pushed to the fore and felt a firm hand upon her lower back, boosting her upward. With her chin low, the Scholar clawed up the eroding embankment as knight and ranger enclosed her sides.

The bleak karst landscape was now heavily shrouded in further drear. Terrific gusts of wind snaked throughout the recently risen bog water, appearing as great leeches savaging the surface. Calliandra's woolen hose instantly grafted to her skin the precise second she entered the downpour. Her shins churned the mire as her sodden boots reached peak saturation. Surprisingly, the ground beneath did not feel as uneven as she had expected. It was eerily sponge-like and forgiving all at once. Perhaps she may have had an easier time had she opted to make the run bare foot. Then a series of icy spikes ruptured ahead, and she immediately rejected that notion.

Now that she was clear of the forest, Calliandra saw that the embankment was part of a greater barricade that hemmed the remains of a vast keep. The first tower that Sprael had indicated now lay a mere fifty yards distant. A great charcoal mist, along the torn wall of what Calliandra believed to have been a bailey, continued to rise.

That must be where the spellcaster was positioned, thought Calliandra. *Or may still be positioned.* She could not detect any life along the wall or beyond as blearing raindrops pelted her squinted eyelids. Abruptly the ground gave beneath her, sending her off-kilter, but the sheer weight of her boots managed to correct her following steps. Rushing across karst land meant hollow earth below, and that misstep may have been a sinkhole, the depths of which were impossible to determine.

The ranger and the knight purposefully maintained their distance ahead of Calliandra, being much more adept to the terrain. And also leagues faster.

All around, but thankfully not quite near, more ice spears ruptured, some the diameter of a child's wrist, while others may well have been fitted for a ballista. The vast majority resembled fear-stricken saplings that terminated drastically into barbed points. If the tips had not culled the victim instantly, then the hook would prevent escape. A horrid, horrid making, but its efficacy went without question.

From over Calliandra's left shoulder an arrow arced the sky, landed amidst the smoke screen, and skillfully recharged the lessening plumes. The tower that had loomed at a great distance moments ago was now near enough for her to clearly perceive its more wind-abraded components.

Sprael flicked his chin to the side. "Follow behind!" he shouted, pointed a course sixty degrees to his left that led toward a narrow gap in a waist-high retaining wall.

As Calliandra swerved toward the wall, the ground suddenly receded beneath her feet. Then a scream, trimmed short by a baritone thud of impact, jolted her attention to the right.

"Leave me!"

Calliandra turned to the shout and saw Sir Kathryn being consumed by an expanding sinkhole. In vain, the knight struggled to pull herself free from the ever-eroding rim. "Don't slow!"

Then, like an unseen tentacle, Calliandra's right ankle was encased within the sinkhole's influence. Desperately she struggled backward, but the sinkhole refused to part with her. Just before her other boot succumbed to the downward flow, Sprael's arms issued from beneath her armpits, and tugged her free.

Sprael spoke not a word while he locked eyes with the sinking knight. The sudden stillness that followed, once Sir Kathryn disappeared, gripped Calliandra about the throat, and rendered her speechless. Then, both ranger and Scholar turned, and made for the gate.

As they sprinted the final leg, the bog rapidly solidi-fied, forming a sheet of solid ice beneath them. Calliandra knew that if Sir Kathryn had not fallen completely through the sinkhole by now, she would most certainly be shorn in half. *The top layer of ice would serve as a swift guillotine!* Calliandra dispelled those thoughts and instead focused her footing to avoid spilling onto her backside. Sprael had a much easier time of it; he simply pivoted his body and glided the remaining distance.

"The gate lies at the base of these stairs!" Sprael shouted urgently, gesturing for Calliandra to enter ahead. "They're completely covered in ice! Just sit and slide down!"

Not needing to be told twice, Calliandra lowered herself down upon the slick landing. When her rear was just above the step, both of her heels slipped at once, aiding her that last inch. She then scooched over the lip, gazed down into the darkened hollow, and closed her eyes. The first three or four steps registered as bumps, easily managed, but her body gradually tilted backward as she gathered momentum, and soon every protrusion lashed her tailbone. At the base of the staircase, the entire floor slab was a sheet of ice. Unnervingly, her momentum had not diminished, and she found herself sliding on her back, unchecked. She attempted to slow herself by rolling onto her belly and digging her fingernails into the ice, but to no avail. She panicked, digging her nails deeper, fearing that she would be sent flying over a ledge.

Believing her death imminent, Calliandra took the chamber's flickering torchlight for granted. Then her boot soles halted upon a form much less solid than a wall.

"I have you!" a voice grunted.

Calliandra was shocked.

"What took you so long?" A second voice that filled the cellar arrived in a grating, distinct alto. "And what is happening up there?"

Calliandra rolled to her side, felt a hand at the bend of her elbow, and was soon upon her feet. It was at that moment Sprael joined, having descended the staircase as though it were comprised of gritted crafter's paper.

"Marius?!" The laif cried out in surprise. His head jerked to the right. "Primula! Bryant!" He peered around their shapes. "Laekar is not with you?"

"No," replied Marius, stepping from Calliandra. "She departed our company after Bryant survived his transformation."

Sprael nodded. "Well done to you both."

Of a sudden, the room dropped several inches. Primula released a shriek and Bryant cursed as misted droplets sprayed upward. The ice spell had broken and the water returned to its liquid state. The storm had not let up, and the staircase continued to act as a waterfall, rapidly feeding the chamber.

Now up to their ankles, Marius informed Sprael and Calliandra that a drain must exist somewhere, as the water's surface never rose higher than the current level. "I assume it lies somewhere beneath that great stone door," he continued, plucked a torch from a sconce, and strode beside the flowing water. Primula rushed to his side, sloshing droplets that sputtered his torch. "A most ominous-looking gate, if ever I could conceive." When he hovered the torch close, a human-shaped indent became instantly apparent, as if the door were a sculptor's mold. "There are words in plain script scrawled along the top. It's a riddle of sorts, I believe."

"It theemth ath nonthenth," opined Bryant. The Healer, now a lampyr, had yet to grow accustomed to speaking through his newly grown fangs. "We thpent the better part of an hour trying to find a latch, or keyhole, or anything that would let uth through."

"Then it began to rain, and we got distracted," Primula explained. Unlike Bryant, her fangs were hardly an impediment. "But I recall seeing this riddle once before..."

Calliandra read the riddle to herself as Primula recited it aloud.

BY WILLINGNESS OR NAUGHT,
THROUGH THROAT OR BY THE HEART,
ONE OR THE OTHER,
THEN AFTER A TURN,
A FINAL BREATH PANTED,
THY ENTRY BE GRANTED

The scent of damp fur struck Calliandra's nostrils the same moment Vaskar tore through the chamber. Now that he was free of the storm, water flowed from his mantle in great sheets. Salve hurried close behind, favoring his left hind leg, a meek crimson trail slithered in his wake.

Right after Primula concluded the phrase, *"One or the other,"* Vaskar gripped Bryant by the collar, forced him into the gates indenture. The lampyr hissed and swatted the mercenary's wrists and forearms. "Releathe me!" he squealed.

"Vaskar! What are you—" Marius' voice cracked.

The party watched in shared stupefaction as Vaskar's dagger penetrated the newly made lampyr's throat. Keeping his hands locked on the dagger, with a violence Calliandra had yet to witness, Vaskar wrenched his torso to the side. Over the sound of Bryant's gagging, a resounding click issued from somewhere within the stone gate. Vaskar stepped back, leaving the dagger lodged, and nodded his head slowly as though he were counting a muted rhythm.

The frantic desperation on Bryant's expression began to soften as his eyes gradually drained of life. The moment after his soul departed, a second click resounded, sharper than the first.

No one dared move for the span of several heartbeats.

"Why?!" Primula whimpered through her rictus of agony. Marius, by her side, held her fast about the waist, fearing the same fate may befall her. "Why did you—!" Her wail was cut short by a feline growl, distinctly predicating a roar. The sound froze the blood in Calliandra's veins, and no doubt it held the same effect for the others.

Vaskar strode forward and pushed the gate forward as though its hinges had been recently oiled. Calliandra locked eyes with Sprael, neither hazarded their thoughts aloud. Their long-awaited destination lay ahead of them, and as they entered, the heavy toll that had been paid stared lifelessly back at them.

When Calliandra was one-step shy entry, she turned back to Marius and Primula. She knew not what to say in the moment to console the weeping lampyr. The phrase "For Camelot" came out unbidden. It seemed as though the words contained a tonic, for right after their utter-ance, Primula rose from her wilt, her mouth tightening into a mirthless smile.

"For Camelot," she repeated, suddenly composed.

Upon their entry into the tunnel, not twenty steps beyond the gate, a wraith assailed them. It appeared as a rail-thin deer, its spectral flesh weeping from its carcass in great leaflets. In immediate response, Vaskar pitched a powdery substance into his torch, transitioning his flames into a bright emerald. As soon as the light flashed upon the wraith, it shrieked and dissolved into a chalky residue. The particles scattered across the stone floor and main-tained their glow long after the party's torchlight passed.

The initial length of the Cavern was a rounded stone-laid corridor, much like an irrigation pipe, that wandered in the same direction as the ice-laden staircase. *The Kar-dowiff must reside in a chamber far from laives or humans, so the further we travel this path, the better,* thought Callian-dra. Lepaskalica lay less than a mile behind them, and if the course continued this way, then perhaps this quest would be at its end sooner than she anticipated. *But if I have learned anything from these past several days, it's best to temper all hopes.*

Along the outer fringes of Vaskar's emerald flare, a conclave of wraiths backpedaled in terror. As a faint tickle upon a spider's web, the gate's clicking must have called out to the wraiths, *"living hosts inbound!"*

How the undead calculated time, Calliandra did not know, but they must certainly feel it. The hunger, the pain, the intense loneliness these wraiths conveyed was nearly heartbreaking. *Almost,* for if Calliandra were not the target of their phantasmic desires, then perhaps she may have felt sorrow for them. Instead she felt grateful for Vaskar, and at the same time hated him.

Poor Bryant! she thought with a pang of misery. *What a waste!* Though she hardly knew the Healer, he seemed a friendly sort—and he had just become a lampyr! *Such a rare and useful trade! And Sprael! The further this journey continues, more and more of his youthful spirit is leeched into the cold stone.* She recalled her first meeting with the laif, his bearing jovial, flamboyant. At all times the variant of a smile played upon his face, even when conversations shifted grim. *And the knights of Orkney! Sir Kathryn!* Though she could not pin all of her grievances on Vaskar, she hated him all the same. *Bryant deserved a better fate—*

Her thoughts were suddenly interrupted by a searing pain that latched about her right calf, akin to the flay of a dampened scourge.

"Sprael!" she cried out in pain, staggered to her right. "My leg!"

The laif caught her and slung her arm over his shoulder, assuming the weight of the damaged leg. The wraiths along the outskirts of the emerald aura halted, and Vaskar turned back, concern heavily etched upon his brow.

"Something sharp lashed my ankle," explained Calliandra. The fresh raw sting constricted her stomach into knots, nearly forcing her to retch.

"I didn't see anything attack her," Marius avowed from behind.

Sprael gingerly adjusted the Scholar's weight beneath his shoulder. "Your doppel must have taken an injury," he speculated. "Can you put weight on your leg?"

"It's just a deep scratch, I think," she said, wincing, presently standing on her own. She eyed the wraiths lingering ahead, their eyes like fiery drops of hatred. "And this is no place for a rest."

Turning forward, Vaskar resumed his march. A shorter wraith that had been caught unaware released a shrill squeak, stumbled upon its backpedal, and was consumed in the light.

"When we reach a safe place," began Primula. "I can relieve your injury, if you wish."

Calliandra glanced back, the slight shift of balance brought a surge of pain. "I appreciate that, but—"

"You'd be my first heal," added Primula hopefully.

"We'll see," replied Calliandra.

The long corridor went on for another hundred paces before its formation widened, opening into a vast multilevel chamber. At their feet, the path they followed gave way to a track that circled the entire space. Wraiths as soft fabric meandered from the ceiling, held their drifting patterns several feet over the torchlight. Without sparing an upward glance, Vaskar strode to a railing, gazed down into the depths of the chamber. The others followed close behind, taking up places along the rail, careful to stay within the green boundary.

"Appears there are three levels," noted Sprael.

Marius eyed a wraith that hung suspended directly over his head. "And we are situated at the topmost," he added, stepping carefully toward the rail. The moment he looked down into the chamber, he grew uneasy. "We have two corridors to choose from up here, aside from the one we just departed. And three on the next lowest level." He readied his torch for a drop to gain a better view of the base level, but Primula stopped him.

"Save your light," she advised, rising on tiptoes, leaning over to obtain a better view of the base level. "There are two passageways at the bottom," she revealed, straining her vision. "Oh, and a third, but I think its gateway is barred." Apparently her lampyr transformation had gifted her the benefit of night eyes.

Seemingly without a reason, a tingle began at the base of Calliandra's scalp and ran down to the tips of her fingers. "In which direction does the barred path lead?" she wondered.

Primula dropped back to her normal height and, after tucking a stray lock of hair, pointed the gate's location.

"It shares the same bearing as the entry corridor?" asked Calliandra. "The same direction, I mean, further away from the village?"

The lampyr nodded. "Maybe it's a continuation of the first?"

"Doubtful," stated Sprael. "For all we know these halls lead back to one another or conclude into barricades of decaying debris." As the party had been gawking, more and more wraiths had assembled overhead and all around. The laif observed a newly arrived wraith that appeared as a rather patient-looking goblin, its hands hidden from view behind its back.

"So which passage should we take?" asked Calliandra.

"Whichever leads back toward Lepaskalica," replied Sprael.

Calliandra's left eyebrow shot upward. "And why do you say that?"

"A hunch." Sprael shrugged.

"A hunch?"

He smiled. "I take it you believe the Nocnik lies in the opposite direction?"

"I *believe* the Nocnik to be the timidest of birds, preferring isolation." Calliandra's tone unwittingly leaned toward condescension. "How else would such a creature manage to avoid being seen by both laif and human for ages upon centuries?"

Sprael shifted his weight, folded his arms. His eyes had yet to leave the goblin ghost. "Sometimes the best hiding places are within plain sight."

Calliandra snorted. "Are you suggesting that we split up, take different paths?"

The laif mulled the notion over for several moments before finally shaking his head. "No," he replied. "My job was to get you here. And Sir Demetrius wanted you to come along for a reason, and that reason was to lead us to the feather." His eyes finally departed the wraith and came to rest upon the Scholar. "So lead on, Calliandra."

~ 20 ~

WHEN A HEALER CAN'T
HEAL

After they entered the lowest level corridor, the floating wraiths returned to the ceiling and several crawlers reluctantly peeled off. Well before that, each member of their wraith greeting committee had turned away; not a single creature from their opening stretch remained.

It seems the spirits are not allowed free range of this place, thought Sprael. *Perhaps, like Fenrirfang, the Caverns are divided into sections and are guarded by invisible wards?*

As they pressed deeper into the corridor, with each step, Calliandra's wound worsened. At this point Sprael nearly carried her.

"Vaskar," Primula called out.

"There will be no rest," replied Vaskar, sounding weary. "There is no shelter."

Primula was taken aback by his response to her yet-to-be-voiced question. "The further we travel, the more distressed Calliandra's wound becomes," she argued, "and the slower we will move."

Vaskar halted.

"Grant me a few moments to care for her," persisted Primula.

Withdrawing his hand from his cloak, Vaskar flung a powdery substance into Marius' torch, blossoming the flames into the same brilliant emerald as his own. "When we pass an alcove, see to her wounds quickly," Vaskar spoke as he turned away. "I won't be waiting."

"If we get separated," began Marius, blinking and shaking his head. His eyes had been thoroughly dazzled by the flaring light. "How will you identify the Nocnik?"

Vaskar looked to the tapered ceiling overhead. "With great difficulty," he replied. "What with the variety of birds we have come across thus far, it will be quite the task to parse through them all."

"Oh, ha, ha," Marius scoffed drily.

"He has a point," admitted Sprael. "Nothing *lives* here. Should we see a bird, *any bird*, odds are that it's probably our Nocnik."

"Not necessarily," moaned Calliandra, her head toward the ground, her untied hair over her face. "It may not be…" Suddenly her voice faded, along with her strength.

Sprael widened his stance to assume the Scholar's weight. Further down the corridor Vaskar's torchlight faded around a bend. "He wasn't joking about waiting for us was he?"

"Vaskar," began Marius, handing Primula his torch so he could assume Calliandra's other shoulder. "Is as far from a jester as one can be."

"How many jesters has he slain?" wondered Sprael. "I'll bet he's put more than one to rest."

"Off the top of my head? I can't recall any."

Marius and Sprael straightened their backs, lifting the Scholar from the stone floor.

"I find that surprising," commented Sprael.

Marius squinted. "I do too."

After rounding the bend, the corridor gave way to an antechamber that provided three optional directions—left, right, straight. When Sprael gazed upward, the ceiling was vaulted so high that he could not make it out. He did, however, notice several other doorways etched into the side of the stone-packed walls, none of which had been connected to a perceivable staircase.

"Wonder where those doors would lead us?" the laif queried, pointed toward the opening above the leftward door. Overhead, wraiths gradually descended from the heights of the chamber and hovered over Primula's torch.

"Might be sluices," replied Marius distractedly, eyes darting all about the space. "Vaskar must have left an indication as to which direction he went."

Turning to face the others, Primula fastened a concerned look upon Calliandra. From the passage at her back, a pair of ogre-like wraiths emerged. Then from the passage to the left, a concert of ghoul-like wraiths bounded hungrily into the room, their cloth-wrapped feet skittering frantic on the smooth stone. Unlike the others, these wraiths ignored the lampyr's light, and entered as if corporeal.

With shuddering recognition, Sprael noticed the darkness that painted the gloom beneath the ghouls. "Shadows!" he shouted, face-palming the nearest encroaching ghoul. "They are not made of vapor!"

A dull crack off to Sprael's left told him that Marius had already engaged the enemy.

"*Mariusssssssss!*" several ghouls hissed as they poured from the entryway.

Outnumbered and encumbered by the Scholar, Sprael and Marius fought as best they could. Soon they noticed with alarm the green light dwindling at their heels as Primula drew back from the fight, and Marius and Sprael surged forward to stay within it.

Over half a dozen ghouls lay slain where Marius had been fighting, while Sprael had claimed merely three. Then an idea came to Sprael. With a great heave he removed Calliandra from Marius' grip and bundled her onto his own shoulder. Now with his burden alleviated, Marius squared his full attention on the ghouls.

"*Calliaaaaaaandraaaaaaa!*" the seven remaining ghouls hissed, their eyes following her arc toward Primula. "*Spraaaaaaaeeeeeellll... Primulaaaaaa...*"

"Here!" said Sprael to the lampyr. "I'll trade you."

"Wait!"

Without further explanation Sprael clasped the torch, pressed Calliandra into Primula's arms, and whirled to join Marius.

The ghouls began to shriek, their movements lending toward panic.

"Marius! Calliandra! Sprael! Primula!"

Finding themselves on the defensive, the ghouls danced frightened jigs beyond the emerald pall. *"Sprael! Sprael! Spraaaeeel!"* One ghoul screamed in frenzy, its features twisted by fathomless hunger. It lunged forward, bent its neck at a most horrible angle, and endeavored a swipe at the laif's ankles.

Sprael avoided the ghoul and riposted with a throat-rending shout. "WHAT?!"

The ghoul swiped the slaver that dripped from its acheilic mouth. *"Sprael, Sprael, Sprael,"* repeated the ghoul as if it were scolding a schoolchild.

"What?!" shouted Sprael again. His torch hand itched for his whetstone.

Off to the right an ill-fated ghoul crumpled beneath Marius' blade, leaving six to contend with. Once dead, the monsters appeared as nothing more than small harmless stacks of soiled, desiccated laundry.

"Spraaaeeel..." The ghoul's tone took on a vulgar, salacious quality.

A fragmented shriek followed by the sound of damp linens sloughing to ground alerted Sprael to the demise of another ghoul.

"She's not healing!" Primula cried. The lampyr knelt with the Scholar's head upon her thigh at an uncomfortable incline. Fresh rivulets of blood trickled to the base of Calliandra's skull from several pairs of fang punctures. It seemed the lampyr was not quick to give up on her new patient. "I've never done this before and I don't know what I'm doing wrong!"

"Well stop trying what you're trying!" shouted Sprael over his shoulder.

With a jarring gasp, Calliandra abruptly regained consciousness. The first she noticed was the ghoul gyrating its hips before Sprael. "Where are we?!" she wailed, skipping the groggy phases. The wetness on the side of her neck drew her hand, and her eyes bulged at the amount of crimson returned.

"I'm sorry!" cried Primula. "I can't seem to heal you!"

Appearing as though she wanted to say more, Calliandra instead staggered to her feet. Upon standing, she teetered on her right ankle in further testament to Primula's failure. Then with her gaze fixed on the lewd ghoul, she sidled next to Sprael.

Well over one hundred leech-like wraiths swirled overhead, the smallest among them as long as a mammoth trunk. And the closer Sprael drew to the outer ridge of the light, the nearer the leeches loomed. If any appendage breached a mere inch beyond, the horrific consequences would be immediate.

A pair of horses cantered an entry from the left, whinnying in irritation, with three translucent huntsman entering close behind. One notched his longbow and let fly an ephemeral arrow that was consumed by the green glow. In frustration, the huntsman torpedoed his longbow at Primula, which yielded the same result as the arrow.

The ghoul taunting Sprael rotated its attention from the laif as more wraiths funneled into the antechamber. *"Calliandraaaaaa!"* Its voice clawed the air angrily in earnest. *"Klonawwwwwwwst…"*

Sprael was taken aback.

"What did you just say?"

"Spraaaeeel…"

"No, the other word," argued Sprael. "Right after *Calliandraaaaaa.*"

The ghoul cocked its head in wonderment, its attention seeming to wander elsewhere.

"Vaskaaaaaar?"

As Sprael shook his head, he noticed his own emerald radiance had somehow doubled. Then Vaskar was amidst them with Salve bounding close behind.

"Run for your lives!" he shouted, lopped the head from the stunned ghoul, and disappeared down a passage.

Sprael underhanded the torch back to Marius and gathered Calliandra into his arms. In his fervor to escape, Marius' feet quickly became entangled in the dead, and before the situation grew more dire, Primula cleverly flung the soggy remnants of a ghoul upon the other ghouls, affording the party enough time to escape.

They caught up to Vaskar leaning against a wall, his back to their approach. He had latched his torch into a nearby sconce and was dressing a forearm wound. Sprael managed to snatch a glimpse of a large welt before the mercenary had finished.

"What did you encounter?" asked Sprael, undoing his hold on Calliandra, allowing her to stand for the moment. Meanwhile Marius and Primula traded gulps from a canteen that they quickly passed back and forth.

Vaskar secured his vambrace and grimaced. "We must keep running." He retrieved his torch, worked his hand upon its handle. "Strysthorns and ghouls do not adhere to this place's ancient boundaries."

"Strysthorns?" Primula nearly choked on her water. "Then what are we waiting for? Let's be off!"

"If we go in that direction," said Calliandra, pointing down the corridor that Vaskar meant as their retreat. "We will be travelling further from the Nocnik!"

"You don't really know that for certain," argued Primula, snatching Calliandra by the wrist and adjusting her finger toward an opening on the second level. "That accursed bird may well be flapping around that tunnel there." She released the Scholar and gestured toward an opening over their head. "Or there, perhaps! We have no clue! But we do know that Vaskar has kicked over a hive of strysthorns, and we haven't time for discussion!"

By Calliandra's startled, albeit agreeable expression it seemed that she had been persuaded. Swiftly, Sprael bundled her back into his arms, and the party ran for the passage that led in the direction of Lepaskalica Village.

Inwardly Sprael was glad to be moving along this route. Why? He could not say for certain, but his instincts told him that *this* was the correct way.

* * *

While Vaskar ran the front and Marius maintained the aft, their torchlights joined together and formed a protective barrier that encompassed the entire party. Within the glow, Primula had taken up place beside Sprael.

To say that Calliandra was sick of being lugged around and treated as a frail damsel would have been an understatement. Even though Sprael was not showing any signs of fatigue, she would have greatly preferred to be running these tunnels of her own accord. And presently, as they pressed forward in the wrong direction, she wanted, more than anything, for her stupid doppel's wound to heal.

Perhaps a passage will open on the right... she thought. *Yes! We need to make two right turns then we'd return to the proper course!*

"Maybe Vaskar has an ointment that would take care of your wound," offered Sprael. The laif had yet to even begin breathing heavy. The same could not be said for Primula and Marius.

"A balm may only help with infection," explained Calliandra. She spoke forcefully so her voice would not be lost in the jostle. "I fear it would not do much for the limp."

Sprael shook his head. "He gave Kathryn a dose of basilisk antivenin that brought her leg back to form overnight."

That's right, he did, thought Calliandra. "What are the chances that he has a second supply?" she voiced with uncertainty. "The value of that tincture could furnish an entire palace."

"And yet he spent it on poor Kathryn," said Sprael sadly, meeting the Scholar's eyes for a moment.

Poor Kathryn.

"It's doubtful that he has more," continued Sprael. "But I think it's worth asking."

Soon the party met a small juncture where two pathways became apparent. One passage weaved toward the right, the other continued forward. Vaskar opted for the onward route, not even slowing to contemplate.

Calliandra heaved an aggravated sigh.

"The strysthorns have not given up yet," said Sprael. "I can hear them buzzing behind us."

Calliandra speculated what it was about these giant wasps that made Vaskar and Salve flee in such fright. Aside from their venomous stingers and gnashing mandibles, strysthorns were simply giant flying bugs. *Why don't we fight them?* Calliandra asked herself. She wanted to voice this aloud, but everyone else was so petrified by the... by the...

The force of the memory surging to light nearly sundered her skull in half.

Come now, Cally! Petrification! How could you forget! Strysthorns prefer to construct their hives in warm stone, so they will often agree to a mutually beneficial relationship with monsters that wield petrification magics. Gorgons, cockatrices, basilisks—in an environment such as this, all the candidates would spell our end.

Calliandra shook her head into Sprael's shoulder armour, drawing his attention. "In order to lose the wasps, we must mask our scent..." she trailed off as it dawned on her as to why Vaskar chose to run toward the village. She hoped to be incorrect but feared the opposite. Vaskar's vast array of weapons, heightened senses, and incomprehensible reflexes were several traits that made him, well, Vaskar of Rhionydd. But the foremost among all was the simple fact that he was exceedingly clever.

"No, no, no," repeated Calliandra. "No, no, no, no, no..."

Sprael cocked his chin downward. "What's the matter?"

Then Primula gagged on a cough. "What is that wretched stench?" she bawled.

"The village sewers," Sprael replied before his sense of irony had a chance to catch up. "Wait, wait." He looked down to a nodding Calliandra. "No..."

~ 21 ~

ROT

At scarcely determinable increments the ceiling pressed tighter while the width of the passage remained wide enough for three to stride side-by-side without scraping the walls.

After another forty yards of dashing, the passage split into a "V", causing Vaskar to slow. He looked to Salve for guidance, and the lion jerked his head to the left.

Within Vaskar's slight moment of indecision, the droning hum of the strysthorn swarm had grown louder, more distinct. Without requiring further encouragement, the party poured into the corridor at a renewed clip.

Even though Calliandra knew that strysthorns could track a scent for fifteen miles or more, she squeezed her eyes shut, and prayed that the wasps would opt for the other route. Perhaps the ever-growing sewage odors would provide an ample shroud?

Unlikely, Calliandra's good sense chimed in as the swarm's diminished buzz returned to its regular volume, fast on their heels.

At some point during the next hundred yards, Primula flagged a step. When the path twisted a hard angled left, the lampyr needed the wall as a means to make the pivot. Calliandra read on Marius' face the desire to call out for a rest, and by the way he bit his lip, he understood the consequences.

Before long the passage opened into a decently spaced cavity. A submerged grotto appeared to the right, a shelf of stone providing overhead coverage. The moat that surrounded the small patch of shadowy ground sheened perilously. Wraiths sharing the same luster as the waters skimmed the surface, appearing as dour fae, no larger than an ogre's knuckle. The passing emerald torchlight claimed a few along the shoreline. Calliandra caught one wraith offer a careless shrug before being rendered into ghostly powder.

Curious punctures in the ceiling allowed streams of light to adorn the flowstone walls above the grotto. It seemed their route had taken a steady incline toward the surface, and without steps nor stairs, they had unwarily increased their elevation.

Still at full run, Vaskar noticed the specks of light upon the cascading flowstone and stuttered a step.

"I don't know how much longer I can keep going!" Primula cried out in desperation, interpreting Vaskar's sudden slowdown as a sign of exhaustion.

"I won't leave you behind," responded Marius, who was not faring well either. "We'll get through this!"

Behind a pained smile, Primula gritted her teeth and ran on.

Three tunnels of varying sizes lay at the opposite end of the chamber. The centermost yawned large enough for a siege engine to trundle through easily, the one to the left passed for a standard door, and the one to the right seemed fitted for a cellar crawlspace. And, of course, Salve darted for the latter; the tightest, rightmost opening.

The slim margins of the cramped tunnel forced the party to run single file. Calliandra tucked her chin as Sprael hunched and bundled her as tight as he could to his chest. Every so often the toe of her boot would skip against the wall, enflaming her wound. After a sharp rightward bend, a patch of radiance glowed at the center of the dark beyond.

"When we reach the end," cautioned Sprael. "We must stay together." Apparently the laif sensed menace ahead.

"Yes," said Marius from behind, breathing heavy. "No fanning out."

If she were not freed soon, confined within the ever-tightening space, Calliandra feared her insides would spill out of her mouth. She winced as her boot clipped the wall for the twelfth time. If she questioned whether she could walk on her own yet, each and every flare of hot pain that lanced up her leg relayed a rather harsh *Don't bet on it, milady*.

There was no mistaking the moment the strysthorns entered the tunnel behind them. The thrum of hundreds of enraged wings rebounded from the walls. When Calliandra hazarded a glance over Sprael's shoulder, she could make out the agitated mass. And for all she knew, a clan of gorgons trailed behind them. She faced this harsh reality with a feeling akin to surrender.

It's so easy to lose hope when grievously wounded and besieged on all sides.

The tunnel ended sooner than Calliandra expected. Her nostrils were the first to alert her of their exit. She had been gazing beyond Marius' torchlight at the swarm that only gained ground. The stench brought a myriad of confusing emotions to light, the foremost among them being an odd comfort concealed within whole-hearted aversion. She had no desire to swim in feces, but at the same time, had no desire to feel a strysthorn latch itself to her skull... Her mind wandered, picturing the sort of damage a strysthorn stinger could wage upon a human eye. Visions of popped grapes and violently stirred pudding flashed in her mind before Sprael's voice brought her back to the present.

The laif had come to a complete stop. Everyone had come to a complete stop.

"This is not the sewers," stated Sprael.

A barb of relief pierced the Scholar's fear.

The vast circular chamber floor churned as if it were boiled lava.

Then the sharp scent of decay plunged Calliandra back into despair.

"We can't cross that!" Primula shouted.

What Calliandra believed to have been some manner of hot simmering liquid, in truth was something altogether different. Then all at once the realization struck her.

This is a sea of feasting maggots!

Then Sprael mumbled at a loss, "The Chamber of Lasting Rot..."

In her studies, Calliandra had not come across anything regarding *The Chamber of Lasting Rot*, but the title felt correct. Certain aspects of laif lore were heavily guarded from humans. And oftentimes, rightfully so.

A balcony spanned the second story of The Chamber, beyond the reach of a staircase. At evenly spaced increments along the balcony meticulously crafted statues of gargoyles and juvenile griffins stared downward, their faces displaying varying shades of horror. Aside from the entryway they had crossed through, the only other doorway lay across the boiling larvae.

Beneath her notice, Vaskar and Salve had plunged into the pit, carving separate paths. The floor beneath them sagged uneven in places, as Vaskar's head would nearly disappear within a step, then return much higher. Salve, remaining in lion form, struggled to prevent his mouth from being overrun.

Sprael chased Vaskar's path, treading the mercenary's wake. To their right, Marius and Primula rushed behind Salve.

"Breathe through your teeth," instructed Marius as his head resurfaced, shaking gobs of filth from his head. The spectral wraiths overhead drew close to the mercenary's torch each time his head went under.

"For Camelot," sputtered Primula.

Calliandra closed her eyes and imagined a gigantic bowl of noodles. Noodles that could somehow wriggle between maille and slither into the deepest crevices of her armpits. A sudden clamping pressure drew her attention to her ankle where she watched a skeletal hand dissipating in Vaskar's emerald light. It seemed more than maggots and worms writhed beneath the surface.

The speed at which Sprael and Vaskar moved was astounding, running across the slippery islands of flesh and gristle as if it were bare floor. Meanwhile Marius and Primula had found labor within each hurried distance, the lampyr falling twice before Marius assumed her into his arms, as Sprael for the Scholar.

A step beyond the Lasting Rot, just on the edge of Marius' torchlight, Salve waited impatiently at the door, eyes transfixed on what Calliandra assumed was the impending wasps.

As they cleared their way onto the dry Chamber floor, sloughing maggots in clotted curds, Calliandra experienced a sharp pain to the back of her shoulder that felt like a well-executed dagger thrust. She twisted in Sprael's arms to swat at the location while the air escaped her throat in a howl that transformed into a whimper. Where she expected to feel a spastic chitinous body, instead found nothing but the narrow space between her shoulder and the laif's collar. She grunted in pain and frustration as her maille prevented the exploration of the wound. It felt as deep as it was wide, but she knew that her senses could betray reality. She tried to tell herself that perhaps it was not as bad as it felt, but she knew better. This was *bad.* The wound seemed to have already festered in her soul, and she could no longer feel her fingertips upon Sprael's arm. Soon she could no longer feel anything.

***

"Calliandra!" Sprael shouted, shaking the Scholar. As they departed the chamber, she had screamed and thrashed in his arms, called his name within a whimper, then fell slack.

A sturdy door had been hung upon the passageway leading from The Chamber of Lasting Rot, which bought a reprieve from the chasing swarm. Gratefully it was not a door that required a sacrifice.

The strysthorns viciously battered the door like hundreds of hammers while their appendages worked feverishly along the spaces between. Fortunately the door's snug fit did not indulge any crossing.

The short passageway gave way to a squarely hewed antechamber that echoed familiar to the one that had sprouted a coven of ghouls earlier. Elevated doors decorated the walls, with no means of reaching them. And at floor level, there was a door for each direction. At the moment there were no perceivable threats, aside from the wraiths circling the torchlights.

Right before the party gathered a collective breath, Sprael thrust Calliandra toward Primula.

"Heal her!" he insisted. "Wake her at the very least!"

Primula had been scrubbing her back against the wall, up and down, in a fervent attempt to remove lingering crawlers. She appeared confused by Sprael's demand. "I already tried," she admitted. A string of maggots fell from her head when she shook it. "She's immune to my skills."

"She sustained another injury," Sprael pressed. "Please try again!"

"All right, all right," conceded Primula, cupping the Scholar's chin and skimming a palm across her forehead. "You may set her down. Surely your arms must be sore."

Until that moment the notion of his own exhaustion had not crossed his mind. He went to a knee, propping Calliandra upright against his leg.

Having exhausted a number of attempts on the right side of Calliandra's neck prior, Primula bared her fangs and plunged them into the blank canvas of her left. Upon insertion, Calliandra's eyes flung open as she inhaled the gasp of a rescued drowning man. When Calliandra shoved Primula away, she gagged on the Scholar's blood, and coughed a small stream out around her chin.

"Is your wound healed?" asked Primula, dabbing at her lower lip as she slowly rose to a stand.

Calliandra reached behind her shoulder and cocked an eyebrow. "Still feels sore, but I can't really tell..." Her fingers rummaged over her mantle for a moment before she gave up. "What good is maille when your doppel persists on getting wounded?"

"If it hasn't healed, we haven't time for stitches," said Marius. "The strysthorns will soon find another way around."

Sprael hooked an arm beneath Calliandra's knees and another around her back, then returned to his feet. As he looked into her eyes, he noticed the renewal of a lost gleam. "How do you feel?" he asked.

"I don't believe I can walk," began Calliandra, "but my shoulder feels *different*. Not certain if it's healed though." She looked to Primula. "Thank you for that."

Primula paused to return a nod as she perused her sleeves for maggots.

"We must move," stated Vaskar. He waited by the door leading to the right.

The party began at a walk, their bodies unready for another sprint. In the distance, perhaps at the end of the corridor, Sprael heard the dripping of water. The stench of the sewers no longer assailed them. His internal compass had been tossed utterly off course by all the twists and turns, but if forced to speculate, his best guess would land them somewhere beneath the karst, their bearing rendered into mystery.

"Do you think all the sludge we just waded through will hide our scent?" asked Calliandra.

"I'm not sure," replied Sprael. "What do your Scholarly instincts tell you?"

Calliandra shook her head. "Such luck as that is not our kind of luck."

"I fear that you're right," agreed Sprael. "To be rid of the strysthorns, we'll need to pay a much steeper price."

~ 22 ~

LIKE SPORES OF MOLD

Their present passage hearkened familiar to that of a palace's upper hallways. Closed doors, spaced at even intervals, lined the corridor. The stain of a carpet long ago decayed highlighted the central walkway. All furnishings and ornamentation had degraded ages from their former beauty, leaving only decrepit remnants.

After passing what Sprael presumed were bedchambers, further ahead the dripping sound of water had grown into a steady drizzle. And for the first time since they'd entered the Caverns, Sprael detected a hint of freshness in the air.

"Did I just feel a breeze?" said Primula skeptically.

"I felt it too," agreed Marius in disbelief. "It came from the chamber ahead."

With a sudden renewal of energy, the party hastened forward. At a steady but surprisingly quick rate, the stale air of the karst was left behind, replaced by a crisper, cleaner variety. Soon the entire atmosphere was overcome by the pleasing scent of freshly fallen rain.

"What if," began Calliandra, "what if instead of pain and anguish..." She trailed away, her pronunciation muddled as if inebriated. Sprael had been so taken with the arrival of clean air that the degradation of the Scholar's health had gone completely unnoticed. "Instead of cuts and bruises, my doppel sister wife and I shared good feelings? Like, if one of us was given a really, really nice neck massage..." She faded off again, her mouth unable to form the words she wished to express.

"Calliandra!" Sprael dropped to a knee while the others continued onward. When he placed a hand to her perspiring forehead, his fingers were nearly singed. "Oh not again!" The laif's mind presented altered images of Prija and Calliandra, melding one to the other.

I must see her wound! Sprael rose into a run.

Upon dashing into the chamber, Sprael noticed a hole in the ceiling, just left of the central pillar. It was not the size of the hole, nor the skeletal adornments upon the pillar that drew the laif's attention. It was the water pouring from the hole and trickling immense rivulets down the sides of the pillar. Marius and Primula had immediately stripped to their small clothes to take advantage of the makeshift showers.

"It's freezing!" laughed Primula, grinning at Marius. "But it's better than having maggots clumped in your hair!"

Marius nodded as his jaw trembled from the chill, holding the torch just beyond the water's influence. A series of fractures in the stone floor acted as sufficient drains, preventing the chamber from flooding.

Sprael hurried toward a raised dais along the opposite wall, its stairs terminating beneath an altar of a fortunate scope. Had the posterior end of the altar seen better repair, the Scholar would have fit from head to heel. But in its present state, her legs were sent to dangle from the knees down.

Immediately Sprael went to work removing her mantle and tunic, while struggling to leave her hair intact. The Scholar's tightly plaited braids had come unlocked, and had managed to flow into every crevice of fabric. After a brief labor that left him satisfied at the lack of bald patches upon her scalp, the laif began to unfasten the three leather straps that secured the Scholar's golden maille tunic.

"She passed out from her wound again," stated Primula sadly from the opposite side of the altar. Her wet hair dripped onto Calliandra's maille as she worked the bottom strap free. "Should we remove her gambeson as well?"

Sprael shook his head. "I'll just cut the section around the wound free," he replied. "Let's get her onto her belly."

With combined effort laif and lampyr removed the maille hauberk, then rolled the Scholar over. Once she was settled, Sprael withdrew his dagger and cut away at the thinly padded gambeson, extracting a square, allowing the lampyr access to the wound.

Primula grimaced. "This doesn't bode well," she began, stepping aside for Sprael to look. "It doesn't appear infected, but it certainly hasn't healed." Suddenly she seemed downcast. "Am I a defective lampyr?"

"Perhaps," replied Sprael honestly.

Primula moaned in despair.

"Or perhaps the wounds are cursed," Marius chimed in, drawing beside Primula and placing a reassuring hand on her shoulder. His eyes softened as they took in Calliandra's most recent trauma. "Is there anything that can be done?"

"I'll clean it as best I can," offered Sprael. "And we should clean the rest of her so the strysthorns can no longer rely on our scent for tracking." He gathered the Scholar into his arms, the feeling of which had become routine. "That's the first sinkhole we have come across," he commented as he strode toward the pillar. "And this chamber is free of wraiths."

"Is there a correlation?" asked Marius.

"My guess is as good as yours."

At great risk, the party unanimously agreed.

"If only for an hour," assented Vaskar.

With frigid, stiff hands, Marius and Sprael worked to hew the roots from a deceased oak. Sprael, being the first to notice the roots protruding from the ceiling, believed that the fibers had maintained an integrity that would provide a decent fire. And he had been correct.

The icy waters had provided an antidote for their strysthorn problem, but it had also brought a prevailing chill that, if not remedied, might see them to an early grave. Though their torches yet burned, the properties within the emerald glow somehow mitigated any sort of meaningful heat. As much as it pained them to admit, they had no other option.

Primula had suggested that they backtrack to the grand hallway to make use of one of its bed chambers. Sensing that the others had no desire to go backward, she reasoned that the smaller room would heat faster.

The small room they selected was a relatively vacant space devoid of wraiths, and the calcified remains of a four-post bed served as excellent kindling. Once the fire was borne, Calliandra was laid before it with her back toward the flames. With the door closed and the party huddled tight, the atmosphere grew cozy rather quickly.

Across the flames, Sprael stared at Vaskar until the mercenary took notice. "Don't think I've forgotten," said the laif ominously.

Vaskar nodded, his eyes returning a singular smile.

"When this is over, prepare for quite the contract."

Marius looked between Vaskar and Sprael. "What's this now?"

"Your mentor here granted me a terrific boon," explained Sprael. "A murder or two on the house. And though I've never really wanted to die before, I really *really* want to survive these Caverns to see him fulfill his oath."

"How intriguing," said Marius. "Care to elaborate?"

Sprael winked at the young mercenary. "You'll just have to wait and see."

"Guess I'll have to make it out alive."

Curled before the door, Salve groaned in agreement.

A somber hush settled in the room. Sprael crouched, placing a palm to Calliandra's forehead. The warmth generated by the fire created difficulty determining whether or not she had cooled from her fever.

"Sir Clarence, Sir Brentin," Marius began reciting names, "Sir Tyrol..." he paused, looked away.

"Brave Sir Kathryn," Sprael completed.

Primula caressed Marius' cheek as the mercenary hung his head. "Toskus and Tari," she spoke morosely. "And poor, poor Bryant." The lampyr looked downward and held Calliandra within her sad gaze. "I'm afraid that we'll be adding another name soon."

The Scholar had not stirred since her lapse into unconsciousness. Last Sprael checked, her heartbeat was strong, but that was all. Should she never wake, the laif would be speechless with anguish, but not surprised.

"While I washed her, I could not help but feel as though I were preparing her for burial," continued Primula. "That water was so exceedingly cold that it would have roused the dead, but she slept throughout the whole ordeal. Her eyelids never once flickered."

The persistent crackle of the fire came to the fore while a thoughtful silence settled. As the quiet stretched, Salve removed himself from the threshold, approached the Scholar and bestowed a nudge to her forehead. A sound resembling that of a *purr* escaped from the depths of the lion, eventually terminating into a sorrowful whimper.

"We won't leave her," said Sprael. "I'll carry her if I must."

Marius glanced to Vaskar and Primula. "Nobody is suggesting that, Sprael."

"I'm only making my feelings clear," explained Sprael. "Before we set off."

"Before we set off," repeated Marius. "Perhaps we could formulate a better way of bearing Calliandra? One that is less taxing?"

"Secure her to my back?" suggested Sprael, looking toward Vaskar. "Rig a harness of some make?"

Vaskar nodded approval. "No matter the way you convey her dead weight," he said. "She will hamper your every step." He offered the laif a tightly bound spindle of webbed chord. "I will not hesitate to leave you behind, should circumstances dictate."

Sprael smiled as he accepted the mercenary's gift. "You don't foresee more doors that require a sacrifice I take it?"

"Perhaps," replied Vaskar.

"You knew about the door all along, didn't you?" asked Sprael. He met Marius' eyes and continued. "It's the reason why you acted so protectively, so out of character."

"Secure the Scholar," instructed Vaskar. "This conversation leads nowhere."

Before it could serve as a makeshift carrier, Vaskar's net required minor alterations. Luckily, a sharp blade was all that was necessary.

With Calliandra presently fastened to his back, the side of her cheek pressed to his shoulder blade, Sprael tested his newly acquired weight. As expected, her extremities jostled a bit as he twisted his torso, but her main core held fast.

This will serve, thought Sprael.

Vaskar stood before the door, torch upraised. He swept a glance over the party before outlining his plan in brief. "Follow me."

With Salve beside him, the mercenary darted to the right the moment he entered the hallway. The others followed behind, Marius at the rear to complete the barrier of protective torchlight. They retraced their steps, passed through the large chamber punctured by a gushing sinkhole. Water continued to flush the central pillar, showing little sign of an end. As he ran by, through a narrow gap in the sinkhole, Sprael glimpsed a sky purpled by nightfall.

Over time, the far end of the chamber had experienced perpetual collapse, which positioned the exit passages roughly ten feet above the slanted floor. Salve surged ahead of Vaskar, lowered a bound before him, and the mercenary used the lion's shoulders as a springboard, vaulted, and cleared the passage. Emerald light filled the void, and within moments Vaskar reappeared to offer a hand to Primula. After Marius boosted the lampyr, his leap required the help of Vaskar to pull him the rest of the way.

"Go on." Sprael encouraged Salve to enter ahead.

Nodding dutifully, Salve joined the others with a casual bound. Even with the weight of the Scholar, Sprael did not require aid clearing the obstacle.

"Showoffs," muttered Marius.

For the span of several steps, the ceiling of the shaft had been inlaid with tiles bearing symbols that Sprael recognized as laif script.

Wait a moment! Sprael turned back, pressed past Marius to gain a second look at the tiles.

"Vaskar!". shouted Marius. "Our ranger has found something." He lowered his voice, addressed the laif. "What do you see? Can you read these symbols?"

"I cannot," replied Sprael. "These are written by the hands of ancient laives, perhaps when we were first known as *elves*." Sprael pointed at a particular tile that displayed a squiggled line that grew faint at one end. "But I think that I recognize that symbol, I just cannot for the life of me recall from where." He then murmured over his shoulder, "If only Calliandra were awake…"

It was then that Primula joined, wide-eyed. "What is it?" she asked.

"Sprael recognizes some of these glyphs," replied Marius.

After staring for a few more heartbeats, Sprael growled. "I can't read them, but that's not the point," he spoke harsh. "That symbol right there! I remember where I saw it, long ago. That symbol was a brand. A brand that indicated the ownership of humans…"

Marius elevated his torch to bring the symbol into better clarity. "You mean to say that these were written by slavers, by *archenlaives?*"

"They were not known as archenlaives then," said Sprael. "But yes, they eventually became what you understand to be *archenlaives.*"

"So the Handsome Death Caverns were constructed by archenlaives," Marius spoke as if he were dazed. "So what does that mean?"

Sprael shook his head. "I don't know if—"

"We should not tarry," Vaskar interrupted.

Upon the mercenary's statement, a dissonant wail combed over them. The party whirled at the noise, stricken with suspicion. Though prevalent and abounding in great numbers, the wraiths did not often make noise. Their arrivals had been deathly silent, which made them all the more startling. It seemed only upon death a few had voiced their terror.

"Was that human?" whispered Primula.

No one gave reply as they continued on. Sprael held several theories, none of which he dared voice. The hallway's conclusion soon arrived in the form of a spiral staircase entirely comprised of red clay. Oddly, the stairs had been fabricated to the cylinder-shaped wall that encased the staircase, and not to the pillar at its center. Within the torchlight's influence, many of the stairs were visibly absent, having come free of the wall. Marius gingerly lowered his torch to ascertain the drop distance, but the darkness greedily inhaled the glow.

Vaskar pressed a hand to the support columnar rising from the center of the staircase. He gave Sprael an ambiguous nod, leapt to the columnar, clung to it, and slid downward. Like a guiding light, the mercenary parted the darkness on his way to the bottom. Sprael perceived the base distance once Vaskar's torchlight became a sustained halo, no longer diminishing.

"He's waving his torch," said Marius, cautiously gazing below, his toes several feet from the edge. "We're safe to follow."

When Primula positioned herself to begin the stairs, Marius flinched.

"You alright, love?" asked Primula, pausing in concern.

Marius shook his head, leaning against the wall. "Heights are not... they're not..." he stammered, handing his torch off to Sprael. "I'll want both hands for this."

"No worries," said Sprael. "Follow my lead."

"Yes," agreed Primula, reaching a comforting hand back to the mercenary. "Just place your feet where we place ours."

Marius closed his eyes, and exhaled a laugh. "I'll be fine," he said, packing steel into his voice. "Go on ahead."

"Once we begin the descent, we cannot stop," cautioned Sprael. "Standing still may cause collapse—"

"I get it, I get it!" blurted Marius. "Let's just get this over with."

The stairs proved surprisingly sturdy, and only a few cracked when weight was placed upon them. As they wound their way downward, Sprael followed close behind Salve, providing light for all. Though it had been some time since they had detected the presence of a wraith, the idea of travelling beyond the emerald glow felt akin to suicide.

When they were nearly halfway to Vaskar's waiting torchlight, Salve came to an abrupt stop.

"Halt!" called Sprael, his shins registering the lion's solid tailbone.

Directly behind the laif, Marius gasped in terror. "We can't, we can't..." he repeated.

"What's happening?" said Primula.

Sprael swept the torch before him. "Salve has stopped for something..." Directly afore the hunched beast, the laif saw a gap of missing stairs, spanning beyond the light, but not beyond his night eyes. "This isn't good."

The stair behind Sprael creaked as Marius shifted his feet. "What is it?!" The question came out as more of a demand.

"There's a sizable gap that may—" began Sprael.

"How sizeable?!"

"Twenty stairs or so," replied Sprael, quickly bobbing his head as he counted the blank spaces. "Maybe twenty-five," he amended.

"Can't we just slide down," suggested Primula. "As Vaskar did?"

"Salve can't slide," Sprael spoke distractedly, deep in thought. "And we must stay within the torchlight." Then an idea sprang to the laif's mind, and he rotated his torso to look below. "Vaskar!" he shouted.

If the mercenary can make his way to us and offer his light to Salve, then me and Marius and Primula can slide...

"Vaskar?!" To Sprael's horror, the bottom was utterly absent the mercenary's protective torchlight. "Where?!" At once, all hope fled the laif.

"Vaskar! Vaskar!" Marius and Primula shouted, Marius' voice growing higher pitched with terror. "Vaskar!"

Oh no! Sprael looked down in time to see the arch of Salve's spine deepen.

In a desperate flurry of motion, the lion leapt the void, embraced the darkness beyond the emerald radiance. The leading stairs denied the beast's weight and collapsed into useless powder. Salve rebounded from the central pillar and advanced the remainder of the staircase in a mad, heedless sprint.

Sprael could feel his stair slowly giving way. He hastened a nod toward Primula. "Go on first!" he directed her focus to the pillar. "I'll follow, and Marius—after me!"

"Wait, wait, wait!" Panic-stricken, Marius backed himself against the wall.

"We can't wait!" stated Primula, balancing her weight ahead of her short leap. "Salve is without light!" With that, she bounded onto the pillar. "For Camelot!" she shouted, her eyes fixed to Marius, her face radiating strength and tranquility toward the man before she was lost from sight.

As the bearer of their only torch, Sprael did not have the leisure of choice. "See you at the bottom," he said, striving to sound encouraging. But even as Sprael descended, the addled mercenary had yet to move.

The trip ended much quicker than Sprael had calculated. Before her feet had met the bottom, Primula had darted from the pillar, thankfully saving them from a collision.

After Sprael dashed from the pillar, he held his torso perfectly still in order to gauge Calliandra's breathing. *Good,* he thought. *She's still with us.*

"Marius!" Primula called after several long moments. "Marius!" She hurried a step back, peering upward in despair. It was then that Salve joined her, head angled toward the peak of the staircase. "What can be done?" she asked.

"Give him a moment," encouraged Sprael. *Any moment now...*

Salve swerved his head, and the fur along his spine bristled. He snarled.

With marked trepidation, Sprael followed the beast's line of sight. "What manner of..."

The vacuous chamber that widened before them, at a gradual downward slope, revealed hundreds of prison cells that spanned the opposing walls, with cages dangling overhead that had accommodated the overflow. The walls were composed of the same red clay as the staircase. Sconces, long ago burnt to cinder, accented the spaces between each cell. Abandoned lifting apparatuses that had relied on chains and boulders lay scattered, their disconnected fulcrums still attached as skeletal tails. Curiously, it seemed as though the cells lining the right side had been unlocked, their caged doors swung open. The cells residing opposite, however, were yet sealed.

Then Sprael caught sight of what had inspired Salve's sudden change of mood.

Skeletons, beyond each and every stage of flesh decay, in staggering number, were shambling toward him from the far side of the dungeon, their ligaments and tendons long since wasted away. How they managed to walk up-right—or walk at all—bested all of Sprael's reasonable guesses.

An ancient curse perhaps? Sprael wondered, baffled as he retreated for the staircase. *Most definitely some sort of fell magic.*

Instantly, Sprael's dagger was in his hands. He adjusted his shoulders and rolled onto the balls of his feet, triple-checking that Calliandra would not come loose.

"Marius!" he called over his shoulder. "Marius!" he repeated with more intensity.

"What is it?" asked Primula. "What do you see?" The gloom beyond the emerald torchlight was far too thick for even her heightened perception.

"Reanimates," said Sprael. This response garnered a puzzled look from the lampyr, so the laif clarified, "walking skeletons."

Primula nodded solemnly, seeming unafraid. "I can hear their scraping footsteps," she stated. "Sounds like there are many."

"And we are few."

* * *

In the four years Marius had trained beneath Vaskar, the mercenary had never gone out of his way to be kind. *But he had never been cruel.* On several contracts, when heights had factored into an equation, Vaskar had the sense to re-calibrate his plans to accommodate Marius' phobia. It was not as if he did such things because he liked Marius, he simply viewed Marius' aversion to heights as a liability.

Standing in darkness inches from an unthinkable height, Marius recalled Vaskar's words. *Liabilities must be minimized if they cannot be eliminated.* Somehow he drew comfort from the grim voice playing in his head.

"If I view my fear as mere liability," Marius reasoned, "I may pluck it out, like a pocket of mold on old bread." On the columnar's smooth surface, the dark green light from Sprael's torch played faint. Then he squeezed his eyes closed for the hundredth time. "My fear is only mold."

He gathered his courage, his thoughts focused on Primula. Her face, the curve of her smile.

His feet dragged forward seemingly of their own accord.

"Only mold..."

"Marius!" Sprael's voice reverberated upward. Marius opened his eyes and the columnar's sudden nearness excised all of his newly gathered resolve.

"Marius!"

The stair crackled threats beneath Marius' heels as he backpedaled to the wall. He lifted his head, panting in fear, wishing his body to be as light as the feather they sought.

There is no rescue coming, he thought, his back drifting downward against the wall. "You've made it this far, Marius," he said to himself, sitting with his chin resting on his knees. "What's it going to be?"

***

"One reanimated skeleton is easy enough to slay," Sprael explained quickly as he watched the horde's gradual approach, which had yet to enter the torch's influence. "Well, maybe 'slay' is not the correct word in this instance."

"I get your meaning," said Primula. Her arming sword, imbued with silver, sparkled in the torchlight. The insignia of a laif craftsman emblazoned the center of the expensive blade's crossguard.

A gift from Marius no doubt, probably procured it in Lepaskalica right after her transformation, thought Sprael. *If only the lad would gift us his presence, perhaps then we would be almost equal...*

"There are hundreds," Primula whispered unnecessarily as her eyes leapt across the chamber. "Is there no way around?"

"We can't backtrack. Our only option is to go through," replied Sprael. "The tricky thing about reanimates, like these fellows, is that they're rather clingy."

"What do you mean by that?"

"If they get a hold of you, they're quite loathe to let go," Sprael elaborated. "And with numbers such as these..."

Primula drew close to the laif. "I wonder what has become of Vaskar?"

At the mention of the name, Salve strode to the front outskirts of the torchlight, gazing into the beyond.

"Maybe he saw the Nocnik and gave chase?"

Primula squared her stance.

Just beyond the torchlight, the first ribbon of skeletons bloomed, their bones reflecting a pastel green. As they lumbered closer, their skulls swiveled intently toward Sprael as if their eyeless cavities still functioned.

Primula gripped her sword in two hands just below her belt. "At least they move slowly," she said.

"Slow acting poison," muttered Sprael, "is still poison."

~ 23 ~

THEY MUST BE CAST ASIDE

Salve had been the one to initiate battle. Splintered femurs and humeri filled the air the moment he streaked into the skeletons' midst. But the horde, in seeming disinterest, gradually eased around the beast. It seemed only the skeletons under direct attack had turned their attention toward him, while all the others honed their focus on Sprael.

"Don't try stabbing them," Sprael cautioned Primula. "Use your sword as a bludgeoning tool instead."

Primula shifted her feet and nodded, raised her sword directly over her head, and aimed a downward stroke on her first encroaching skeleton. If not for the silver properties forged in her steel, the skeleton's skull may have simply cracked, but when Primula struck, she rendered the skull to powder. Severed in two, the remainder of the skeleton collapsed into a heap inside its final step. Lunging left, her sword trailing behind, Primula scored another skeleton's neck with a well-placed arc. By the skittering of her feet as she recovered, it seemed the lampyr had not spent much time in a sparring yard. Her skills were clearly below a novice, but truth be told, enemies such as these made for excellent practice.

If only she were facing half a dozen, not half a thousand, thought Sprael, pressing his torch into a skeleton's chest. *And if only I had a hammer instead of a dagger.* He followed the push with a whirling dagger sweep that saw the skeleton's head sailing clean from its body. A piercing shriek burst from the skeleton, chilling every living bone within Sprael. A wraith had emerged from inside, and instantly disintegrated in the emerald light.

"What the...!" Sprael reeled. That had been his first kill, Primula had claimed more than five at this point, and Salve... *How could you keep track of his numbers?* And that was the first wraith he had seen since The Chamber of Lasting Rot.

Battling the fringes along the skeletons' frontline, Primula chopped another skeleton down. She wielded the blade rather clumsily, but her tactics proved efficient. There was no denying her body count. With all the enemies focused on Sprael, their defenses had been nonexistent, which made dismantling them all the easier. Between the two, Salve and Primula had silently dispatched dozens, but each time Sprael brought a boneman low, he had been met with an ear-rending scream.

The battle continued, and it became blatantly apparent that the skeletons only sought one target. Sprael.

As the skeletons drew nearer, their formation tapered, separating the three defenders from one another. Far to Sprael's right, Salve faithfully enacted his best showing of violence, culling numbers that only seemed significant in the frame, but were mere drops in a vast basin. And to his left, on the further side of an overwhelming migration, Primula cut down the skeletons from behind. Though the party fought valiantly, the tide of bones continued to drift, devouring more and more ground.

Soon Sprael found himself with his back mere steps from the spiral staircase. It was not long before one persistent skeleton scored an indurate hold upon his dagger wrist. Sprael plied an elbow to the reanimate's chin, netting nothing but a disconnected mandible.

In a spray of bone slivers, Salve pressed the horde in a valiant attempt to join Sprael's side. As he bounded before the laif, he combed a dense snarl of skeletons. A series of detached hands decorated the beast's flanks, signifying the number of skeletons he had passed on the way. Thanks to Salve, the skeleton that had been latched to Sprael was quite gone, but the pressure on his wrist had not lessened. Try as he might to shake it free, the entire skeletal arm remained attached.

Salve contorted his body, behaving as a hound afflicted by ravenous mites, gnawing at the disconnected skeleton hands that still gripped him. In a fit of agony, he managed to twist one knuckle free, but in the process purged a great deal of flesh. A torrent of blood poured from the gash, the beast writhed, his attention shifted, and he was overtaken by the horde. It seemed their sheer numbers proved too much for the dragonslayer.

Primula called out through the clacking walkers, but Sprael could not make out her words. As the horde pressed and pressed, the disembodied skeleton hand tightened more and more. He now understood the anguish Salve had endured.

I will lose my hand, he thought as his vision tunneled. In a swing fueled by desperation, he separated another skeleton from its head. *If I can't free myself!* With a thud that registered through Calliandra, he found that he had backed into the columnar.

The Scholar stirred, mumbled incoherently.

The dead hand squeezed, bones shattered.

He grew faint.

Prija.

Emerald light emanated from the floor.

Prija, forgive me.

***

Driven upright by Primula's screams, Marius stood with one hand to the wall. The urgency, the sheer panic in her voice had parsed a bit of the mold from the bread. But he had gone no further. *I'm so sorry, Primula.* He shivered. The sweat that drenched his mantle had cooled.

"What's it going to be?" he asked himself again. "Either you choose when you jump or this crumbly stair chooses for you." It was all a matter of *when*. He just needed to match his stride to the columnar within the perfect rhythm. However, he had found the unearthly shrieks coming from below to be less than helpful.

What are they killing down there? Marius wondered. *Probably something Salve could handle blindfolded.* That was definitely a lie, but he would ignore that for now. As long as he believed Primula and Sprael were doing fine without him then he could cower a few moments longer.

Somewhere within the cacophony, a woman cried out. Her voice began as a tremulous wail but concluded in a distinctly *inhuman* snarl.

Marius finally approached the columnar. He gazed below to see a laif splayed unmoving on the floor. It was all he could see from his position.

"Sprael!" he screamed in fright. *He's dying!* Marius drew a breath, leapt, and at the end of his exhale, found himself beside the laif. The downward slide had been quickly forgotten. "Can you hear me?" The laif did not respond. Marius discovered the netted bindings that had held Calliandra were severed. He looked around, hoping she was alive and safe, but she was nowhere to be seen. He scoured the area for Primula, but all was lost to darkness.

"Primula!" he yelled. "I'm over here!"

Marius returned his attention to Sprael. He groaned as he took in the skeleton arm tightly clamped to Sprael's wrist, contorting the laif's hand at a grotesque angle.

Meanwhile, inches beyond Sprael's fingertips, the torch-light depicted a canvas of motion that defied reason.

Hastening to the reaches of the torchlight, Marius squinted into the darkness where Primula appeared.

"Thank the Creator you're safe!" said Marius, relieved beyond reason. She tightly embraced him, and he grate-fully pressed his lips to her forehead.

The lampyr drew back, looking into his eyes. "Marius," she said solemnly. "You're not going to believe this..."

Over her head, the shadows had fled before his torch.

"Is that?" Marius stuttered, stunned. "Is that?"

At the center of a sea of shattered bones, a bristly sil-houette heaved its shoulders. Then the clicking of feline claws approached and joined the emerald glow. Absent-mindedly, Marius ruffled Salve's great mane.

"It is," replied Primula.

The silhouette turned. The creature's baleful eyes soaked in the green of the torchlight and reflected a cold sapphire.

"Calliandra is awake."

A REAL STUMPER

The sharp prick on the side of his neck woke him ahead of the drain, and when Sprael bolted upright, Primula miraculously held her fangs in place. Cleansing magic pulsated in the laif's veins; flesh mended, contusions cleared, bones restructured. Afresh, as if newly born, feeling as though he could clear the entire dungeon of reanimates all by his lonesome, the potency of the young lampyr's healing magic was undeniable!

Primula withdrew her fangs, delighted. "I'm not defective!" she cheered and looked to Marius standing over her shoulder. "Look now! At his wrist!"

In real time, the observers watched the crunched portion of the laif's wrist inflate to its regular shape, for Sprael it simply felt like a steamed rag had tightly wrapped his wrist. Once he tested it for feeling, the heat dissipated. The distorted portion of his limb had regained its full function, from fingers to forearm. Then it was at that moment Sprael realized he was leaned against the stairwell columnar, where he had fallen beneath the tide of skeletons.

"Where's Calliandra?" The netted chords were absent his chest. "Where's Calliandra?!" he demanded.

"She's, uh..." Marius scratched his head, stepped to the side.

A werewolf loomed on the outskirts of the emerald aura. When the beast turned, the torchlight ignited the fibers of her golden fur. "Hello, Sprael," said the werewolf.

Sprael could not breathe.

The voice wholly belonged to Calliandra, of that there was no mistaking. His mind reeled. *When did... How could...*

"You must have a million questions," said Marius, clasping the laif by his newly mended wrist, and heaving him upward. "But we have more ground to cover."

"Has Vaskar not returned?" asked Sprael, with eyes that seemed permanently glued to the werewolf.

Primula shook her head after drawing a pull from her canteen. Evidently the taste of laif blood was an acquired one for her. "He has not," she replied, her voice more husky than usual. "But Calliandra is back to form, well, back in *a* form." She suddenly appeared as one who had just swallowed a gadfly. Quickly she fetched her canteen for a supplemental swig. "Your blood doesn't seem to want to go all the way down my pipe," she explained, thumping her chest.

Marius stepped forward. "Now that Calliandra is back, we have a compass of sorts." He administered a friendly nudge to Salve's cheek. "Though it's not as if Vaskar had any idea as to where he was leading us." The lion seemed surprisingly hale after sustaining such a heavy procession of wounds. "Honestly, he seemed to rely on Salve for guidance."

"You don't seem overly concerned about your mentor's well-being?" Sprael surveyed the party. "None of you seem overly concerned."

Marius cocked a speculative eyebrow. "Are you?"

Not really, thought Sprael, shaking his head despite his inkling of worry. *But he better survive.*

Swiftly, they navigated their way through the bone lagoon, leaving behind the dungeon and all its misery mysteries. The cells lining the left wall had contained long-decayed skeletons, purposely overlooked by the re-animate spell. Sprael deduced the story behind the scene, but such woeful thoughts only lagged his steps.

Sprael found the corridor they had entered appeared as though it were pleasantly flooded with daylight. For the time being, the laif's senses had been elevated by the lampyr's bite. For how long it would last, he did not know. He noticed the way every granule of dirt scattered along the stone pathway cast a tiny shadow. He also noticed an ogre wraith clumsily loping toward them in a chamber beyond their corridor, brought up short a few steps from entry. Presumably the spirit was barred by one of the long-ago placed boundaries.

"I wonder why those cells on the one side of the dungeon were open, and the others shut?" said Primula. She looked to Marius near her elbow; the proximity of his torch forced her to squint. As the sole torchbearer, Marius strode at the center of the party. "You think Vaskar opened them?"

Marius shook his head. "The opened cells had rusted open," he replied. "Someone had opened them long before we ever darkened this Cavern."

"Huh," Primula said with a shrug. "So Vaskar just walked right past them. Makes sense. They only seemed keen on killing our ranger. The skeletons just walked right over Salve after he fell down and didn't even bother him." A sharp click came from inside her mouth. "Well, except for the graspy skeleton hands that shredded some of his coat. But we took care of those nasty gashes, didn't we, Salve?"

The lion favored the lampyr with a glance.

"It was a most cruel punishment," Calliandra answered.

Sprael winced.

The golden werewolf did not elaborate.

Primula's mouth gaped, appearing as one who expected an explanation. "A punishment...?" she asked, irritably shaking her head.

Calliandra opened her answer with an *I feel it was quite obvious* sort of tone. "Well, it was a punishment, or more likely a sentence that was passed down to all the prisoners." She sighed. "One side had been released and granted everlasting life, while the others remained shackled behind bars, unable to leave. The prisoners bestowed immortality had been forced to watch as their loved ones slowly starved, died, and decayed."

Primula sneered. "Yeah? And how come those skeletons only attacked Sprael?"

"Easy." Calliandra shrugged. "The skeletons had all once been humans, and laives had meted their sentence. And after shedding all other desires, it seemed that only vengeance remained."

"Got another for you," said Primula, her eyes narrowed. "How did you become a werewolf?"

"Oh, a real stumper," Calliandra remarked. "My best guess: my dark sister got herself entangled with some werewolves, and one managed to score a bite."

As Primula considered Calliandra's response, her face contorted bitterly. "Explains why I couldn't heal you," she reasoned at length. "But how did the curse transfer..." she trailed off at the sight of the ogre wraith frantically backpedaling away from the torchlight.

They entered a chamber that was wider than it was long. From end to end along each wall, nearly sixscore steel-banded trunks had been abandoned upon an equal number of shelves. Each one had been built identical, roughly measuring the length of a prostrate schoolchild. The ogre wraith had fled toward the deepest corner of the chamber, huddled at a generous distance. He was accompanied by several other wraiths; a hob, a human, and a mule. The grouping had ostensibly assembled the primary components for a real sidesplitter of a joke.

The momentum the party had gathered kept them moving past the room and its frightened wraiths. Any curiosity wrought from the possible treasures buried inside the chests was batted aside, forgotten.

They passed through an entryway, three steps in length. Remnants of a forgotten gate clung to the heavy iron hinges still bolted to the slab. A series of stone hewn counters and tables filled the ensuing space. Several walk-in crannies along the outskirts fed into larders, the abandoned jars within greeted the passersby with lids tipped at affably jaunty angles.

"That was all so very wrong," began Marius, standing upon the central worktable, allowing the others to navigate the maze within the torchlight. Stray wraiths, appearing as bats, floated in the uppermost corners, eagerly awaiting an opening. "What the archenlaives did to the people in the dungeon."

"From my research," said Calliandra, "that's just a light scratch upon a much broader bulwark. I can recall an instance—" She suddenly halted, her ears locked toward the exit. Then, another emerald light bolstered that of their own.

"Vaskar!" Primula cried out in relief.

The mercenary stood at the threshold. "We must hurry," he said. "She is not faring well."

"*She?*" Marius and Calliandra said as one.

But Vaskar had whirled from sight, leaving the question suspended. As they departed the chamber, two wraiths hurtled for Primula. Had it not been for the faint tail of green light that managed to screen her heels, she may have fallen victim to their evils.

"Watch your footing," Vaskar cautioned from a great distance within the neighboring chamber. His voice resounded and dislodged the flakes of crusted filth clinging to the vaulted ceiling. "This one has seen some collapse." He swiveled his torch to reveal a chasm one-half stride to his left.

Sprael felt overly exposed, walking single file in a room expansive enough to accommodate an army.

"Could you cease that scraping for now?" said Calliandra, angrily side eyeing Sprael. "You're setting my teeth on further edge."

Unaware that he had drawn both his dagger and whetstone, Sprael hastily resheathed them. "Apologies," he stated. "Habit."

The chamber offered a great many options for escape, most of which involved a drop into fathomless darkness. The more sensible alternatives appeared as open doorways. Generously sized gates adorned the opposing wall, while a much smaller gateway lay at the end of a meandering walkway that spun toward the right with edges chewed by centuries of erosion. And by this brittle pathway, Vaskar waited.

A startled shout issued from beyond the mercenary. Sprael found the sound more curious than cautionary.

Warily they crossed the chamber, briefly descended a tidy set of stairs, and ducked through a cramped anteroom to find their feet coming to rest in a vast chamber that had, without a doubt, once been an armoury for a great laif dynasty.

None of this makes any sense, thought Sprael with a hand to his forehead. *Not one ripple of sense.* The space appeared organized, and not as if it had been quickly abandoned.

Shining battleaxes sprung up along the right wall, numbering well into the hundreds. Ensnared to arming stands, suits of fearsome armour loitered, most plated in a rich shade of green, while others bore dreary hues of red or blue. An endless arrangement of longswords, dipped and readied in functionally elegant scabbards, hemmed the opposing wall.

The central walkway was comprised of a smooth, deep amethyst that reflected clear images of the party, as if alternate purple versions of themselves walked the same path upside down just beneath their feet. The space where Primula trod, however, was blank, as if her copy had not survived this far into the Caverns.

As their shadows, thought Sprael in brief. *Lampyrs also shed their reflections.*

Further ahead, the walkway diverged around the base of a great statue that depicted a rearing laif-bred destrier arraigned in brilliant green armour. The beast's rider was present from the waist down, its upper portion had top-pled and returned to rubble long ago.

Wraiths darted circles over and around the statue, as kapreta to blood-tainted waters. Vaskar had run ahead, his torchlight keeping the fell spirits at bay.

Portions of these Caverns seem eldritch, daemonic, while others are wholly archenlaif. Sprael drew closer to the laif-horse and half knight statue. *Yet this room depicts a structured laif society.* Beneath its helm, the horse glared back in noble defiance. *Just what happened here?*

"You can't stay!" A woman shouted. Her voice came from beneath the swirling wraiths, her identity obscured by the statue.

"Give me ten good reasons!"

"If you go, I will never forgive you!"

The argument was carried by one troubled voice that varied its pitch upon each statement.

"You never think of their sacrifices anyhow!"

"How could I not? We were meant to touch the stars to-gether!"

The woman bristled as she came into Sprael's view.

Impossible! Sprael's chest constricted all breathing. Though she was hunched over, incensed by some kind of internal agony, Sprael could not mistake the tall, lean fig-ure of Orkney's knight commander.

"Kathryn!" shouted Calliandra, her arms flung wide. But the knight's sudden repulsed facial contortion brought the Scholar up short.

"Who let the daft hound in from the rain?!" sneered Sir Kathryn. A string of red spittle quivered from her bottom lip. "It reeks!"

"She's crazed!" Primula claimed, clutching Marius' torch arm.

The party joined Vaskar's side, opting to observe the knight from a healthy distance.

"She has been possessed," Sprael corrected despondently. "By a great many wraiths it seems."

Vaskar nodded. "My torch expelled a number of them, but she is yet assailed by tenfold or more," he said. "But we only need the one."

"Only need one?" questioned Calliandra. "One for what?"

"Why, one for the fowl," answered Sir Kathryn coolly in a voice that belonged to another. She had straightened to her full towering height, seeming in a state of calm. "The Warrior abides, sheltered in her mind, but she revealed what you seek before she scurried off and hid." Her accent rang peculiar, hinted toward that of ages past. "Is that not what you seek?" One corner of Sir Kathryn's mouth deepened into a vulpine grin. "A bird from fables, a creature of myth?"

"That voice," said Vaskar, pointing directly at Sir Kathryn. "That's the voice that can lead us to the Nocnik."

"Or lead us to our deaths," argued Sprael. "That's the voice of an ancient laif. And if you might recall the dungeons, these ancient laives treat humans in very *specific* ways."

"The hour grows late," said Vaskar. "And I have already brokered the deal."

The possessed Sir Kathryn placed a hand upon her hip, cocked her torso in an uncharacteristic manner.

"A deal?"

"I will lead you to the *nest* of this Nocnik," explained the manifesting spirit. "In exchange, I shall be granted passage from this purgatory."

"While masquerading as Kathryn?"

"Yes," replied the spirit, her chin upraised primly. "Until I find a more *suitable* host. This physique is most unbecoming a true lady."

"And how does Sir Kathryn feel about this bargain?"

"I believe her words were," the spirit began, cleared her throat. "*For Camelot.*"

Primula inhaled sharp and backed a step.

Sprael's lip twitched. Dealing with daemons seldom yielded the fruit one sought, and often brought about the unintended. "If we must," he groaned. "I cannot offer further argument if Kathryn has stamped her approval." The laif exchanged a glance with Calliandra, then turned back to the knight. "But if I may be so bold, how should we address you? It feels most odd to call you by your host's name."

The spirit attempted a majestic curtsy but found the knight's sculpted musculature resistant to such a bend. Instead she bowed. "You may call me Zaotrice."

This is a very bad idea, thought Sprael, smiling and nodding.

When Vaskar brought his torch closer, an ounce of fear passed behind Zaotrice's eyes. "Lampyr, exorcise the knight," he stated plain. "This helpful spirit will force the others from hiding. The moment she taps you upon the forehead, relinquish your fangs."

Primula clutched her chest. "You want me to perform a controlled exorcism?" She laughed dryly. "I've only healed lacerations and splintered bones."

"You're competent," said Vaskar. "You will succeed."

"I may become possessed as well! Or worse!" Primula shook her head vigorously. "What's the harm in setting off with Kathryn as she is?"

"Not part of the deal," said Vaskar. A coldness crept into his voice. "The hour grows late."

Primula gave Marius' hand a rueful squeeze. The young mercenary was reluctant to release, and the lampyr gently shook her hand to free it from his grasp.

As Zaotrice knelt in preparation for the exorcism, her eyes danced between the torches.

Sprael had fallen witness to scores of healings, been the patient on the good end of many. But he had never seen an exorcism. It was a procedure reserved for seasoned lampyrs—laives with over a century of experience—and even then, most refused to even try. At Primula's level of experience, Sprael wagered that this was akin to a novice archer instructed to strike a bullseye while blindfolded, with the distance and location of the pell an utter mystery. Also, if she missed, the pell would spring to life and pile drive her into oblivion.

Sprael recalled the damage Elshur sustained from healing Calliandra.

And that was merely from onion soup, thought Sprael. *Even if the Healers of Lepaskalica successfully heal him, he'll never be the same again. A mind can endure only so much torment.* Sprael smiled and shook his head. *Such a bad idea.*

* * *

Marius had witnessed Primula's bite suture Salve's gaping wounds and heal them within the blink of an eye. *And curing beasts is tricky business,* he thought, reassuringly.

As he watched Primula steady herself over Sir Kathryn, the knight's possessed body assumed the pose of one prepared for a dubbing. A position she had taken once before, under considerably different circumstances.

She also brought Sprael back from the brink! Marius continued, trying to think positive thoughts. *And his wrist looked like it had been mangled by ghouls.*

Never before had Marius felt such a connection with anyone so quickly. At first, it had been Primula's beauty that had captivated him. But as time went on he only wished to be near her, wished to know more. He had surprised himself by finding he was planning a future with her, imagining years into a shared future. More surprising, perhaps, was that he had broached the subject with her and she had enthusiastically bolstered his hopes.

Perhaps I'll finally be able to settle down, mused Marius wistfully. *Leave the mercenary life behind.* He paused and repositioned himself near Primula, angling his torch as close to her head as safely possible. Every fiber within him wanted to ensure her success. He was doubtful it would make a lick of difference, but perhaps the flame would act as a better disintegrator than the light alone? No matter the case, he was determined to slay the escaping wraiths before they had the chance to inhabit her. The thought of any harm befalling her created a hollow in his chest.

Vaskar watched, his torch at a more measured distance. Salve, beside him, casually preened the back of his paw, rubbed it behind an ear. Calliandra's features, though werewolf, betrayed curiosity. Sprael trembled, deeply affected, absently scratching at the traces of lampyr bites upon his neck.

Without further preparation, Primula plunged her fangs into Sir Kathryn's neck.

Sir Kathryn pleaded, her eyes shut tight. "This is not the way!" she shrieked with her arms locked to her sides as if bound. "You will never be—" The phrase was cut short as a phial-sized amount of ghost powder spilled from the knight's forehead. The first spirit had been vanquished without harm to Primula!

Primula continued to consume, and more powder spilled onto the floor, each one in dissimilar quantities. It seemed as though Zaotrice was systematically rooting the spirits and pushing them off some ethereal ledge.

Please, Creator, prayed Marius fervently. *Guide her to safety.*

After what felt like hours, Sir Kathryn grunted in the timbre of Zaotrice, and a spoonful of powder cascaded from the knight's temple. "There remains only one more!" she cried out, panting in near exhaustion. "Aside from the anchor."

Marius turned a look of panic toward Calliandra, unsure of what Zaotrice meant.

"Kathryn's the anchor," assured the Scholar.

Good. Marius nodded. He turned his attention back to the women. Though Sir Kathryn was the person being drained of blood, Primula's complexion had become alarmingly pale.

"Let's be done with this!" Marius pleaded. "This is hurting her!"

Sir Kathryn's eyes cracked open as her left arm suddenly sprung from her side, clenching Primula about the throat. The lampyr's eyes registered panic as she struggled to swallow.

"Get off her!" shouted Marius. With his offhand he clasped Kathryn's wrist at the vambrace, attempting to wrench it from Primula's throat. Primula gagged, unable to contain the flow, and blood burst from the corners of her mouth. "Please! No!" Marius begged as Kathryn applied more pressure.

Vaskar's torchlight flickered and, in a blur, Kathryn's arm fell away. Her cleanly severed hand tarried lifelessly for a moment before Primula swiped it from her collar. She tucked her chin and swallowed. In disbelief, Marius watched her return her lips to Kathryn's neck to resume feeding. The glistening stump where Kathryn's hand had been quickly healed.

Marius glanced at Vaskar. Never before had he felt such appreciation for his mentor's decisive brutality.

"You shan't slay me!" an incensed male voice crackled from Sir Kathryn, jerking Marius' attention to the knight. "Not without a reckoning!" Sir Kathryn's left arm suddenly adhered firm to her side, and a cloud of dust blasted Primula between the eyes.

With a wail, Primula released her fangs, and wheeled toward the floor. "My eyes!" she screamed, raking her face. "They burn!"

Marius dropped to her side, his insides contorting with dread.

Sir Kathryn stood over them, displaying a grin that was explicitly Zaotrice.

"Is that all?" Marius cried out over Primula's weeping. "Are you finished?!"

Upraising her left arm, Zaotrice glanced at the place of separation with clear amusement. Her attention then filtered toward Vaskar. "You came to a rather hasty decision, human," she crooned. "Were this vessel more than a temporary vessel, I might have been cross with you."

~ 25 ~

JUDAS

According to Zaotrice, the Nocnik's eyrie was not far from the armoury. After describing the route, she had not been forthcoming with further details. It seemed the exorcism had sapped nearly all her energy.

Sir Kathryn rocked back on her heels, as one just woken from a deep slumber. "You warned us," she muttered absently, eyes rolling to front. "Sprael... I had no idea..."

Sprael approached the knight and took her remaining hand into his own. He had no words.

Meanwhile, Primula had regained a semblance of composure, explaining to Marius over and over that *something* felt very wrong inside her. "Do you think my sight will return," she asked as she clung to him. Her eyes matched the sickly pallor of her flesh, while the rest of her appeared gaunt, sickly thin. "I don't think I did it right."

"I think you did very well," Marius consoled her as he tenderly guided her down a seemingly infinite staircase. "I'm sure you'll see the world again very soon. Trust me though, right now you need to take it easy! The next step is much steeper—you're not missing much."

After twenty steps, the landing ricocheted a hard right turn, then after another twenty steps, another hard right angle, and so on. Marius could not help but notice how the increments, the distances between stairs and landings, were so precise. Though battered and chipped, even the risers were uniform.

"It's getting chilly," Primula murmured, "and I can hear what sounds like the gurgle of a flowing spring."

Marius heard nothing of the sort. "You're right," he agreed. "And the air is definitely growing much colder." He caught the piteous glance Calliandra offered from the landing ahead. "But we'll make it there all the same."

"Marius," Primula whispered, stopping to feel the mercenary's face. "I don't think I did it right."

Fighting tears, Marius gripped the hand brushing his cheek. "You did just fine, Prim." He sniffed, trying to regain a semblance of control. "We're almost there."

The ensuing stairs proved a struggle for Primula, and Marius entertained the notion of carrying her.

"Do you like Judas?" asked Primula, endeavoring the next step on her own.

"I've never known anyone by that name."

"Me neither," said Primula. "I meant as a name for our first-born."

No longer able to contain his tears, Marius moaned, gripping the stone rail. "I think that's a beautiful name," he admitted. "Has a real trustworthy ring to it."

Soundlessly, the mercenary carefully gathered the frail woman into his arms.

"Glad you like it," whispered Primula. "I'm so tired. I think I'll just close my eyes for a little bit."

"You do that," said Marius. "I'll be right here when you wake."

* * *

Sprael stood upon a landing with the others, pausing for Marius and Primula. Their pace had slackened gradually, and now it had finally halted. Calliandra had ventured to the outskirts of Vaskar's torchlight to catch a glimpse, and had returned sullen, unable to meet Sprael's eyes for longer than a moment. And that was all he needed to know.

"We once travelled with so many lampyrs," said Sir Kathryn, sounding wistful, her eyes glistening. The knight had not spoken for some time. "Did we not?"

No one replied.

Soon the emerald tongues of Marius' torchlight played upon the stone handrails. The mercenary came into view, carrying Primula in his arms, his torch beneath the crook of her knees. "Calliandra," he said, gestured for the werewolf to relieve him of his torch.

"How is she faring?" asked Sir Kathryn.

Marius scowled, more from sadness than anger. "Unwell," he replied. "Let's bring an end to all this, eh?"

"Marius," began Calliandra as the party renewed their descent. "If you want to take the torch and leave this place, no one will blame you. Perhaps you and Primula could make it back to Lepaskalica before..." she trailed off. Marius behaved as though he could not hear her and continued on.

As they plunged the depths, the noise of rushing waters increased dramatically. From what Sprael knew, the nearest source of fresh water lay within Lake Humiel, but that meant that they had travelled several leagues eastward? *Impossible.* Perhaps these waters were fed by aquifers? Sprael shook his head. But from where? Where would their origin be? Sprael had long ago given up attempting to divine their location and would soon see himself joining Sir Kathryn in the company of the mentally afflicted if he continued.

Eventually the staircase ceased its spiral routine and became a flight of steps that terminated onto solid ground. The final stairs had experienced erosion, their shade an unpleasant green, and seemed unwilling to take on weight. Vaskar and Salve leapt the distance and the others did the same, save for Marius who strode the steps as though they were whole. With each step he seemed to sink just a bit, his boots leaving distinct impressions in their wake. Surprisingly not one stair gave way, and instead accepted the combined weight of both mercenary and lampyr.

According to Zaotrice, once the stairs concluded, a most obvious gateway would become evident. Her description had been accurate regarding the existence of the gateway, however, she had omitted a rather crucial detail: a tremendous whirlpool spanned nearly the entire inner dimension of the chamber. Only the base of the stairs lay beyond its breakers. Its waves roiled and churned, daring only the bold to enter. Even the outer rims of the pool, at its presumable weakest, furiously lapped the fringes.

Sprael combed their surroundings for a means of bypass. Judging by the rings of erosion along the walls, he figured this whirlpool increased and diminished, fed by an unknown source. The boggy bottom stairs were further evidence of the pool's penchant for expansion.

"We have half an hour," said Vaskar. "Before the shores become passable."

Sprael had only begun his calculations. *That probably checks out,* he thought, his equations dissolving. "Marius, would you like us to rig a harness for you and Primula?" The laif looked to Calliandra. "Like the one we used?"

The way Marius gazed through Sprael made him feel as though he may have spoken in an incomprehensible foreign tongue.

"The time may be better spent taking stock of our provisions," suggested Calliandra. "And replenishing our canteens. This pool should be drinkable." With a nod she indicated Sprael pass her satchel in trade for her torch.

Salve waded into the harsh churning shallows to lap the quickly moving water. The others, not quite as bold, dipped their canteens without hazarding a step within.

Confined in a hollow behind the staircase, Sprael discovered a dry patch of stone. With torch in hand, he decided to while the time away there, chewing on strips of dried meat. After a few minutes spent in solemn contemplation, Calliandra sat down beside him. She unstoppered her canteen and drew a dainty sip. "It was a stroke of luck, that was," she said with a heartfelt sigh, but failed to progress her point.

"Care to be a bit more specific?" Sprael asked at length. In the silence he had assumed she remarked on her new lycanthrope status.

Calliandra rifled in her satchel. "At some point while I was unconscious," she began, quickly finding what she sought. She withdrew a glittery bundle. "Somebody removed my maille."

Sprael was confused. Was the Scholar upset about her undressing? "Yes," he said, his voice taking on a defensive stance. "Primula removed it when she bathed you. Nothing unseemly occurred..."

Calliandra recoiled with a laugh. "No, no, Sprael," she said. "I might not have survived my transformation if I had been wearing this!" She tossed the maille into Sprael's lap. "It may have rendered me into a heap of extruded werewolf skins! So that was quite the stroke of luck, I'd say."

With all that had happened since, Sprael had never stopped to consider that detail. *That is most fortunate,* he admitted inwardly. "Too bad that luck didn't extend to your clothing as well."

"Oh, well," said Calliandra, her shoulders deflated. "Just gives me an excuse to stay in this form and grow more accustomed to it." She settled back against the recession of stone, stretched her legs before her. "Speaking of luck, it seems that only one of my archenlaif scroll spells survived."

"Of how many?"

Calliandra tucked her chin in thought. "I thought that I had packed five, but it seems the Creator granted us a small boon. You see, after everything that's happened, the daemons, the wraiths—the *waters*, it all proved too much for the paper. Makes sense, seeing as the ancient serifs were hardly legible, nearly faded before we even set off."

"But?" Sprael's eyebrows topped his forehead.

"But," began Calliandra, lifting a clawed index finger. "A sixth scroll had been accidentally bundled and wrapped, courtesy of our careless friend Earon, within the last of the scrolls. The outer scroll acted as a water barrier, protecting the smaller scroll within."

"Ah, Earon," said Sprael. "The lad may have just saved the kingdom, and he doesn't even know it."

"Sadly, this is probably the most he will contribute to the war."

"More than most can say," added Sprael. "Even if we manage to translate the spell, I'm more likely to hand it off to a Royal Caster, or a more established mage. No offense to our beneficiary Sir Demetrius."

Calliandra hummed a single note as she nodded. "Absolutely." Then her demeaner shifted, her gaze grew distant. "Although, I once had a premonition about Earon—" Whatever she was about to reveal was curtly bitten short.

"The vortex has narrowed!" Sir Kathryn's head invaded their hollow. "Zaotrice tells me that we have only a mere junket before we reach our..." The knight blinked in rapid succession, appeared ready to vomit. "Goal," she struggled to conclude. As she backed from their presence, one of her eyes stayed shut. "Salve and Vaskar have already crossed." The knight mumbled as her footsteps faded off toward the whirlpool, "Wraiths enter through the eyes..."

"Can't say that was my favorite interaction with Kathryn," admitted Sprael, rising and making certain his daggers and traveling paraphernalia were yet in place.

"I fear that's what we should expect from now on." Calliandra's snout crinkled. "Even after her body has one soul residing in it again, I don't think she'll ever be the same." With that said, she gave Sprael an oblique glance and departed.

"As if any of us will be the same," muttered Sprael as he performed a final cursory check. Once satisfied that all was in order, he strode out onto the rocks, faced the extravagant gateway hovering beyond the noticeably smaller whirlpool. "Best not waste any more time."

After they navigated the whirlpool's boundary, deftly avoided drowning, the party was voluntarily swallowed by the portal that led closer to the Nocnik. It was then they were greeted by a generously spaced cobbled walkway, where the wraith activity remained at a comfortable zero. Aside from the spirit dwelling within Sir Kathryn, their ilk had last been seen at play in the armoury.

"I can't help but notice the lampyr's graceful bone structure," Zaotrice said to Sprael. Before they had crossed the whirlpool, the spirit had awakened and taken full control of the knight's body. Now they strode behind Marius, treading in his torchlight. "She would have turned a great many heads during my time. Of course, she would have been preserved from the fields, or the mines, or any sort of hard labor. No doubt she would have found herself servicing a great laif household—"

"All right," interrupted Sprael. "That *lampyr* is the reason why you're here right now and not fluttering above a broken statue."

"I am only declaring," persisted Zaotrice, "that the human is comely." Irritably she shook her head. "I meant it as a mere compliment."

Sprael leaned close to the knight, lowering his tone. "It's probably best to keep such observations to yourself."

No doubt Marius had overheard the conversation, and Sprael applauded the mercenary's restraint. A needless confrontation so near their destination would only serve as a detriment. And adding to Marius' credit, this was not the first instance Zaotrice had offered comment on Primula's appearance.

Further ahead of Vaskar's torchlight, Sprael noticed a conical slab of stone upheaving the floor's structure. Since crossing the gateway, they had been enjoying a gentle downward slope, as the soft roll of a meadow, but as they approached the disruption, the laif knew another amazing obstacle was readying itself for an introduction. He hurried ahead to join Salve and Vaskar.

A few steps shy of the slab, the three stopped and peered cautiously around its crumbled, serrated sides. Then at the same moment their gazes dropped downward.

Where a bridge had once connected the pathway, a great chasm stretched. Centuries had passed, calmly overseeing the structure's gradual decay and eventual collapse.

Even with Sprael's gifted vision, the depths were far too dark. As he turned from the chasm to speak with the others, his eyes snagged on an aberration along the cliff face. Upon a second glance, he noticed an anchor wedged between a crevice. "What manner..." The laif crawled to the edge of the precipice. "Of climbing hook." Then further below, he espied a dynamic series of scaffolds presumably rising from the core of the basin.

For how else would the scaffolds stand on their own? thought Sprael, gingerly returning to his feet. "I can't foresee a means of crossing," he admitted, nervously addressing the party, purposely avoiding Marius. He sighed while he prepared to drop the bad news, then Zaotrice spoke up.

"We won't need to cross," she said. "Congratulations. For your quarry lies beneath our collective feet." She folded her arms, licked her lips. "*Far* beneath."

Resolutely Marius strode to an outcropping, dropping to a knee. Primula, in his arms, did not stir as he peered across the expanse. "Have we any netting or rope to spare?"

Vaskar shook his head.

Suddenly Marius' face came undone with despair. "How else can we bring her along?" He looked to Sprael, but the laif could not offer a solution. Calliandra was equally useless, carrying only a small traveler's satchel.

"I know of a means of transport," said Zaotrice slyly. "It would require a return to the armoury..."

A spark of hope kindled in Marius' eyes. "You know of a supply of rope and chord?"

"Not exactly," Zaotrice purred, sweeping closer. "There is a most suitable spirit that lingers there, who would fit perfectly inside this vessel." She coiled a lock of Primula's hair around her forefinger. "You will find that this spirit during its lifespan amassed a rather diverse set of *climbing experiences.*"

Marius squinted, mouthed the phrase *climbing experiences.* "I don't know what that means," he admitted.

"Possession is out of the question," Sprael cut in. "And you're grossing everybody out. Can you give Kathryn control of her body until we're done here?"

Zaotrice lazily relinquished Primula's hair and used that same finger to trace a slow circle around Calliandra. "She agrees with me," she stated. Her smirk creased the lower portion of Sir Kathryn's facial scar. "I can tell. Don't lie."

For a moment, Calliandra appeared indignant. Then she shrugged, raising her palms. "What other options do we have?" she asked. Sprael and Marius launched simultaneous protests, slinging varying phrases of disagreement. "Aside from leaving her here," Calliandra growled, abruptly calling for silence, "what else can we do? Should we magically obtain proper climbing equipment, how long do you wager the descent would take? And the ascent afterward?"

Marius and Sprael exchanged troubled looks.

"I *wager* your war would be over by then," crooned Zaotrice, seductively tracing a finger across her collarbone. "Your kingdom long fallen to your enemy."

Calliandra scowled. "That hardly seems accurate."

"She's right!" spat Marius. Despite the glare he received from Sprael, he continued. "We haven't time for debate! Primula would do anything for the kingdom. *'For Camelot'* she'd say if she was awake. But we also don't have time for a return to the armoury." Grim-faced, he turned to Zaotrice. "Why don't you do it?"

"Why, me?" Zaotrice feigned surprise rather poorly. "I would have never considered that," she spoke coyly as her eyes appraised the lampyr from nose to shin. "I suppose I could be persuaded..."

"No more negotiations." Vaskar was suddenly among them, his hand gripping the back of Sir Kathryn's skull. "Possess the girl, or you will be the first to the bottom."

Zaotrice laughed though her eyes expressed turmoil. "Surely you joke?"

"Your use to me has expired." Vaskar pressed the taller woman toward the ledge.

"I relent! I relent!" she shrieked, digging her heels into the stone, to no avail. "I'll take the girl!"

Sprael wholeheartedly believed that was the last he would see of Sir Kathryn, and the last he would hear from Zaotrice. Admittedly, his feelings were mixed. He had grown to admire the knight commander's ferocious grit and loyalty, but Zaotrice, on the other side of the coin, was simply awful.

Unexpectedly the mercenary withdrew his fist from the small of Sir Kathryn's back, curtly stepped to the side. Another half inch forward would have spelled her demise.

"Thank you, thank you," muttered Zaotrice, teetering, clearly shaken. She wiped the sweat from her brow as she plotted an unsteady course from the abyss. "Kindly, if you would, remove the torch's dreadful light from the girl." She fanned a trembling hand at Marius. "This won't take long."

THE SOURCE

Vaskar had led the descent, Salve the shadow behind. The beast had no use for the climbing hooks, and instead employed his claws. For this reason, he was the first to reach the top platform of the scaffold before the others.

Sprael climbed next. Marius followed behind. The well-placed hooks zig-zagged down the cliff face, providing adequate hand and footholds. Rung by rung, hook by hook, Marius ferociously plunged to the depths. It seemed as though the gravity of his emotions overshadowed his fear of heights.

After endeavoring the short drop from the final hook, Sprael quickly side-stepped to allow Marius space for his landing.

"Wasn't so bad, eh?" asked Sprael.

"Nothing," replied Marius tonelessly. "As mold from bread."

The rest of the climb passed without incident and without conversation. Calliandra and Sir Kathryn had been too focused on the climb to utter any phrases beyond the sort meant for declaring movement. Marius seemed elsewhere, in a daze. And Zaotrice, marionetting Primula's body, was still rattled by Vaskar's threat. Though the lampyr's eyes remained a sickly shade, the spirit's influence magically alleviated her blindness.

The skeletal scaffold frames had hardly swayed or bucked. The crosspieces fashioned to the ladders held true. It appeared as though the structure had been secured to the cliff face by craftsmen who knew what they were about, but they had disappointedly run out of time before they could repair the fallen bridge.

At the bottom, the air was a warm thick mist, drenched in sulfur. Partway down, the air had suddenly taken on the unfortunate aroma, and had yet to dissipate.

"Follow." Zaotrice parted the haze, leading the group into a fissure in the adjoining cliff face. Once within, the scent of rotten eggs went away, and with its desertion arrived an intense chill. "It will pass," stated Zaotrice through chattered teeth.

Brilliant blue lights shimmered upon the jagged stalagmites, emanating from the chamber beyond. As they strode further within, a calm and tranquil sort of quiet settled. An aura of this kind was exceptionally rare, leaving little doubt in Sprael's mind that they were entering a space that had been kissed by the Creator. For all of Zaotrice's many flaws—and there were many—it seemed that she had upheld her end of this bargain.

Sprael's outlying senses dulled, as if whatever lay ahead prevented external influence. This created a rather odd sort of blind spot. At the very least, he had grown accustomed to knowing the scent of a chamber before its entry. Now he was rendered just as clueless as the humans he was surrounded by.

The chill then evaporated like the fleeting images of a dream and was replaced by a warmth that flowed upward from the lush soil beneath him. An arboreal garden scape, veiled by flourishing vines, glimpsed Sprael's view. *Impossible,* thought the laif.

"Impossible," voiced Calliandra.

With dagger in hand, Sprael hacked at the vines that barred entry. Beneath each strike, more and more blue light filtered into the chamber. Soon the impossible scent of springtime melded with the clamor of a thriving forest—trickling streams, chattering beasts, the belting of bird songs—the latter of which sent Calliandra into an urgent sprint. Fast behind her, Salve darted into the newly cleared breach.

A hound and a cat, thought Sprael, stepping aside as the others entered. *Who better for this hunt?*

Sir Kathryn was last in line. "Is this it, ranger?" she asked timidly as she peered into the sanctum. The cheer emitted by the chamber did not seem have an effect on her. "Have we finally reached the end?"

"I certainly hope so," replied Sprael.

With a listless nod the knight entered. Even now that her body contained its rightful owner, she did not seem quite herself. No matter her proximity, a distance prevailed around her.

Sprael breathed deep, closed his eyes. "Let's see if the old fae legend proves true," he muttered, making his way into the sanctuary.

A brook, in an absurd shade of indigo, slithered its way through the grass, surrounded on all sides by trees that offered blossom and fruit all at once. Though shielded from sunlight, the chamber found illumination by way of an array of stars, spanning an indescribably high ceiling. Sprael stared into the vacuous skyline, and found his periphery swallowed as though he gazed into a tunnel. Disoriented, the laif averted his eyes, and was immediately drawn to the gold of Calliandra's fur.

The werewolf, on the short side of a thicket, resided upon her knee, intently observing an oddly spotted songbird. Upon first glance, the bird's plumage appeared as an auburn field dappled in black, but as Sprael approached, the shades morphed into greens and grays, the spots unexpectedly giving way to diagonal stripes.

"Is this the Nocnik?" whispered Sprael, hunkered beside Calliandra.

The werewolf shook her head. "Nay," she spoke at a conversational volume. "That's a leonic thrush, a most rare specimen, not native to Fenrirfang."

The thrush cocked its green-capped head toward the werewolf.

"That explains why I've never seen this sort of fellow before."

Calliandra rose and turned, meeting Salve's eyes upon the opposite shore of the brook. "Any luck?" she called out.

With downcast eyes, the beast flicked his chin off toward his left. Calliandra replied with a nod and set off to where the beast had insinuated.

"How would he know what to look for?" asked Sprael.

"I told him that it would *look* like a bird, but all his other senses would tell him otherwise."

"Huh," said Sprael. "That reminds me, when you were on the brink of death, you said something to me—"

"Which time?" asked Calliandra without slowing. "I've been placed upon Death's doorstep more than once in recent memory."

"Uh, the time Elshur shot you with a poisoned arrow," amended Sprael. "You told me not to expect the Nocnik to be avian at all."

"I did?"

"I think you might have died right after you said that."

The werewolf slowed a step. "That would explain my lapse in memory," she reflected. "At some point I began to feel things differently, sense the forest, sense the world for more than what I had believed it to be. As if I had sorted a great riddle, and understood the reason behind existence."

"Nothing pries the eyes wider than the fingers of Death."

Calliandra groaned.

"Or so I have heard."

"It wasn't death that gave me such insight—" Calliandra was readying an explanation but was interrupted. A series of pillars punctured up from the ground, terminated into the fathomless heavens. If Calliandra had not so quickly braced him, the laif may have joined the stars in a most unromantic way.

"My thanks, Calliandra," wheezed Sprael.

Calliandra chuckled. "There's something that may rival Death in his game of *eye prying.*"

"And bumhole clenching," added Sprael, suspiciously approaching the broad pillars existing at even intervals, spaced wide enough for a shoulder to squeeze between, but not much else.

I had no idea these pillars were dormant beneath the ground, wondered Sprael, then voiced, "How did you sense this mechanism, and I did not?"

"That's how it was designed," replied a regal voice confined beyond the pillars.

Sprael started.

"Hello?" Calliandra called as she peered in between the spaces afforded her. "Hello? Who is—?" Her eyes widened as saucers. "Creator's kinked, curled tail..." she murmured, pressed her snout deeper. "Sprael, are you seeing this?"

Sprael leaned forward to see a lavish bed chamber furnished in crimson. A hearth exhaling flames roiled in its background, pitching textured shadows onto walls dressed in elegant tapestries. A laif casually stood upon a thick fur woven carpet, its curls rising above his ankles. Long dark hair flowed from his scalp, rendered invisible when it entered the black of his simple tunic. Aside from the tunic, the laif wore no other raiment—no jewelry, no armour—merely a tunic laced with a blue that projected odd against the upholstery around him.

"I see this," replied Sprael.

"Good," said Calliandra. "I feared for a moment that I had died again."

"Not unless I have died with you."

"Rest assured," began the laif in blue and black, "you have not passed into another life. Those pillars are meant to keep me contained, and they only sprout when a mortal draws near to me. Otherwise, I am invisible. A nobody."

"Hold a moment." Calliandra sounded as one on the verge of discovery. "A nobody..." She drew a step back, opened her mouth, but only appeared at further loss.

"Who are you, friend?" asked Sprael.

"In life, I did not have many who called me *friend*." The laif smiled, strode from the carpet. "When I lived, I was known as Lhaewyn, the first son of Famyl." His smile revealed fangs. "But after I perished in battle, betrayed by those I held dear, I found myself in another realm where I was offered a choice." His smile faded. "A gift by some descriptions, but others may argue it a curse."

"He's the first lampyr..." intoned Calliandra, still working through her puzzle. "But still a nobody..."

"What manner of gift?" said Sprael, glancing sideways at the werewolf. "Or curse?"

"For all eternity, I offer my blood as a *gift* for those worthy to walk the path of a lampyr. I am the source that fuels the fount far above our heads." A great water wheel, that had somehow gone beneath Sprael's notice loomed in the far corner of the room. A tight stream of water, as a ribbon, flowed from far overhead down to where the wheel spun, sending a second stream back up to the surface.

Tremendous magics are at play here.

"And the curse?"

"Come daylight," said Lhaewyn, his eyes darting sharp behind Sprael. "*You* are welcome to find out." Sprael felt as if the laif addressed another.

"Welcome to find out what?" asked Marius tentatively. No doubt the others had noticed the pillars and had come to investigate. "Who is this laif?"

"Claims to be Lhaewyn," replied Sprael as an aside to the mercenary. "*The* Lhaewyn."

Marius observed the imprisoned laif with skepticism. "Do you believe him?"

Sprael nodded.

"Then why did you preface that with '*claims to be*'?"

Before Sprael could offer explanation, which may have taken awhile, Lhaewyn had drawn near. Standing in the presence of this relic from a bygone age had hamstrung his clear thinking.

"One among you has recently received my blessing," began Lhaewyn, scanning the party. "I sensed you the moment you entered, but I also sense a great *conflict* within you." His attention came to a rest upon Primula. "Zaotrice, it has been some time, has it not? Did you believe that I would not recognize one of my betrayers?"

Sprael sensed a tremendous amount of malice rising in Lhaewyn.

Zaotrice appeared abashed. "I had held that hope."

"You are most fortunate, for if these obelisks were not taking up ground between us, then..." He trailed off, focused his attention elsewhere. "Words are a waste on you." Then he closed an eye and favored both Salve and Calliandra with a wry smile.

"A Kardowiff," Sir Kathryn stated. Lhaewyn opened his other eye, gave the knight his full attention. "We have traveled a dangerous road, lost many along the way, in search of a feather from the wing of a Kardowiff."

"Some have lost more than others," said Lhaewyn sadly. Self-consciously Sir Kathryn obscured her severed hand behind her back. "There are a great many birds in my demesne," Lhaewyn continued. "Regrettably, none of which bear that moniker. I fear you may have journeyed in vain."

"Perhaps you know where we could find this bird?" pressed Sir Kathryn. "We cannot return empty-handed. The Kingdom is in the balance. As we speak it is preparing defenses for war."

Lhaewyn blinked in disbelief. "And a *feather* will ensure victory?"

"The feather from a Kardowiff," said Sir Kathryn, nodding emphatically.

"How?"

Calliandra eased into Lhaewyn's view beside the balking knight. "It is said that the feather, in anyone's hand, has the ability to decode a foreign written language into the wielder's native speech," she explained, offered a rolled parchment. "You see, this scroll contains an ancient enchantment, and we believe that if we could only decipher it, we could either use it against our foe, or perhaps use it to render their spells inert."

"Why are you giving this to me?" asked Lhaewyn, accepting the scroll.

"Because," said Calliandra. "Even if we don't find the Kardowiff, maybe you could decipher this one spell for us?"

The ancient laif's lip curled with revulsion. "You beg this of me? When one amongst you could have performed this task long before your arrival here?" Though he replied to Calliandra, his ire was solely meant for Zaotrice. "You have ventured all this way, and have already paid a steep price." His features softened as he seemingly gazed through Zaotrice, saw Primula. "I wish that I could rid you of this curse, dear one, but alas, I cannot. You are lampyr, one of my children, and the magics would not take. However, it is not in me to turn you away without aid. Your Kingdom lies in peril, so I imagine every fragment of a moment counts." He extended his hand. "I will do this for you."

Unraveling the scroll, the laif strode to his bureau, dipped a blue feather into a small inkwell. Solemnly he pored over the scroll, leaning an elbow, foregoing the chair. After a few scrapes of his pen, the decipher was complete. Sprael felt a thrill course through him as Lhaewyn returned, a scroll in each hand. Though it was merely one spell, he equated its earning to the shattering of a fortified enemy gate.

Small acts such as these, thought Sprael, *can sometimes be all that is needed.*

"Gramercy," said Sir Kathryn as Calliandra accepted the scrolls, reverently stowed them in her satchel.

"You should be on your way," urged Lhaewyn. "Farewell."

~ 27 ~

WHAT YOU ARE, AND WHAT YOU ARE NOT

After leaving Lhaewyn's sanctuary, Marius could not shake the incessant nag that he had forgotten something. As if he had left something behind. Something so obviously important, that in a short amount of time the loss would become apparent, and if only he had that one *thing* with him, then he would be fine. The sensation continued to fester, as he climbed the scaffold, overtook the anchor hooks, and, at Zaotrice's behest, bypassed the armoury for a shorter route to the outside. She claimed it would place them half a day's trudge north of Lepaskalica.

They hurried toward the night shaded gateway exit, Calliandra leading the way, victoriously clinging to her satchel. The end was nigh, but only *just* so. That alone caused Marius to falter again.

What could we have possibly forgotten? thought Marius. All of his belongings were accounted for. He had checked nearly a dozen times. It had to be *something* that had been forgotten by the collective.

"Night is still fallen!" exclaimed Calliandra. She had slowed several steps ahead of the gate, wary of traps. "There's still time!"

Not for the first time, Zaotrice used the lull to reach for Marius' hand.

"Will you quit that!" Marius spat, recoiling.

"What's the matter, love?" asked Zaotrice, batting her eyelashes in a manner alien to Primula. "Are you not attracted to me anymore?"

In that moment, Marius wished he could extract a page from Vaskar's book—bury a dagger in Zaotrice's eye and be done with it. Vaskar loved nothing, was attached to nothing. But Marius could not claim ownership to that level of ruthlessness. Besides, Primula was still alive somewhere in there. At least, that was what Zaotrice claimed. Marius could not be the only one suspicious of her claim. If she admitted that Primula were dead, then Zaotrice would lose all of her leverage.

A draft that carried the cool of night entered Marius' collar. He shivered despite his warmth.

"If you're nice to me," Zaotrice purred, "I'll reveal a secret to you." She attempted to tug a lock of Marius' hair and was quickly rebuffed. "See, that's not very nice."

After Salve set his claws to work, freeing the opening from decades of accumulated mud and dirt, the outside world became visible. *An open world that offers many hiding places,* thought Marius, lingering his steps while the others made their exit. Then suddenly Marius fastened his hand to Zaotrice's throat and pressed her to the wall. "You want to negotiate?" Marius seethed. "Let's begin with your secret, and maybe I'll ponder not crushing your larynx."

Zaotrice struggled for air as she pulled at Marius' vambrace. After a moment, the mercenary loosed his hand wide enough for the entry of a single breath.

"Primula lives!" croaked Zaotrice. Tears lurked along the far rims of her eyes. "She does!" she added quickly, sensing the pressure's return.

"Prove it," insisted Marius. He could feel his mentor's influence.

"One moment, one moment," begged Zaotrice, her eyelids flickered as her pale eyes rolled back. The ancient laif knew better than to venture an impersonation of Primula. The girl's voice was far too distinct. "She lives, she lives," she mumbled.

"Talk is cheap," said Marius, employing his other hand. "The next voice I hear must belong to Primula."

This is Vaskar's way.

Immediately Zaotrice tightened her lips, and her countenance fell. Her eyes rolled forward, and the blatant fear that played out upon her face made Marius gasp, release his hold.

"I still can't see anything, my love," Primula panted. "And my throat hurts. Why does my throat hurt?"

"Forgive me," said Marius. *This is not my way.* "I lost myself for a moment."

"You should stop doing that," said Primula drowsily. "I'm tired." She shuddered. "Promise to be here when I wake again?"

Marius collected Primula's hands into his own. "I promise."

As swift as the dropping of cloth, the softer contours of Primula's face became hardened lines. "See!" shouted Zaotrice. "I told you true!"

The swiftness of the transition jarred Marius a full step backward. "You did," he agreed. "Now tell me your secret."

Zaotrice shook her head, beckoning Marius closer with a smile. "After a kiss, then I shall reveal my secret."

"That's off the table," Marius spat.

"Just pretend I am your beloved," cooed Zaotrice. "It should be easy enough. After all, I am garbed in her lovely flesh, am I not?" She stepped toward the mercenary and placed her hands upon his chest. "I promise, it will be worth it."

Marius wondered if perhaps her secret held a balm for the itch that nagged him, telling him that he had forgotten something important. Telling him that he had left something behind.

"You haven't blanched from my touch," drawled Zaotrice. "It seems we may be getting somewhere?"

Vaskar would be withdrawing his hilt from her chest about now, thought Marius. *But I'm not Vaskar.* He cradled Zaotrice's chin and joined his lips to hers. For the first sweet moments, she felt like Primula. The fantasy ended when she began to rake her fingernails over the back of his scalp, her kiss growing ravenous and violent.

With a bit of force, Marius freed himself. Her fangs had drawn blood.

Zaotrice withdrew and rose on tiptoes. "Now the secret," she whispered, pressed her mouth to his ear. "Lhaewyn *is* the Nocnik."

Marius did not remember leaving the tunnel. He did not remember crossing into a pine forest. He could not recall the first words that came forth when he finally caught up with the others. Next he knew, he found himself with Sprael's mantle bundled into his fists.

"That's not possible!" argued Sprael, striving to unfurl the mercenary's hands.

"It was all there!" insisted Marius. "The blue feather! The ease of his translation of the scroll! How quickly he changed subjects!" He watched the doubt slowly seep from Sprael's face. He took a step back and addressed the others. "*Come daylight*, he said, one of us was welcome to find out what happens. *What* happens? He didn't say, but what we do know—"

"At night, I am nobody!" shouted Calliandra. She was met by a breeze of bewildered stares. "He said it himself! He's a nobody!"

Sir Kathryn appeared in pain from her confusion. "What does that mean?" she asked.

"Apologies, apologies," said Calliandra, attempting to calm herself. "Nocnik loosely translated means 'at night,

I am nobody,'" she explained. "When Sprael and I first approached him, he revealed that to us. In the moment, it rang some bells, but I couldn't quite put my finger on it."

Sprael nodded. "Until now," he said. "I recall how you seemed to be puzzling at something."

"What does that mean to us now?!" said Sir Kathryn, seeming on the verge of rage. "What difference does it make? We have the spell! Whether Lhaewyn transforms into a Questing Beast or the All-Father of Goblins during the day, what difference does it make to us *now?!*"

A quiet fell for a moment. Marius looked to Sprael, and he could see that he too agreed with the knight's point. *It's not as if we're venturing all the way back—*

"Makes all the difference," said Vaskar.

Oh no, no, no, thought Marius. "We're done, Vaskar!" Marius stood before his mentor. "We have the spell!"

"The pinion was the bounty," stated Vaskar. It was then that Salve joined his side, aiming to venture back to Lhaewyn's chamber with him.

"You can't be serious!" pleaded Marius. Vaskar strode past, uninterested in argument. "That's madness! We have the spell."

"But Camelot needs you!" Calliandra rushed beside him.

Surprisingly Vaskar slowed to look her way. "Purefoy commissioned me for a pinion."

"He'll pay the seven hundred farthings for what we've done!" said Calliandra. "He'll understand!"

"Are you his mouthpiece?" stated Vaskar, divorcing himself from the werewolf's side.

"We've done enough!" Calliandra shouted.

In a blur Sprael cut ahead of Vaskar's departure.

"Don't waste your time," said Vaskar.

"Don't," began Sprael, jabbing the mercenary's chest. "Forget your green torch. I can't have you getting possessed and dying. We have unfinished business, you and I. So, wrap this up and meet me right afterward. You owe me a contract."

Vaskar gave a solemn nod, and Sprael cordially stepped aside.

When Sprael returned to the others, a look that began as concern quickly grew into distress. At first, Marius believed the laif was unexpectedly forlorn at the loss of Vaskar and Salve. Certainly, the road back to Orkney held its perils, but after surviving the Caverns, the route seemed manageable. Then he met the laif's eyes, and in an instant knew what brought such disquiet.

"Where's Zaotrice?" voiced Calliandra.

28

REMEMBER ME

Marius and Sir Kathryn essayed south, running through a lifeless, silent forest populated by petrified trees. Of the place's terrible history, Marius had no idea. Calliandra may have been able to offer explanation for why the boulders embedded in the soil glowed as crystals in the waning moonlight, but she had taken her leave with Sprael. Seeing no other alternative, the party had split; the laif and werewolf would return to Orkney, seeing the quest's end, while Marius and Sir Kathryn would seek Zaotrice in Lepaskalica.

Sir Kathryn's history with Zaotrice gave her a bit of insight on how her mind worked. The knight knew for certain that the ancient laif would break for the village as fast she could, the moment she could. "As pretty as she finds Primula," explained Sir Kathryn, slowing to clamber the steep grade of a hillside, "she would greatly prefer an immortal body, and Lepaskalica holds many such options."

"Well, it is a laif village," agreed Marius. "In truth, I'm not unhappy about Zaotrice carrying her all the way to a village renowned for its healing arts."

"I had not considered that," said Sir Kathryn with a smirk. "You mercenaries are a clever bunch." She cleared the ridge ahead of Marius, shielded her eyes from dawn's first rays. "Even from this side, it all looks familiar." A bell tolled off in the distance, signaling morning's arrival.

Though he was focused only on rescuing Primula, Marius was gladdened to see glimpses of Sir Kathryn's former self arriving more and more. *Perhaps this chase has given her fresh purpose?* he thought, hurriedly clambering the bank's final stretch. "Are you certain you wish to cross straight through it?" he asked, his voice devoid of humor.

"What other choice do we have?" said Sir Kathryn.

"Last time you ran across this karst, you fell in a sink hole." Marius set his jaw, inhaling sharply. "And once we start running, I don't plan on stopping."

Sir Kathryn inhaled as well. "Last time I crossed this karst, a spellcaster was involved." She waved the stump of her hand over Marius' eyeline. "And like you, I don't plan on stopping either." With a twitch of her head, she concluded. "Let's be off, that wraith in pretty skins can't have journeyed far."

The terrain was pocked with ankle-twisting craters, holes that hitched both heel and toe. Soon their approach led them astride the ruins where Bryant had met his untimely end. Further ahead, Sir Kathryn abruptly altered her course, describing an arc around a noticeably sunken patch of earth. In the gradually nearing distance, Lepaskalica loomed into view, and somehow, they had yet to detect any sign of Zaotrice.

Marius understood that Zaotrice was a powerful entity. Even in Primula's over-weakened state, she had flooded the lampyr with vibrant energy. *What are her limits?* he wondered. *We have been running at near full speed, and she only had a few minutes' head start!*

They ran on. Marius was not sure where his strength came from. Soon they were within hailing distance of Lepaskalica's north-facing sentinel towers.

"Slow yourself, Marius!" exclaimed Kathryn, sounding winded, her breaths arriving fast. "We can't afford to be brought down by friendly arrows!" The remainder of the karst lay planate all the way to the village and the expanse between was utterly barren.

Marius scowled, reigning his legs to a walk. Though he wished to press onward, he recognized the sense in Kathryn's words. *I'll be no use to Primula with a throat torn apart by quarrels.*

"Before we cross aneath this gateway," Sir Kathryn went on as she slowed beside the mercenary, "there are things you must know about Zaotrice."

"Go on," said Marius tersely, glancing for the ramparts. The first tower appeared empty, not a single outline of a sentinel shifted beyond its unshuttered windows.

The knight cleared her throat. "My memories after the sink hole are just snippets," she began. "After I fell, I recall a short drop, then there were voices... soothing voices at first. My limbs operated of their own accord, leading me somewhere. A chamber of wraiths had entered me..." As she spoke, her eyes became slits. "I recall a dungeon with heaps of skeletons piled atop one another, and a fiery green light that sent a tremor of fear throughout my body." Her head twitched violently, and she waved a dismissive hand. "Forget that, forget that. Never mind." She straightened, swiped a hand across her chin to collect herself. "All that matters is that while Zaotrice possessed me, I also possessed her. My mind was laid bare before her, and in like kind, hers was bared to me. You understand what I'm saying?"

Marius nodded.

"Well, for all her bravado and pride," Sir Kathryn continued, "there's still an insecure laif child dwelling in her. A part of ourselves that we find impossible to shake. A trait that both our races share, I suppose." Her head twitched again. "I'm fine, I'm fine," she insisted. "Point is that Zaotrice nurses quite a grudge against Lepaskalica, and there's a particular blood line that she wishes would end. And if she were she able..." The knight trailed off, gestured for their pursuit to recommence. "I'm not certain of much anymore, but upon Tyrol's grave, I swear to you, Zaotrice is somewhere within this village." She then stiffened, lifted her eyes to the ramparts. "Hail!" she cried out abrupt, lifting her hand in courteous salute. "Good tidings!"

The ramparts were silent, not one soul stirred.

"Where are the guardsmen?" asked Kathryn, scrutinizing the tower as if it had just lied to her. "When you departed the gate yesterday, were they manned?"

Yesterday? thought Marius. *Had it only been yesterday that me and Primula had set off for the Caverns?* He shook his head for two reasons. One was disbelief at the passage of time, the other was in response to the knight's question. "I can't recall," he said. "Wait, a moment. Yes, it was. There was a single guard there. I remember. Yes."

"All right," said Sir Kathryn slowly.

"Perhaps we caught them during a change in shift?"

Sir Kathryn returned her gaze to the tower's heights. "Relief comes to the guards upon the ramparts," she explained. "Not the other way around. In that way, vigilance remains unbroken." After a moment of thought, Sir Kathryn shifted her weight, made for the village postern.

They entered the north gate and were met with a silence that permeated deep into Lepaskalica's vitals. The other day this square radiated with commerce, and now the streets were barren, the shops unmanned. Wares and produce had been left unattended on the exchanging sills, free for the taking. Not even a lark could be seen roosting upon the row of cottages that Marius and Sir Kathryn strode beside, making their way toward the village center.

Laives rarely slept, so trade merely lulled, it never concluded.

"This is not good," said Marius.

Sir Kathryn nodded and as she was about to reply, the shout from an overhead balcony cut her off.

"Oi! Did you not hear the alarm ring?! There's a daemon loose! Find shelter from its sight!"

Marius peered up in time to see a laif woman disappear into a doorway, and bar it behind her.

If Zaotrice is loose... Marius' conclusion hit him like a slap to the face. "Primula!" he screamed, dashing for Lhaewyn's Fount, the only point in the village he could locate. "Primula!" he cried out again. A loose wraith meant that Zaotrice had abandoned her.

Pivoting left, Marius sprinted down a familiar avenue. Soon he could make out the banners emblazoning grand houses that lined the courtyard overlooking Lhaewyn's Fount. Houses of this magnitude in Rhionydd would constitute a cathedral, but in Lepaskalica, they were home to the eldest laif families.

Like the guard tower, the market square, and the streets, the courtyard was barren. But unlike the previous locales, Marius heard voices here. They came sharp, intermittent, not quite complete; pitching from a great house on the far side of the courtyard.

Marius ran through the orchard surrounding the Fount. Fruit lay scattered as though the boughs had been disturbed recently. Dampened voices rebounded throughout the courtyard making it impossible for him to pinpoint from where they came.

"Tell me where!" a hysterical voice plunged down into the courtyard.

Instantly Marius recognized to whom it belonged, and within the same breath, drew a bead on which building it had come from.

"I'll find her myself then!" Zaotrice shrieked.

An anguished chorus cried out in reply, begging the wraith to cease whatever she intended.

As Marius drew closer, he reached into his satchel, sought what remained of his emerald powder. Though he did not fully understand its efficacy beyond its use in torches, he felt certain that it would bring Zaotrice a measure of harm.

Maybe it's all I'll need, he thought with murderous hope, readying his shoulder for the door.

"Oh, not this!" Sir Kathryn cried out from behind Marius.

The mercenary whirled around, looked to the knight standing among the orchard. Her head was inclined toward a crumpled silhouette taking up space at the base of a tree. The morning's light brought the knight's expression into full clarity; however, what she beheld was yet concealed in shadow.

This can't be happening! His walk to the tree would never be remembered. The crunch of trodden fruit, the things of imagination. The small shadows cast by the sunbeams at play upon the grass would remain forever overlooked. *This can't be the end!*

"Oh, Prim," was all that Marius could manage before collapsing to his knees.

At the sound of his voice her pale eyes seemed to brighten with life. Passively her hands concealed a wound just below her chest. A fresh streak of blood stained her tunic, ran sideways from the manner in which she sat. The exposed flesh of her face, neck, and arms were marbled in burns.

"I tried, Marius," began Primula. Her voice weak beneath shallow breaths. "I really tried. I fought her, but at the end..."

"Don't try to speak!" said Marius gently, craning his head around the courtyard. "Lampyr!" he cried. "Lampyr!" He wanted to rise and run for aid, but he could not bring himself to let go of her hands. "Kathryn! For all that's sacred! Find a lampyr!"

"I fear that I'm beyond repair," confessed Primula, lifting a blistered forearm. "I'm cursed. Daylight now burns me. I was cursed to die the moment I bit Kathryn."

"You'll pull through," said Marius as the world blurred. "You'll see." He pulled his gaze away. "Lampyr!" he screamed. "Lampyr!"

Then with as much strength as she could muster, Primula removed her hands from Marius' grip, brushing them against his cheeks. "I wish that I could see your face," she whispered. "Remember me."

"How could I forget you?"

She brought her hands to grasp his. "Promise me."

"I won't forget you!"

Primula shook her head. "Not that." She smiled. "Promise me that you'll hunt her like Vaskar would," she said, her hold on his hands loosened. "But bring her to justice in your own way. Nothing would please me more."

Marius could no longer breathe.

"For Camelot," she said, resisting the beckons of Avalon for a few moments longer. "If only I could have seen your face…" With those words, her body grew slack, and upon her final breath, her feet brushed the shores of Avalon.

Marius lost the will to move. He had fooled himself into believing that he had finally found a love that would last, found the simple life he had been longing for. The gold no longer mattered. Demetrius could stow it in a hole for all he cared. Every farthing spent would remind him of what he had lost.

If only…

Marius wept.

Then the sound of shattered glass brought Marius' eyes from his despair. More screams came from the house. More pain wrought. More senseless suffering.

Hunt like Vaskar… Marius rose, his countenance hardening.

His instincts told him to breach the front door, confront Zaotrice face to face. After that, see what happens, then when an opening presented itself, bring harm with the emerald powder. A simple plan without an exit strategy. *This is not what Vaskar would do.*

He recalled how the Fount behaved beneath the earth, recalled Vaskar's patience, and his initial thoughts quickly spiraled into motion.

He was alone in the orchard. He had sent Sir Kathryn off in search of a lampyr. Which was all well and good, except that the success of his plan required another person.

Change of plans, thought Marius, running for the alley between the houses. The breeze brought a chill to his face, as it seemed his tears had yet to dry.

Another scream reached down to Marius through the windows. Another life lost. Marius wanted to confront the evil face to face, but he needed to be ruthless. These dying laives were mere distractions. He must focus on finding a point of vantage to see inside.

On the neighboring house he noticed a series of ornate stone corbels that flowed upward from an arched window and led toward a covered parapet. The parapet eventually concluded into a cylindrical turret that offered well over a dozen arrowslits. *This'll do,* he thought, leaping to place his boot upon the ledge of the window. Nearly halfway to the parapet, Marius recognized that heights no longer held sway over him. He forewent the final corbel in a surging leap, placed a hand to the top stone of the parapet, heaved his legs over, and slipped down into the walkway.

In the cool shade of the turret, fully concealed from sight, Marius withdrew his spyglass and peered through the arrowslits. *What's happening next door?* A well-dressed laif came to a hurried stop, awkwardly pressing the tip of an arming sword to the soft of his own chin. His mouth moved, but Marius could not read his words, nor make out whom he addressed. The laif then backed from the narrow viewing margin, and a few moments later three laives crept into view, their hands raised placatingly, each face ruined by fear. Then as one, they whirled toward something at their backs and slipped from sight.

Marius lowered his spyglass to seek a better perspective. Quickly he tested several arrowslits and found that none offered a decent angle. As he backed from the leftmost slit, he glimpsed movement on the ground floor through a small decorative window. Snapping the spyglass to his eye, he discerned the running of boots, their toes pointed for the front door. The window had been placed upon the wall of a staircase, affording Marius a downward view of treading heels, but nothing more.

In frustration, Marius dropped to a knee, angrily clenching his spyglass. His mind returned to his sorrow, his tears renewed.

At some distance beyond the Fount, a voice filled with a commander's wrath lilted through the air. Marius' spyglass wavered against his tear-stained eyes. With a swipe he cleared his face, steeling himself again as he returned the glass to his eye. "Kathryn," he whispered before compressing the spyglass and stowing it.

The moment Marius' boots found solid ground, a tumult erupted from the front stoop. All over the square, the windows suddenly flared with spectators. Marius rushed to the corner of the house's foundation, not wishing to intervene yet. Upon the lawn, seven laives faced a demure laif child, no older than ten winters, threatening suicide with an arming sword pressed to the side of her own neck.

One laif stepped from the others, offering a hand. "Give up the weapon!" he begged. "My daughter has nothing to do with any of this!"

The girl's head rocked back with a sharp laugh. "She has everything to do with this!" the voice of Zaotrice shrieked. "Yours was the family that passed final judgment on me and mine!" With a slight tremble, the edge of the sword drew a scarlet line beneath her ear. "These are the consequences for your actions!"

"She is only a child!" pleaded the child's father.

"Exactly!" countered Zaotrice. "Extricate the weeds before they can sprout!"

"But none of us were even born when my grandfather passed his sentence upon you!"

"What difference does that make?!"

While the laives bickered, Marius had slipped into the orchard. His passage had gone undetected by Zaotrice. Presently he found himself kneeling behind a tree several feet from the laif child's unsuspecting back. *I must cover her eyes,* thought Marius, recalling Sir Kathryn's words. *For that his how a wraith enters.*

"Why haven't you killed us already?" the father shouted, stepping forward as Zaotrice stepped back. "And be done with it?"

Marius could sense the stand-off neared its end.

"Because I want you to suffer! And it's not like any of you can stop me!" The muscles surrounding the child's sword hand grew taut. "Say good-bye, poppa."

The father's eyes ignited with hope as Marius broke from the tree and, in three swift actions, struck the sword from the girl's hand, concealed the girl's eyes, then bundled her to his chest. The child wriggled with a fervor greater than what her size portrayed, seeking to remove her captor's hand from her face.

Swiftly he ran for Lhaewyn's Fount, ignoring the searing pain blooming from the heel of his hand. Along his route between the passing trunks, he espied Sir Kathryn with Laekar fast behind her. Then he heard the little girl spit, and he sensed a good chunk of his hand missing.

"Let me go!" yelled the child in her own voice. "The bad lady is gone!"

Marius was not one to be fooled so easily. "Who do you take me for?" he said.

An astonished pause clung to the air. But Zaotrice had taken too long, for Marius had reached the basin of the Fount. The pedestal rising from its center spewed water in all directions, collected in the basin, and twirled with centrifugal wrath before it was suctioned into the depths. The villagers had erected a barrier that prevented small children from taking a tumble, believing the Fount to be bottomless, but Marius knew better.

That's one thing about Architects...

With the back of his legs pressed to the Fount's barrier, Marius adjusted his hold on the girl, gripped her at the collar, spun her to face him. She hung crooked, her left foot dangling closer to the flagstone than her right.

"This won't end well for you, you little whelp," threatened Zaotrice. "You've overstepped and overstayed!"

Marius met Sir Kathryn's eyes, sent a nod that conveyed, *Farewell.* Then he removed his hand from the girl's face, gazed deep into her eyes.

"You fool!" screamed Zaotrice, writhing, finding her present angle quite unpleasant. "I shan't be taking hold of you! I'll inhabit this wretch's body until I bring its end!"

By the time people stop underestimating them, it's too late.

The moment after Marius stripped his hand from her eyes, he brought that hand to his waist, unsheathed his dagger. The curdled scream began as Zaotrice, then as it grew faint, sounded as a child. His dagger had passed clean through the child's abdomen, and from sheer panic, Zaotrice leapt into Marius' eyes. Before the wraith assumed full control, he had released the child, and whirled toward the Fount.

An exquisite pain crackled inside Marius' head while the Fount's tremendous suction overcame him. Lifelessly he flowed along with the waters, allowing them to take him back to the depths of Halodwyth.

Whatever it takes...

29

CALLING OUT THE DEAD

Marius came to, looking out through his eyes, but held no control as to where they darted. He ran, but did not feel the strain. His body and breath were his own no longer. He had no control. He was merely a passenger in his own body.

Moss-coated walls went by, the bricks beneath barely visible. His heel slipped as he made a sharp turn, and he heard the strike of his knee onto the ground, but suffered none of the pain.

"Fack!" hissed Zaotrice.

She felt that, thought Marius. *Good.*

Zaotrice, wherever she was heading, was headed there in a hurry. "Relish my discomfort while you can," she seethed, resuming her run with a noticeable limp. Her voice quavered, unmistakably anxious. "Once I am free of these wretched Caverns once-and-for-all, I will have my pick of a host body. Rest assured, for your treachery, I shall leave your corporeal form in quite a state of disrepair before I depart."

"I sense your fear," Marius commented. "What has you so scared?"

The daemon hurtled down a narrow corridor comprised of damp stone, glancing behind at regular intervals. Through her rapid breaths, Marius could smell the scent of damp cellar. If there was a ceiling, he could not tell, and the same could be said for its ending, as the path appeared endless.

"I am not *scared*," replied Zaotrice, a tremor in her voice. "I am simply out of breath. This body is most inadequate."

"Lies," said Marius. "You're running like someone being chased."

The wall on the right abruptly concluded and Zaotrice gazed into the darkness. Her eyes shot upward, where there was a canopy of faintly lit stalactites. Bats flitted between the columns, screeching and chirping, chasing one another through the cavern.

"Silence!" hissed Zaotrice. Her eyes locked onto a pinhole of light hovering in the distance. "There it is! I cannot tell you the number of times I have hovered here only to be rebuffed inches from freedom!" Her panic had receded, giving way to elation. "I cannot wait to stab you in the stomach right before I leap into the next body I see!"

Unlike the right wall, the left wall concluded gradually. For a length of steps the wall rose to shin height before it eventually ceased. Her exit was now well in sight, well in hand.

"What a fool!" shouted Zaotrice. "He thought he could catch me! As if he knows these Caverns as well as I do! I have lived *centuries* here!"

Marius felt her thrill, bore her excitement. It was infectious and tasted of sweet victory, but burned like poison. Beyond words he hated Zaotrice, wished for nothing but her downfall.

"Who are you speaking of?" asked Marius.

"Why, your infamous mentor, of course" replied Zaotrice. Marius saw his arms pumping, caught the rapid flash of his kneecaps rising and falling. The pinhole widened, growing more substantial with each step. The stalactites were gone now, only soil existed in their stead. Dangling roots hung overhead like long dead tentacles, and the sudden arrival of fresh air purged the staleness around them. "Last I saw of him, he was standing still, almost too still." Her voice had quieted introspectively before she continued with a renewal of zeal. "But! I could see that he was preparing to give chase."

"How could you tell?"

"Why, after Lhaewyn snatched me in his dreadful bird form, your mentor ran to see my condition. His steed followed close behind. You see, I feigned injury, and attempted to mount his lion to make my escape, but the beast would not have me and I was quickly unhorsed. Though he threw me aside, I enjoyed the final laugh." Marius sensed the daemon grin. "I felt the beast preparing to shake me loose, so before he threw me aside, I plunged a dagger into his neck!" She barked out a laugh. "Your mentor was exceedingly wroth. His body went rigid, like a man struck by an arrow—"

It was Marius' turn to laugh. "You hurt Salve!" Marius cackled, unable to bridle his laughter. "We are going to die! You stupid, stupid daemon! You've doomed us both!" If he had control of his body, tears would be streaming down his face. "You stabbed him in the neck! In the neck! You are the dumbest of creations!"

"Enough!" shrieked Zaotrice. She punched the side of her head. "Still your tongue! If it comes to that, I will claim him in the same way that I claimed you, and the same way I claimed your beloved!"

You took her from me, thought Marius, knowing the daemon was able to hear him. *Now you will reap the consequences.* With difficulty, Marius stilled his mind. He did not wish her to read his thoughts any longer.

Zaotrice scoffed, casting her eyes to the right. Faint light trickled across the rim of a chasm. Its depths were unknown to Marius, but he sensed dread in Zaotrice and knew the fall must be great. Her eyes strayed to the left, and a matching chasm abounded there. It seemed the route they trod had slowly filed itself down to a narrow path, both sides hemmed by a great abyss.

Her eyes darted back to the front. The exit passage lay one hundred paces ahead. Marius heard her breath intensify, sensed her relief. He took it all in, all while painting a portrait of Primula's face in his mind. He refused to think of aught else.

A squeak came abruptly from Zaotrice's throat, her pace slackening for but a moment. Her head shook. *Just an insect bite,* she reasoned.

Marius etched the juncture of Primula's nose and the space between her eyes.

Light met the stone of the ground beneath them. Her long-awaited egress was now within reach. Her exhilaration was palpable.

At long last! thought Zaotrice. Suddenly she listed hard to the right. "What manner of—!"

Marius finished sketching one corner of Primula's mouth.

Zaotrice's right leg faltered and she screamed in guttural frustration. Her left leg followed suit. She fell forward, palms smacking the ground, prevented her face from disfigurement. Her eyes went forward, gazing toward the exit. The threshold lay merely three steps away. She squinted into the daylight where the outside world beckoned. Birds trilled their mid-summer songs as emerald stalks of vegetation loomed just beyond reach.

Zaotrice's cheek met the ground, and her fingers clawed the stone. She cried out for the world to come to her.

Marius dulled Primula's complexion with dry brush strokes.

An overwhelming brume slowly encroached, dimming the daylight and filling the space with darkness. Behind them Marius heard the hiss of a smoke device relieving itself. Zaotrice's coughs became rasps as the fumes filled her throat. Her breathing grew strained, coming out as whimpers.

Vaskar's spurs jangled violently as he approached. Her eyes darted to the sound, but suddenly the world went to black. What remained of the light Vaskar had stripped away with his scarf tightly wrapped around her face.

"Vaskar, why?!" pleaded Zaotrice, attempting to sound as Marius.

"Save it," came Vaskar's voice. "I know what you are." Marius could hear the sound of a dagger sliding free of its sheath.

Zaotrice groaned. "What have you done to me?" she demanded. "I am so close to the outside!"

"It's called a paralytic," replied Vaskar. "This is called revenge. And I'm calling you dead."

As Marius tenderly rounded a distal curl of Primula's hair, Zaotrice wailed in the purest of agony. For him, the ordeal was rather odd; listening to the sounds of his orbital bones being scraped and rooted by a dagger. As his eyes were pitted and extracted, he felt nothing at all. The shearing of fiber, the slicing of tissue, he could hear it, but experienced none of it.

After some time Zaotrice's wailing receded, and Marius heard the sound of a body dragged through dirt and stone.

For a great span of time, that was all he heard aside from the daemon's howling.

At length the sound of dragged heels gave way to the softened brush of grass and soil.

"Please do not take me to him!" pleaded Zaotrice. "Think on it! I can take the form of any maiden you desire," the daemon bargained. "Simply point her out, I will become her, and I will allow you to play out all of your wildest desires without consequence!"

The dragging ceased.

"Does that notion please you?" Zaotrice's whimper lilted with hope. "I can make that happen endlessly for you with any number of women."

Marius heard a hand patting solid flesh, and Salve's grating purr arrived in response. The beast sounded quite hale, and very much alive.

"There is always a consequence," replied Vaskar. "The werefowl will be yours."

Zaotrice screamed, her fists beating the soil.

Quite suddenly Marius felt *something*. It began as the prick of a pin to the side of his neck. Pain flared through him, feeling like searing daggers plunging into his flesh. He could not help but join his screams with Zaotrice. As his mind returned to his body, his screams became his alone. His eyes healed, reforming in their sockets like rapidly filling puddles. Shooting into an upright position, he stripped the scarf from his face and found Lhaewyn standing over him. Two rivulets of blood flowed down the laif's chin, originating from his fangs.

"You are rid of Zaotrice," Lhaewyn said, wiping his chin clean with the back of his hand.

"Along with the rest of the world," said Lhaewyn, brushing his chin with his wrist. "You are rid of Zaotrice."

Marius reclined in the grass and closed his eyes. "I'm free," he whispered. "I'm free, Primula." As he spoke, he noticed that his upper lip moved peculiar. He brought a hand to his mouth feeling the newly elongated teeth.

"You have survived my bite," continued Lhaewyn.

Marius opened his eyes.

"You are also lampyr."

30

THE WAY THEY ARE

"Sprael," began Calliandra. The two had been travelling through Fenrirfang Forest in relative silence. Their southeastern route would carry them for two days, maybe less if they only stopped when necessary. "Are you familiar with the habits of the plaevian drowerswing?"

Sprael observed the creek water funneling into his submerged canteen. "I can't say that I am," he replied. "Are they the territorial little orange blokes that murder bats and squirrels?"

"You're thinking of sempiternal wingjacks," said Calliandra with a shake of her head. "Not sure how you'd confuse the two..." She scratched behind her ear, then continued. "Anyway, the plaevian drowerswing is a rather curious specimen. Native to these parts of Fenrirfang I daresay." She lifted her chin, surveyed the surrounding poplars. "Adults grow no bigger than your knuckle, but the females lay these eggs that are as large as a raven's, believe it or not."

"Oh, I believe it," said Sprael, feigning interest.

"It's remarkable really." Calliandra smiled. "And are you by any chance familiar with the crested craven?"

"Does it share any relation to the kravatica?"

"They are one and the same," said Calliandra, impressed. "Kravatica is their given name, but some Scholars like to playfully refer to them as cravens. You can't say that we're all a bunch of fuddy duds all the time."

"Oh, we certainly cannot," said Sprael, securing the cap of his canteen. "And I know that the kravatica is quite the troublemaker."

"Indeed," agreed Calliandra. "But they are also quite lazy, can't be bothered with the challenges of child rearing. They spend most of their lifespan at play, so they don't often have time to build nests, and will bully other birds from theirs."

"Little pricks," commented Sprael, raising his eyes toward the skies. They were now several hours past dawn and making remarkable time. At their current rate, the laif wagered they would breech Fenrirfang's boundary before the following noon. In his original calculation he had factored in the hours for sleep, but had neglected to discount the fact that Calliandra no longer required such consideration, as werewolves required much less sleep than humans. *We may just pull this whole thing off*, thought Sprael. Shaving off an entire day was entirely possible.

"Well, as I was saying." Calliandra cleared her throat, "though the craven is quite larger than the drowerswing, they never bully them. Not ever. The drowerswing prefers isolation, and they tend to mate for life, so it's their nature to avoid most other creatures. The craven, as we both know, is quite the opposite!"

Maybe this trek will take us the full two days, thought Sprael, folding his arms.

Calliandra continued. "As I mentioned beforehand, the craven does not like to work, but they *do* like to breed, if you know what I mean. So, in the springtime when the Mrs. Drowerswing lays her clutch of big blue eggs, sometimes, while she is away from her nest, Mr. Craven may be lying in wait to replace one of her eggs with one of his own."

"What a prick," said Sprael half-heartedly.

Then Calliandra's ears flattened sadly. "Thing is," she began, looking to the creek, unable to meet the laif's eyes, "Mrs. Drowerswing is a canny lady. She has grown wise to Mr. Craven's tricks, so before she takes wing, she makes note of the *exact* position of her eggs, and if any are even remotely out of place... then she..." she trailed off dourly.

The unforeseen shift in the Scholar inspired a sudden dash of curiosity. "Then she what?" Sprael wondered.

"She disowns them."

"They are birds after all, Calliandra."

When Calliandra finally looked to Sprael, the fur beneath her eyes had grown damp from tears. "Do you think my family will behave as the plaevian drowerswing?"

The point of her tale resonated within the laif. He paused, gazed into to the creek where a spotted salamander scurried beneath a flat stone.

"You could hide it from them?" he said at length.

"Not possible," replied Calliandra, slightly irked. "You know me better than that. I couldn't keep such a thing from them." Then the coarse hairs around her snout slowly parted as she smiled. "Besides, I'm a terrible liar."

Sprael looked to the trees, the creek held no more inspiration. "I can't say for certain how your parents will react. I have never met them. I do not know them," he said, rubbing his chin with the base of his dagger. "But I do know you, and if that's anything to go by, then you have no need to fear."

The laif's words offered a measure of reassurance, but the Scholar's ears had yet to lift. "Do you think so?"

"I do," replied Sprael. He turned his head to the southeast, sheathed his dagger. "And if it would make it any easier, I'll be right there with you."

"I'd like that," said Calliandra.

With that, the two resumed their journey.

* * *

Yet deep within Fenrirfang, Sprael slowed his run upon a steep hillock overlooking a wooded glen, and a peculiar feeling overcame him. "Remember earlier when I inquired about your doppel?" he asked.

Calliandra simply nodded.

"And you said that you could sense her, but couldn't quite tell exactly where she was?"

Calliandra's nod became a curious tilt.

With a sweeping hand, Sprael gestured to the bottom of the glen, its view obscured by a tight accumulation of trees. "Can you sense her down there?"

"No," she replied. "But I do smell *something*."

"Yeah." Sprael wrinkled his nose. "I can't smell anything, but I have an odd sort of feeling about the area."

"Should we go around?"

"Nay," replied Sprael. "This little valley is an amazing shortcut. Figured I'd see if it was your doppel that sent up the flare."

Calliandra batted an eye behind them. "The moment we fled the Caverns, I felt her exhilaration at my freedom. It was as if our connection had been deadened while I was underground, and now that I'm free, it has only grown stronger."

"Do me a favor," began Sprael. "If she's about to make our acquaintance, please let me know."

"Will do," said Calliandra. "She's changed, you know. Advanced, progressed. Maybe those are better terms to describe her growth?"

Sprael scratched the side of his nose. "How comforting," he said drily, slowly treading toward the glen, preparing his legs for the downhill run. "Have you given her a name?"

"She already had a name," Calliandra replied.

An icy chill went down Sprael's neck. *Of course she did.*

After squeezing between the trees, they discovered the glen enwrapped by a terrific quiet. As far as Sprael could deduce from where he stood, the entire length felt as somber as the closing notes of a funeral dirge. The over dense coppice that reefed the basin provided shelter for smaller creatures, like wisps and fae. Ordinarily, upon entry, Sprael had been met by the sweetest of rackets. On one such occasion he had happened upon a Fae wedding ceremony midway through its proceedings, and he recalled promising the captain of the excursion a discount if he allowed a rest so he could watch. Of course, the lout refused.

Those marked by the Warrior, thought Sprael with a sneer. *Are rarely marked with a sense of wonder.*

"What is it?" said Calliandra. "Why are you making that face?"

Sprael shook his head, dispelling the memory of the scowling knight and his stupid moustache. "It's not usually so quiet," he replied. "Something is amiss. Let's make sure that our next steps fall with great care."

The hush persisted as they worked their way south. The snapping of a frail twig was magnified a hundredfold, the crunch of a leaf was an obnoxious herald to their arrival. By and by the valley walls began to flatten, the terrain broadened, but the quiet persisted. When they were less than half a league from the valley's end, Sprael and

Calliandra, at the same time, caught the hint of a tiny whimper on the wind.

Quietly they crept, hunched low. If not for the pervading silence, they may not have heard the distinct sound of mourning.

"Best to avoid getting involved," whispered Sprael.

Calliandra disagreed with a slight nod. "What if they need help?"

"We haven't time," came Sprael's hushed reply.

They progressed closer, and soon from the distance, Sprael detected the scent of werewolf. Without a doubt Calliandra sensed the same. She froze as the hairs trailing along her spine raised up.

If we can smell them... thought Sprael.

At that moment, the weeping curtly ceased.

They can smell us!

"To ground!" Sprael commanded hoarsely, darting behind a protruding boulder. Calliandra joined his side a heartbeat after.

"Werewolves travel in packs," explained Sprael.

"You don't say," said Calliandra, pointing an obvious claw to her chin.

Sprael blinked, shook his head. "It's too late to travel round," he continued, "so we'll hold here and observe."

Calliandra raised her snout, sampled more of the air. "They don't seem to be moving," she relayed. "It's a rather stagnant aroma."

"Doesn't smell of decay," added Sprael.

"Perhaps they're wounded?" offered Calliandra.

"We'll give it a bit more time," said Sprael, easing his head to the side of the boulder. "But I think you're probably right."

I hope she's right.

A few more minutes transpired, the intensity diminished with each passing breath. Sprael waited for the crying to resume, told himself that would be their cue to abandon cover. But as time wore on, his sense of urgency escalated, and he decided to scrap that plan.

"Let's be on our way," said Sprael, with a nudge to Calliandra's elbow.

The werewolf spasmed as though she had been startled awake. "They have not moved since we began this watch," she revealed distractedly. "So we're probably safe."

"Good," said Sprael, leaning his stomach against the boulder, gazing at the surroundings. "Glad we agree."

Circling as wide an arc around the core of the scent as they could, Sprael and Calliandra managed to pass without kicking up any werewolves from hiding. Just as the scent began to dwindle into obscurity, Calliandra muttered an aggravated growl.

"They must be wounded." She turned to Sprael, an apology churned behind her eyes. "I won't be able to live with myself, Sprael." She dipped her shoulders and ran directly toward the werewolves, and shouted in her wake, "I'll only be a minute!"

Sprael was frozen in awe from the sheer stupidity on display. It was not until she disappeared beneath an overhanging furrow of bracken that he finally stirred.

"Unbelievable," he whispered. *We were making such good time.* How could a person be so staggeringly brilliant, greatly accomplished in the knowledge of history, the minute nuances of birds, yet was somehow devoid of all common sense? *We are so close to the end...*

Following her steps, Sprael caught up to Calliandra in a narrow vestibule of a clearing. The way in which the trees clung tight to one another created a barrier of sorts, and only the staggered ribbons of sunlight streaming from overhead provided any meaningful light.

Calliandra knelt beside a man whose face was overtaken by deep abrasions. A thick, metallic band enwrapped his neck, secured to heavy chains tethered to the tree that he was propped against. The collar and chains shared the same metallic glimmer, as if they were composed of the same material.

From Sprael's standpoint, it seemed no other creature occupied the clearing. The werewolf scent must have originated from the wounded man. Once the laif was ten steps shy the scene, he recognized the man's affiliation. From a distance it had been hard to make out, as his tunic had been so heavily marred in blood and soil.

"He's a Royal Knight," stated Sprael angrily. "He's no good, just like the others we encountered." He turned a step to leave. "Don't waste your time on him."

"He needs my help," argued Calliandra as she tipped her canteen into a cloth.

"Leave him," said Sprael, nearing the harsher tones of a command. "If those turncoat werewolves chained him up like this, that means he's probably worse than them. Likely a rapist."

"He is not," said Calliandra. "He's like me."

"He is not like you."

With her cloth, Calliandra cleared a patch of grime from the side of the man's neck. "See." She nodded at the symbol of the Architect that was now plain to see. "They chained him like this because he stood against them. He's not like them. He's Marked. He's like me."

Sprael crossed the clearing, gave the man a dubious look. "Did he tell you this?" he asked.

Calliandra shook her head, pointed to a lower bough. "He did," she replied.

An armoured wisp bobbed upon the length of a branch, his helm tucked into the crook of his arm. The scabbard at his waist was empty. For whatever reason, the small knight had withheld his scent from Sprael; a trick performed by fae when they sensed danger. "This werewolf has lost his voice for the time being," explained the wisp. "When he attempted to transform, the collar evidently damaged his throat. Luckily he had enough control to bridle a return to his human form."

"Were you the creature we heard weeping earlier?" asked Sprael.

Calmly the wisp nodded. His head resembled that of a nightjar.

"You knew we approached," Sprael continued mistrustfully. "Why did you hide from us if your friend needs aid?"

"I do not know you," replied the wisp. "At times like these, it's often best to err on the side of discretion." The wisp gestured toward the man. "This werewolf's entire pack turned on him inside the blinking of an eye, ferociously slaying the knights posted at Fort Navarene. One moment they were happily sharing supper, and the next, their throats were torn out by the claws they believed they could trust." His eyes wandered a trail along the forest floor. "Few even had the time to draw their blades—"he paused, abruptly focusing his gaze on Sprael. "So forgive me if I am not overeager to flag down some random passersby."

"We haven't time for this!" exclaimed Sprael. "I'm sorry that your friend got himself double-crossed, but right now *we* have much bigger stakes to contend with. Much greater than a single chained-up werewolf." He indicated Calliandra join him with a frantic wave. "If you'll excuse us, we have *an entire Kingdom* to pull from brink of ruin!"

While Sprael and the wisp conversed, Calliandra had been furiously trying to free the man of his collar. The muscles of her back rippled beneath her fur as she strained.

"I fear that won't work, my lady," cautioned the wisp. "My fruitless attempts claimed my adamant sword. The clasp is locked fast, and as you can see, there is no keyhole. Therefore, no key. We require a tremendous force of impact to free him, I wager."

Calliandra settled back on her heels. "Such a force would kill him," she panted, exhausted, her tongue draped across her lower fangs.

"Calliandra!" shouted Sprael. "We can't tarry here while the archenlaives knock upon Camelot's doorstep!"

"We must free him!"

"We must depart! Now!"

"If this were Prija, what would you do?!"

Sprael staggered back. "How do you know that name?"

"You think I haven't overheard your mumbled apologies over and over?" began Calliandra, rising. "And you'd have me abandon one of my own, as you abandoned Prija?"

"That's not fair!" Still recovering from his shock, Sprael could not formulate a better reply. "This is different!"

Calliandra's snout twitched while the rest of her bristled. "Explain," she demanded.

"We don't have time for stories!" shouted Sprael, shifting from the defensive. "Think about all those we have lost! If we don't deliver the scroll, their sacrifice will be for nothing!"

Calliandra growled, whirled for the collar, employing her renewal of rage. Then all proper thinking escaped Sprael as he bolted forward, bodied Calliandra from the man, and angrily insinuated his whetstone into the collar.

"Careful! Careful!" warned the wisp, fluttering over Sprael's shoulder. "I tried that already! That won't work!"

"Stop it!" yelled Calliandra, maintaining her distance. With such a sharp implement so near the man's throat she was wary to intervene. "You'll only harm him!"

"For once," growled Sprael. "Let's all pretend that I know what I am doing!" He wedged the whetstone into the clasp and withdrew his dagger, flipped it so the pommel faced the whetstone's pommel. The man casually rolled his head to the side, undaunted. Then with what seemed a tap, clicking pommel to pommel, the whetstone shattered and, with its breaking, the collar came undone.

Sprael stepped back, gave the man room to stand. "I have already seen more winters than you will ever see, and throughout my life, I have been placed in chains more times than I care to admit," he directed his speech toward Calliandra. "*Maybe*, just *maybe* I might know a thing or two about the breaking of locks. Sometimes it's not a wicked impact that you need, just a calculated nudge."

"Your whetstone," began Calliandra.

"Think of it as an exchange," said Sprael with an up-raised a palm. "My whetstone for the scroll."

Calliandra seemed like a mummer who had forgotten her cue. Her mouth moved but no words came forth.

"Werewolves are drawn to one another," Sprael said. "It's how you are." He pursed his lips, watching Calliandra retrieve the scroll, extend it his way.

"I can't explain," Calliandra began. "I can't explain this feeling."

"I know," said Sprael. *It's not something you'll find with me.* The laif understood that a werewolf's demand for a pack was truly powerful. The pull, undeniable.

As Sprael made his way through the tunnel of trees, he fought the urge to offer a final glance. Instead, in his mind he pictured what transpired. And these imaginings always ended the same. They always forgot him.

I guess, in a way, in the end, I was correct when I told her the Forest would claim her. Sprael picked into a run, eyeing the eastward rays of sunlight piercing the crowded foliage. *Indeed, it has.*

31

AN HONEST MISTAKE

Blaine did not enjoy the taste of betrayal, nor did the flavor of battle sit well on his tongue.

He was the son of a Warrior, his mother a great knight serving under the banners of Ghore. His father was born Marked as well, beneath the Runner. His three siblings, one and all, took after their mother—Marked by the Warrior. But Blaine, the last born, had been born without a Mark.

"Right after you came mewling and screaming out of mother, they wanted to name you 'Blank'," his eldest sister related this to him on more than one occasion. *"They were so disappointed. But they changed their minds at the last minute."* During the one instance he had brought this up to his parents, they dismissed his sister's claims. But he had caught their traded glance, and noticed the distance in their eyes when they assured him it was a falsehood.

As the years dragged on, the disappointment deepened. It deepened so greatly that the chasm between himself and the rest of his family had grown distinctly visible.

Eventually his siblings grew to become knights, following in their mother's footsteps. Daily, in secret, since the day his parents lied to him, Blaine had trained. He tested the limits of his body's endurance, even though his siblings had surpassed him years before. By the age of eighteen his prowess was equal to his eldest sister's when she had barely reached ten winters. This disappointment had then led him to the tavern, and the tavern led to drinking, and drinking promised oblivion.

One sunny sweltering afternoon, as he stared into the bottom of his fourth tankard, he overheard a conversation that would forever alter the course of his life. Apparently some blokes in Benwick had discovered a way for poor Unmarked bums to become savage fighters, equal to those born Warriors. He had kindly asked the gents where exactly he could find these blokes, pounded back a fifth round, and departed the pub. That very same day, while the sun yet blistered the skies, he had become a werewolf.

After that he fell witness to great and terrible things.

That glorious moment when Corbin felled the karbaled, thought Blaine. *And we rescued Benwick before King Arthur even arrived. But, afterward, after Arthur dubbed us knights of his Court... it was the betrayal at Navarene—the way my pack slew those unsuspecting knights. Knights we had only just called friends...* His eyes fell to the tree roots that jaggedly snaked between his feet. *There is no atoning for that.*

For that reason, he had done the unthinkable. He had abandoned his pack, running as they slaughtered their allies.

"Hey Blaine, can ya spare another pinch of that pipeweed?"

He had deserted his pack.

Blaine nodded. "Yeah, Carlis," he replied to the grinning jikavos, handing over his soft leather satchel. "Take as much as you want."

"Careful with that kind of generosity," said Larik, a cheerful noctym. "You've heard the old adage about jikavos, haven't you?"

Trekking through Fenrirfang along his route home to Ghore, Blaine had come upon Larik and Carlis seated in a clearing, enjoying a few bowls of pipeweed. Perhaps a few bowls too many, for despite his appearance, the creatures welcomed Blaine into their company. The three had fast become friends, and for the past several days they had traveled north through Fenrirfang together. Blaine had wanted to go home, but now, standing upon the edge of Fenrirfang, he was not so sure if he really wanted to return.

To his east, the war between the archenlaives and Camelot had been joined. Blaine recalled with a shudder the only battle he had been a part of. *Perhaps the Creator knew what he was doing when he denied me a Divine Mark.*

"Give a jikavos a scratch," continued Larik, "and he'll want a full belly rub. Heard that one before, eh Blaine?"

The werewolf did not seem to be listening. "Eh, Blaine?" The noctym distributed a few playful jabs to Blaine's ribs. "Eh?"

Blaine recoiled with a start, focusing bleary eyes on Larik. "What was that now?"

"You alright, mate?" asked Carlis, concern marring his porcupine face. "It's just a silly old saying."

"No," said Blaine. "It's not that at all." He looked between their faces to find an unexpected solace waiting there. For the first time in his life, Blaine felt like he belonged. "I just, I'm just not so sure that I'm ready to go home yet." He smiled, shrugged. "What do you guys think if we—" The harsh rumble of hooves and the approaching cries of war abruptly overtook his words. Overhead, leaves unclasped and twirled around his companions.

"Blaine!" shouted Carlis, launching himself into the werewolf's arms. "Protect us!"

In spite of the jikavos' spiny quills painfully blistering his inner arms, Blaine squeezed Carlis all the tighter.

"We're surrounded!" Larik shrieked with fright, his voice rising several unbelievable octaves. "Archenlaives are flanking us!" He pointed toward the shadowed depths of the Forest. "See! See!"

"Save us!" wailed Carlis, burying his forehead deeper into Blaine's armpit.

"I see hundreds of them!" quavered Larik.

Though Larik indicated there were many, Blaine smelled merely one.

One is dangerous enough on his own, thought Blaine. He would die before he would allow any harm to befall his friends. He vowed to never again aid in betraying those who had put their trust in him.

From the murk, a figure blurred into view.

"Stay behind me," instructed Blaine, stepping forward with claws bared. His companions' pitiful whimpers had effaced all of his lingering fear. "Not a single hair on your heads will be harmed this day."

* * *

Hurtling down the forest hillside, Sprael careened a gentle slope that would see him all the way to Benwick's northern border. As he drew closer toward Fenrirfang's end, the unmistakable ring of steel upon steel filtered clear through the trees.

The war has been met, thought Sprael, devastated. *We are too late.* He hurried to the thicket to behold a battle in a most frenzied state. And to his sincere exhilaration, witnessed the banners of Camelot leading the wave, driving the archenlaives west! The tide of battle swept across his view, but less than a league further west, he noticed an expedient gathering funneling from the Forest. To his horror, he recognized the figure standing in the foreground, stark against pitch-black archenlaif arms.

It can't be! This soon?! thought Sprael. *That's the ice spellcaster from the karst! And the archenlaif force we witnessed upon our departure from Lepaskalica!*

Sprael swung his head back to the thick of the fight where his eyes snagged upon King Arthur riding a beast much like Salve, culling his enemies with savage efficiency. In the wake of their King, Camelot's bannermen pressed behind, the surety of victory spurred their mounts, bolstered their blades, unaware of the doom lying in wait.

"He must be warned," murmured Sprael. But as he made to pivot on his left heel, a werewolf sprinting in his direction arrested his movement. The beast bore the tunic of the Royal Knights, and instantly Sprael knew him to be a traitor. Sprael eased back upon his right heel, drew his dagger, but when he reached for his whetstone, found the sheathe wanting. In that moment, Sprael's heart rapidly descended.

"Archenlaif!" screamed the werewolf. "You die this day!"

Upon first glance, Sprael had noticed the werewolf was substantially smaller than Calliandra, and regrettably, for this reason, he had underestimated him. The laif attempted to parry the incoming claws with his whetstone, then instantly the ponderous sensation of burning ice spread upon his left side, and his hip unwillingly gave way. With surprising ferocity, the beast was upon him.

As Sprael experienced the sensation of fangs sinking into his collar, tearing flesh from bone, his mind flashed a reel that opened with his parents, went to Prija, then shifted to the removing of the Celliwig executioner's bag from his head, and, after that, flashed to Calliandra. Blood began to well at the back of his throat and, as he gagged, his thoughts went to Arthur and the scroll buried within his satchel.

He began to laugh.

Abruptly the werewolf ceased dining on the laif's shoulder. Perhaps it dawned on him that archenlaives did not often give into laughter. Or maybe he was confused by this unexpected spark of humor? No matter the case, he withdrew his fangs and backed from his prey with eyebrows hefted in shock.

"He's not an archenlaif!" claimed an overly distraught jikavos. The creature had presently joined the werewolf's side.

"What have we done?" said another voice. It was labor for Sprael to look up any longer, so he would never know who had spoken. "Look! He's reaching for his satchel!"

"Is that a scroll?"

Prija, if only I could have avenged you.

"Why does he offer a scroll?"

The werewolf had returned to his human form and pressed an ear close to Sprael's lips.

"Sir Demetrius," the laif managed to whisper over a gurgle. He chuckled, and all faded to black.

Whether it had been five minutes, or five hours, Sprael had no idea. The three chaps were gone. In a display of care, or perhaps contrition, they had propped him up-right against a tree so he would not choke on his own blood. Try as he might, he could not shake this over-whelming sense of... *odd*. He could not identify the feeling, but it was an *odd* he had never experienced.

Oh, yeah, thought the laif, slumping his chin. *This must be what dying feels like.*

To his elation, he discovered that the scroll was gone from his hand, but the sounds of battle quickly stripped him of his joy.

It seems that it has been closer to five minutes. Sprael sighed in dismay. *All will be for naught if Arthur dies, and the kingdom falls to the archenlaives.* "But there's not much you can do anymore, can you, you old idiot," said Sprael. His blood had receded enough to allow voice for his thoughts. But when he moved to rise, a tremendous pain erupted from his collar, as though that section clung by mere threads. *Just be happy that you can breathe for a few moments longer.* Sprael laughed. *Let's not get greedy now.*

What was meant as a soft nuzzle to the side of Sprael's elbow translated into the purest agony. The laif inhaled. Over the clang of steel and the screams of war, Sprael had not heard the creature's approach. He believed that it must be the werewolf and his companions returning to check on him.

"Found him!" A familiar voice called out. "Good work, Salve."

Salve? It pained the laif to crane his head, but he was grateful that he did.

"How'd you find me?" the laif asked, smiling into the sad eyes of a lion. "You probably followed my scent. My, you guys work fast."

Marius lowered himself down to Sprael's eye-level. "Looks like somebody did a number on you," he said, somehow beaming. "But I'll get you patched up in no time." It was then that Sprael noticed the distinct curve of lampyr fangs protruding from the young mercenary's mouth.

"Don't waste your time," said Sprael. "Werewolf."

Marius nodded gravely, rose to a stand. "Werewolf attacked him," he addressed someone out of Sprael's view. Aside from the fact that Marius had somehow become a lampyr, Sprael detected another distinct change in the mercenary; a distance pervaded his eyes.

It's quite deep and quite sad. Wonder what happened to him? thought Sprael with a painful shrug. *Guess I'll never know.*

Then Vaskar was before him, cupping Sprael's face in his hands. Without realizing it, the laif's head had drifted back to his chest. "Your contract," he stated calmly. "What do you need done?"

Visions of Prija battered Sprael's mindscape. Then one image held longer than the others, clung to the front, played out as if it were happening now—days after Prija had learned to walk, Sprael remembered the way the lad would totter behind him, reaching his arms out to the laif, only wanting to be held. Suddenly, Sprael's eyes went elsewhere. He saw Prija standing on the shores of a white sand beach, his arms reaching out for him. Reaching in the same way he always did. *Always reaching for me... my son, my Klonost.*

As Sprael was about divulge the names of the untouchable laives responsible for Prija's murder, his damaged arm somehow lifted, and he pointed off toward the ambush. "Arthur," he rasped. "Protect Arthur." Then he looked to Marius, chuckled. "For Camelot."

32

FROM THE DEPTHS

Without knowing that a substantial force of archenlaives had amassed, King Arthur drove his forces westward. Not only did archenlaives wait there, but there was also an ice spellcaster, presumably the same caster that had assailed Sprael and Calliandra at the karst.

Before bounding into the forest, Vaskar had instructed Marius to restrict the archenlaives nearest Arthur, then work backwards.

It had become commonplace for Archers to compare their skill to music. They would say, *"Ol' Henrick? When he takes the stage, it's a four-string concerto. The geezer's fingers are as nimble as a cat on a wire."* From the obscurity of the Forest, Marius had picked his shots, selecting the mounted archenlaives first. The saddles emptied as quick as his quiver, and, as his symphony concluded its final refrain, the mercenary found himself down to his final three arrows.

The final three, he thought. *The arrows reserved for a stand-off.* Vaskar had provided that nugget of wisdom early on. A wise archer does not empty his quiver while enemies remain.

The archenlaives Marius had brought down registered a significant loss, but it was not nearly enough to secure the King's safety. As he planted his final three into the soil, an archenlaif spearman drove his weapon into the King's mount. The dragoon destrier reared on its hindquarters and, in a sinuous sideways movement, splintered the spear with its jaws. Upon the beast's downward return, Arthur cleaved the spearman's helmet in two.

"Where were you on that one, Vaskar?" Marius whispered, looked to the treeline ahead, where his mentor had been releasing his magnum opus. In a similar fashion to his own, Marius witnessed three arrows protruding from the ground, but Vaskar was nowhere to be seen. Then Marius realized that it had been a few moments since he last witnessed an ice mechanism havocking the field.

Right at the beginning, Marius had ignored Vaskar's instruction and fired his first volley at the spellcaster. This had proved most unwise as the caster simply erected an ice bulwark in immediate response, rendering his arrows a waste. After that, a dozen ice missiles spat from the bulwark, postmarked for Marius' skull. This spurred an instant desire for a change of scenery, and Marius tucked a roll, narrowly avoided a missile to his ankle tendon, and sprinted for the outlook he occupied presently.

"Where are you, Vaskar?" said Marius, drawing his arming sword. He waited for the right moment to strike.

Without a knight's heavy armour, he would not last long in the thick of things, so he planned to flash into the fray and exit twice as fast. *A true caitiff technique*, thought Marius with a smile. *Kathryn would be proud.* Unbidden, he recalled the eyes of the child he had slain; their absurdly greenish blue tint, and the way she had whimpered...

Laekar saved her, Laekar saved her, he told himself over and over. Though he did not know this for certain, it was the only way to quell these sudden attacks. *She is not dead, she is not dead. The only one who died was Zaotrice,* he reminded himself. *When Lhaewyn sank his fangs into your neck, he slew her screaming.* "But Zaotrice wasn't the only one who died..." he whispered, recalling Primula's ashes swirling beneath the apple tree.

When Marius finally gazed up, every ounce of Arthur's remaining momentum had halted. The forces of Camelot were surrounded, having pushed their advantage too far.

Marius shook his head. *Sprael must have seen this coming,* thought Marius dourly. *His fears have come to fruition.* His knees gave way, and soon Marius discovered that he was kneeling, his sword prostrate beneath a canopy of bracken. His sorrow had overcome him. This life, the life of a killer for hire, was no longer for him.

Marius watched on in helpless melancholy as a werewolf chased a disarmed Ghore foot soldier. The woman's pleas came to an end the moment she fell. A wall of vegetation gratefully hindered Marius' view of the killing. And just beyond that piteous display, an archenlaif masterfully twirled a heavy-ended halberd, and skewered several horses that drew near to him.

"There's a bloke that needs a reckoning," said Marius. He lazily glanced sideways at the shimmer of his weapon but did nothing. As he returned his eyes to the archenlaif, a sixth knight was freed from his saddle, and instantly faced his unexpected end. Within a single blink, the archenlaif cracked rigid, dropped to his knees, and died reflecting the same pose as Marius. The arrow protruding from his throat had been fashioned with the most brilliant blue fletching.

An arrow from the depths Halodwyth. Lhaewyn's gift to Vaskar. This evoked a sudden spark within Marius. He traced the arrow's journey, knowing that it would lead back to his mentor. "Where are you, Vaskar?" he mumbled, not for the first time. Somehow Marius managed to catch a glimpse of Vaskar's green gray mantle disappear behind an ice barricade. A brumal gust of ice shards sparkled in the daylight, struck where the mercenary had been a moment before. A desperate barrage of such magnitude could only have been inspired by Vaskar. And then Marius realized why Arthur had not already been impaled by an ice spear. *Vaskar has been keeping her at bay,* thought Marius. *All by himself.*

"How do you do it?" wondered Marius aloud, reaching for his fallen sword. Along the hem of the forest the same werewolf who had brought down the Ghore soldier now stalked another—a golden knight of Tintagil. "Guess I'll be coming out of retirement."

With eyes keyed on the werewolf, Marius staggered over toward his final three arrows. The beast's fur was a ruddy brown, easily lost among the sodden field. A horn bleated off to Marius' left, and he ignored it. The werewolf was now within lunging distance of his target. The Tintagil knight, like the other bannermen, fought a battle on all fronts. He whirled a bloodied spear, unaware of the single threat looming nearby.

Without even trying, Marius had nocked his bow, angled it for the werewolf's spine. He loosed before his weary mind had given permission, and the premature shot pelted the mud beside the werewolf's heel. The splash, coupled with the dazzling white and yellow of Marius' fletching, grabbed the beast's attention, wrested him from his stalker's trance.

"Wish I'd have done that one better," mumbled Marius as he reached for another arrow. The werewolf had finished scouring the treeline for the archer, having discovered him almost instantly. Under the impression that it would take Marius several moments to reload, the beast hurtled forward with a frenzied abandon.

Perhaps my horrible miss told him that I'm easy prey? Couldn't blame him if it did.

Marius smiled faintly, straining his back muscles to full draw. At the end of his exhale, the perfect time for release, Arthur's mount unleashed a deafening roar. The air rippled with the sound, causing Marius' elbow to lift by a hair's breadth.

Missed! thought Marius. White-hot fury sizzled from his fingertips as he reached for his final arrow. The werewolf had not altered course and seemed just as eager as ever to reach the mercenary.

"Better make this one count," voiced Marius. Suddenly his eyes strayed upon a fell glimmer in his periphery. Arthur, in his radiant golden armour, lay upon the ground, his mount slain by thousands of ice spears. Ten steps shy the King, the ice caster conjured another working, folded at the waist, quaking. Vaskar and Salve were nowhere to be seen, and Marius had no time to search for them. He barely had the time for recalibration, but he did it any-how.

At the same moment the acrid scent of werewolf pierced his nostrils, Marius released his final arrow.

For Camelot.

The sorcerer shrieked her final breath as the merce-nary's arrow found rest inside her chest cavity. For the re-mainder of Marius' life, he would never forget that sound.

~ 33 ~

DETERMINING CROPS

3 days later...

Vaskar's needletail had arrived at some point during the pre-dawn hours, a message secured to her leg. The thrill Dafne had experienced from the sight of the bird roosting upon the top back of her dining room chair had sent her into a pirouette. And, upon the reading, the mercenary broker's impossibly high expectations had only been further solidified.

"*Locus Castle, Orkney—tomorrow, midday,*" the message said. Short, succinct, and obviously Vaskar.

"He's done it!" Dafne screamed at the needletail. The bird flinched, raised a wing to shield her face. "The impossible! He's done it!" She scooped the stunned bird into her hands and spun several more pirouettes. "Where do you think Marius will build his estate?" she inquired. The needletail had yet to recover and simply blinked in response. "I think you're right, little friend—Tintagil will suit him just perfect!" Then she stopped mid-spin, held the bird to her ear. "What's that? What will I do with my broker's fee and the winnings from that greasy gambler's den? You think that I should build an estate of my own? I like the way you think!"

Since the quest's fateful inception, Dafne had sent missives of inquiry to Sir Demetrius Purefoy, hoping to pry some gossip. To her dismay, not one of her messages had been given any sort of thoughtful reply. Day after day she relayed her disappointment to her fellow brokers, all of whom waited upon bated breath for the tiniest scrap of news. A seven hundred farthing bounty was explicitly unheard of and had rivaled the war in topics of conversation. Most, if not all, believed the quest was destined for failure, but that did not stop the odds-makers from assembling a central betting pool. In truth, the quest had lent a bit of a reprieve from the doom and gloom brought by the debates associated with the archenlaif invasion and the impending war. And with Camelot's seemingly impossible victory, of course, the seeming impossible had to have been accomplished by...

"Vaskar of Rhionydd," stated Dafne to herself, shaking her head. "Who better to make the impossible a reality?" Dafne shouted the question to the needletail from her bed chamber. After sprinkling an assortment of seeds on a plate for her guest, Dafne began parsing her wardrobe for the perfect attire. "This situation calls for something a bit..." She chewed her lip. "Garish?" Her eyes played upon a gold-laced bodice with a dipping neckline that invited overtly observable glances. She shook her head. "No, perhaps we should lean more toward..." A purple ball gown embroidered with black pearls that flowed down into a frilly petticoat seemed to bat its lashes at her. Once again, the broker shook her head. "Not the right occasion for you..." She thumbed through a dozen more contenders before she passed a red and blue squire's tunic, paused, and returned to it.

"Marius will get a kick out of this one," she said with a grin. "After all, Creator knows, the lad has probably been through it, and could use a good chuckle." She then lifted her voice. "What say you, needles?"

Unexpectedly, the bird chirruped a sprightly reply.

"That settles it then."

The atmosphere that swirled throughout Locus Castle was of a most peculiar sort. Some folks were in the throes of gaiety, skipping in hand-held circles, while others simply could not lift their faces above the cobblestone beneath their trudging feet. Ultimately, and above all, the war had been won. Which meant humankind would not be seeing a return to forced slavery, at least for Dafne's lifetime, and on the heels of Vaskar's success, may have seen an end completely. But with a victory that reaped such a heavy toll, there would be many vacant seats found around the feasting tables. For Orkney, not only had the land lost many souls on the field of battle, but it had also lost its greatest knights whilst fetching a legendary feather within a cursed Cavern far beyond its borders.

Their Duke-Knight had brokered an outrageous gamble, and it seemed, for the most part, that it paid off, thought Dafne solemnly. *But I suppose, it really depends on how you look at it.* Presently, she stood beside the portcullis that funneled commoners into the Castle's central bailey. She had met Vaskar at this entry point once or twice in the past, so she concluded that this was as good a place as any to await his arrival.

"Has your knight already gone inside?" inquired an Orkney squire that had seemingly appeared from nowhere. "I only ask because you are welcome to join him, is all."

How many times will this happen today? Dafne forced a smile. "I'm not a squire," she replied curtly. "Thank you."

"My mistake, milady," said the squire, abashedly raising his hands. "It's only that your garb betrays you as a peer..." The squire's voice petered off as Dafne's smile became less friendly. "I shall take my leave. Good day." And with that the lad pretended to acknowledge a passing cart and scurried off.

"It'll all be worth it," Dafne explained, offering a sunflower seed to the needletail on her shoulder, "just seeing Marius laugh. You'll see. Your master on the other hand, I doubt he'll even notice."

It had become customary for Dafne to arrive several hours before a meeting with Vaskar. She knew from his past that the mercenary would part ways with brokers he found less than punctual. For Dafne, being on time was not a struggle, as it could often be for others. Though she wondered Vaskar's personal opinion of her, she knew that he approved of her work. If he did not, he would have dismissed her years ago.

On this particular morn a greater number of carts had entered beneath the portcullis than exited. Which made sense to Dafne, seeing as the majority provided fresh edibles for Sir Demetrius' victory festival. Until now Orkney had foregone scheduling any sort of celebrations, and were probably going to forego them completely, but word of Vaskar's success had brought a sudden change to their rhetoric.

As the morning carried on, the thoroughfare jammed tighter from the latent arrival of commoners that had recently rolled from their cots. Amongst the jumble of faces, Dafne strained her eyes to catch Vaskar's arrival. While she leaned against the stone barbican she had kept tabs on the length of her shadow, and it seemed that high noon's arrival drew nigh.

Three pushcarts overladen with melons arrived, and as the exchequer paid them careful scrutiny, the guards at his back began to stir and mumble. Their attention had been drawn to a disturbance at the rear of the throng. The youngest of the vendors noticed something as well, and furtively began whispering to his fellow melon farmers. The exchequer continued to nose through the wagons, inspecting the fruit, unaware of the behaviors around him.

Vaskar and Salve drew closer, and Dafne could not make out any other shapes beside them. Her heart caught in her throat. *Surely Vaskar and Salve are not the only survivors?* Over the past week, she had been caught up in the discussions and the gambling and the story telling, that she had forgotten the reality of it all. The Handsome Death Caverns was not a fae tale. Nobody had ever returned from that place.

"Where's Marius..." murmured Dafne, striding to meet Vaskar.

Upon the bridge the crowds shifted to the left, hushed deathly silent. Under breaths the message had passed, traveled from the rear to the fore. They all knew who *he* was and what he represented.

A plague of blood arrayed the mercenary's tunic and mantle. Shoulders that refused to display an ounce of exhaustion were marred, overtaken by filth. In contrast, his lion companion appeared fresh, in exemplary form, faithfully padding along beside him. In defiance of the mud caked to his flanks, Salve's fur glistened in the daylight.

"Where's Marius?" asked Dafne. The needletail tussled her hair as it abandoned her shoulder. "Are you the only survivors?"

Vaskar looked down, acknowledged his broker with a brief glance. "As far as you're concerned," he replied while he affixed a tiny scroll to the leg of his needletail. He had not bothered to stop his horse and pressed onward toward the Castle. Within his next steps the needletail sped from his hand, disappeared from sight.

Dafne may have been crestfallen, had she not been so outraged. "What of the knights? What of the Scholar? What of the ranger?" she angrily peppered Vaskar as she tromped at his horse's flanks. "And what happened to Marius?!"

Unsurprisingly, each of her questions was met with silence.

The moment before Vaskar arrived at the exchequer station, the clerk graciously swept an arm toward the Castle. "Our Duke-Knight anxiously awaits your arrival," he stated. "Along with the remainder of Orkney."

Vaskar leapt from his horse, placed a hand to Salve's flank, and strode beneath the portcullis. Dafne trailed behind, her emotions ripping her into shreds. She was about to become the richest mercenary broker in all of Camelot, which was beyond exhilarating. She had helped arrange this record-breaking bounty and was moments before witnessing the haul. Seven hundred gold farthings was beyond *unheard of.* Then it suddenly occurred to her. *If Vaskar is the only survivor, that means...*

Midway through the bailey, Dafne froze. "He won't be splitting any of it."

She followed Vaskar as he was led into a refectory that was bereft the ornamentation commonly seen throughout the keep.

The remaining knights of Orkney, including Sir Demetrius, encompassed a central round table, standing at their wedges of honor, taking up vigil. Their longswords had been placed upon the table before them, set to shimmer beneath the splendor of a blazing cathedral chandelier. Longswords, dressed in scabbards, lay before each vacant seat, signifying those that had fallen in battle, or otherwise. The arrangement of the longswords drew the eye toward the center of the table, where seven stately strongboxes resided. Huddled along the outskirts, several steps from the table, a coven of robed Scholars tarried, their cowls drawn in shared solemnity.

"*The* Vaskar of Rhionydd," declared the herald positioned to the left of the port. "Accompanied by his intermediary, Dafne Chivington of Garlot." Salve had opted to curl up for a nap just outside the refectory. Along the hallway, the beast had stopped to circle a patch of sunlight scribed upon the plush carpet. Dafne imagined the servants giving that stretch of hall a rather wide berth for the time being.

Sir Demetrius gazed upward from his seat on the far side of the table. "See the price we have paid, mercenary," he stated humorlessly. Last Dafne had seen of the Duke-Knight, his hair had only been accented with waves of gray, but now his crown was completely donned in flint.

"Once twenty-seven sat here. Hale, healthy, prepared for the wilds." His beard merged with his moustache as he scowled, cast sad eyes to the sword before him. "Now only five remain."

Dafne noticed Vaskar passing the herald a small rolled parchment.

"Our mage, Earon, perished on the frontline of the battlefield," continued Sir Demetrius. "Died a hero, slaying a karbaled, so I am told." Then his demeanor shifted humbly. "They all died heroes! Forgive me, my knights. It's only that I had such different hopes for Earon, for Orkney. Every day I pay a price of my own, and now it seems my lands have finally been afflicted by my suffering."

"The only price that concerns me is the one sitting on top of your table," said Vaskar, tossing an opened satchel upon the tabletop, scattering a handful of brilliant blue feathers. "Had you selected a better crop, you may have avoided such hardships."

Within the shadow of a moment, Sir Demetrius's expression slid from outrage to confusion. "A better crop?" he puzzled aloud. The knights of Orkney instinctively rotated their stances, reached for their scabbards.

"Your herald has the location for the delivery of my portion," said Vaskar. "Make certain it arrives no later than dusk tomorrow."

Before Sir Demetrius had the time to recover his thoughts, the mercenary had already strode from his chamber.

Dafne, ludicrously donned in the surcoat of a squire, suddenly found herself standing alone in a chamber of troubled knights and stunned Scholars. She felt it impossible to feel any more awkward.

"So," began Sir Demetrius, dropping into his seat, folding his hands beneath his chin. "That was *the* Vaskar of Rhionydd." He paused to smile at each of his knights. "You get what you pay for, I suppose."

Dafne stepped forward, and as she was about to offer a concession for her client's behavior, Sir Demetrius lifted his palm. "No need for apologies," he said with an unexpected grin. "Spirits such as he do not require forgiveness. That is simply who he is. A tool." Sir Demetrius turned his head to scratch beneath his chin. "Albeit a tool of exceeding efficiency."

Since Vaskar had pitched the feathers onto the table, the Scholars in the corner had been champing at their respective bits to feast more than their eyes upon them. The tight circular arc the feathers had tumbled into seemed to have locked a few of the Scholars in some sort of mesmerizing spell.

"In the absence of Vaskar, I suppose I shall address you, Maid Chivington?" asked Sir Demetrius. "It's up to your discretion whether you relay what I say. Please forgive that I cannot offer you a seat. Circumstances dictate contrarily." He indicated the vacant seats with a slow wave of his hand.

Dafne stared down at the longsword before her, at rest in its scabbard. "I understand," she said. "I don't mind standing anyhow, been doing it all morning. Why quit now?"

Sir Demetrius offered a perfunctory nod. "I see," he said, then glanced toward the Scholars. "Alright, Prebis, go on ahead! I can *feel* your slavering over them."

"Thank you, milord." The Scholar broke from his ranks and scurried forward to gather the feathers back into their satchel. Afterward he fixed a meaningful gaze in Dafne's direction, not quite meeting her eyes. "The other day we came into possession of a translated scroll, brought by a noctym, a jikavos, and a werewolf—most unusual messengers, I daresay. A true gift, and a grand piece to a missing puzzle. With these pinions, we shall ensure this *latest* archenlaif invasion is their *last*. Humankind will never again need fear the yoke of slavery." With his declaration made, the Scholar bowed three times, and returned to his place among his peers.

"Well said," Sir Demetrius applauded. "I pray this knowledge serves as adequate consolation for our losses." He paused. "The evening last, I was made aware of a messenger bird hailing from Fenrirfang that brought a sealed missive bearing the insignia of your Knight Commander."

All the attention in the room shifted to a wedge in the table that was absent a sword. Until that moment, this detail had gone beneath Dafne's notice.

"Sir Kathryn is alive," began Sir Demetrius, rising to his feet. The knights and Scholars clapped and cheered. One knight bowed forward and placed both hands upon the table and released a cry of relief. "She recuperates in Lepaskalica," continued Sir Demetrius, his tone brightening with each passing syllable, "and other than her regret from her failure, her missive did not reveal much further. Evidently, she is unaware of the quest's success. It's safe to assume, whatever obstacle had slowed her return, must have been of the gravest import. But in all this, take cheer, my friends."

Dafne could not help being overtaken by the joy of the moment.

"This is a boon," began Sir Demetrius. He then cleared his throat as a signal for calm. "This is a boon arriving ahead of the coming days set aside for remembrance. Before we begin to rebuild, before the farmers plant..." The Duke-Knight's voice faded, suddenly lost in thought. "*Crops... Not of good crop...*" What began as a simple chuckle, suddenly vaulted into uproarious laughter. The Duke-Knight collapsed onto his chair, and none could tell whether he wept or cackled. "Not of good crop! Had I selected a better crop! I knew it!" Whether he was enthralled by delight or regret, no one could yet determine. "I remember the lad now. As he walked into *this very room*, I felt a tremor of remembrance, as if I'd met him before. It was in his shoulders, the way he sauntered into *this very room!* It was exactly like that day!"

The knights and Scholars appeared speechless by this sudden turn.

"What are you talking about?" hazarded Dafne in their absence.

"Why Vaskar of Rhionydd of course!" explained Sir Demetrius, his beard now drenched in tears. "He arrived as a suitor for my sweet Elodie, all those years ago! As I recall, the two of them got along very well, and Elodie favored him quite heavily. She had even begged me to select him above the others!" Demetrius now stared at the strongboxes as if they were speaking to him. "But he was a poor lad of far lesser means. No title, no family, no lands. He seemed a vagabond at the time, employed as an archer, as I recall. My pride dictated a dismissal. I turned him away with that old phrase I once tossed around from sheer habit, designated for those I deemed unworthy. *'Not of good crop.'*" Burying his face in his hands, Sir Demetrius then heaved a tremendous sigh. At length he seemed unable to muster the wherewithal to continue.

After several moments passed, and the time for departure seemed appropriate, Dafne performed a silent bow and took her leave.

Though Vaskar didn't win Demetrius' daughter, she thought as she weaved through the festivities that had sprouted up all around Locus Castle, *he did obtain her dowry.*

~ 34 ~

EPILOGUE

Three Seasons later...

For now, the room was empty. Save for him. Marius sat alone, contemplating his life. His eyes searched the space for ghosts, sometimes hearing their laughter at the tail end of a breeze. The fire in the hearth kept the chill at bay, but soon the weather would change. He shivered and smiled. Moments like these were rare. Moments of stillness. When his mind would wander to the Forest, to shallow dug graves, a village with a grove of—

"Is the good doctor in?"

That voice! How could he forget the sound of it. In the quiet, in the stillness, it was one of the multitude that assured him he had served an adequate penance. And now it seemed winter's thaw brought more than just the hope of days spent beyond doors.

"Calliandra?" Marius rose from his stool.

Framed within the doorway, the woman gave a nod.

"I thought, I thought you were dead..." Marius stammered, opening his arms.

"You must have me mistaken for someone else," said Calliandra, furtively glancing toward a dark spectre beneath the trees behind her, then stepped forward into Marius' embrace.

"No," said Marius. "No, I'm fairly certain that was you." He had assumed that she had been with Sprael in the northern fields of Benwick and had met his same fate. In the hopes of finding her, he had joined the burial crews, but her body had never been recovered. Poor Sprael had perished before Marius had been given the chance to ask of her whereabouts. Lastly, all news relayed from Tintagil claimed that she had yet to return.

"So many things have happened," admitted Calliandra. "I have so much to tell you."

After several moments, they separated. Calliandra withdrew a step, placed a hand beneath her woolen mantle.

"This belongs to you," she stated. Pommel first, she offered Marius the dagger he had gifted her in the Forest, the day their fated quest had begun. "I told you I would return it to you when it was all over."

When Marius smiled, it seemed to hurt. "I can't accept that."

"Come, now," encouraged Calliandra. "We both know that I don't have much use for a dagger these days." From

Marius' expression, she could tell he was not going to relent. "Come." She edged the pommel nearer. "Why not?"

"Because it's not over," said Marius sadly. "I fear it will never be over for me. That quest held no end for me."

Calliandra strode to the front window, placed the dagger upon the sill. "I can't imagine what you have gone through. Kathryn told me about the passing of Primula—"

"Kathryn?" Marius interrupted. "You've seen Kathryn?"

"I have," said Calliandra, turning from the window. "I ventured to Lepaskalica and spent some time there. That's where I heard the tale of a mercenary who saved their village from a terrifying daemon. Right at the onset, I believed the mercenary they described *had* to be Vaskar. When they told me the mercenary had slain a child in order to defeat the daemon, I knew for certain they were speaking of Vaskar. But when they further explained that the mercenary had done that in order to assume the wraith into his own body, and then sacrificed himself by leaping into Lhaewyn's bottomless fountain... that's when I knew it could not be Vaskar. It smelled every bit of Vaskar, but that morsel at the end?" Calliandra shook her head. "That had to have been a mercenary cut from a different cloth."

"A mercenary no longer," said Marius as he calmly gestured to the room around them. "I left that life behind." He tried his best to hide the tempest roiling inside him.

Calliandra nodded, taking in the space with folded arms. Where Marius' shadow should have danced in the candlelight, instead bare hardwood planks stared back at her. "You're a Healer now, I see. Using your lampyr gift to rescue others. Saving lives, not ending them. Primula would approve greatly." As if Marius' torment were visible, she added. "You know that little girl survived, right?"

Marius flinched, froze still.

"What did you just say?"

"The laif girl," said Calliandra. "Javaema is her name. She didn't die. You must know this? Laekar was mere steps away and healed her almost immediately. She claimed that you met their eyes right before..." Calliandra trailed off, holding her breath. "You had no idea."

Before her eyes, Marius came completely undone.

Calliandra knelt by his side. "She barely has a scar."

Marius sobbed on all fours. His tears gathered a puddle on the hardwood beneath him. "At first I would tell myself that she'd survived," he explained. "Then after a while I somehow convinced myself that had to be false. The Creator must have stripped me from his favor. Luck such as that was not meant for me. I *knew* that I had killed her. I *knew* it in my bones, Calliandra. In my bones."

"You lost so much," said Calliandra.

"We lost so much," amended Marius. He lifted his hands from the floor and settled back onto his knees. "I knew you and Sprael were close..."

Calliandra straightened, tucked a lock of hair behind an ear. "Like you," she began, her face solemn. "I am seeking atonement. Which is partially why I am here."

"Go on," encouraged Marius.

"Marius," she said, her eyes finally finding his. "Can you recall a name that Sprael would mutter? Oftentimes, when things were most dire—"

"Prija," said Marius immediately. "He even spoke it under his dying breath."

Calliandra clapped and brought her hands beneath her chin. "Yes, that very name." She then beamed sadly. "When Sprael and I parted ways, it was not on the best of terms. There were many things left unsaid... so for the better part of a year my dark sister and I have been chasing Prija, trying to discover the story behind the name. I owe Sprael that much, and perhaps much more. But to cut a long tale short, this question, *who was Prija*, eventually led us to Sprael's homelands, The Gentle March. Oh, Marius, we discovered such great and terrible things while we were there." Dourly she shook her head. "Prija was Sprael's Klonost, a human who forms a strong familial bond with a laif. It's far more complicated than that, but I'll spare you the details for now. Anyways, at that time, humans in The Gentle March were strictly forbidden from leaving the land's boundaries, upon pain of death. I tell you this because, before Prija aged thirteen winters, I was told that he decided to disobey the law and wandered beyond the borders. His sentence and execution were carried out by the elders simultaneous."

As he listened, Marius had gone to his cupboard to retrieve a bottle. "So that's what happened to Prija," he said, passing a wooden cup to Calliandra. "No wonder Sprael seemed so guilty. Probably blamed himself for all of it."

"That's not the thing, though," said Calliandra, placing her cup aside. She leaned forward. "Prija never left the borders."

"Wait," said Marius. "What are you saying?"

"I'm saying Prija was falsely accused. The lad had never broken the law."

"But why?"

"Now, *that's* the thing," said Calliandra. "The trail leads all over both Camelot and Fenrirfang, but I can't seem to get any straight answers from anyone. And when I do get anywhere in a conversation, the person clams up, and dashes away. You must understand, this all goes deeper than just the murder of an innocent child. We're talking ancient laif family conspiracies here, Marius. Families that go back to the very beginning. Families with wealth beyond measure, wielding more power than we could even begin to fathom. I'll bet my summer fangs that Sprael was wise enough to understand how hopeless it was to even attempt to bring them to justice." She reached for her cup and took a long pull from it. Her face contorted in pain for a moment, then she recovered and continued. "So, what do you say, Marius? Want to help me avenge Prija?"

Thoughtfully, Marius beheld his room. A room for healing. A place for the dying and broken to find care. He thought of all the lives he had already saved, and the ones he was destined to preserve. Suddenly he found himself trapped in the middle, snagged between righting an old wrong, and preventing further harm.

He thought of Primula waiting for him on the shores of Avalon, imagined her nodding in approval at what he had already accomplished. In that beautiful moment, Marius smiled.

Then his thoughts wandered up to a funny laif ranger that had perished beneath a tree while saving a kingdom that was not his own.

One day a lampyr and a werewolf went off on a journey...

"For Sprael," said Marius.

ACKNOWLEDGMENTS

My gratitude to Hiram Ring and Scott Telle.
Without your guidance my books would be garbage.

To Jonathan Myers—Your talent is undeniable, and
I truly can't thank you enough for your contributions.
The paintings, the words of encouragement,
it all means so much.

Gina— Admittedly, without Hiram and Scott (and my
host of other supporters) my books would not be of such
quality. But without you, they would not exist at all.
I will love you for all of time.

Mary—Though the Almighty never gave me a sister,
you were the closest I ever got to experiencing one.
And what a sister you were.

Eric—Such an incredible man with a countenance of a
caliber that I fear will never again be matched.

To Both Mary and Eric—The day you went away some
might say a light went out, but for me it was a beacon.

ABOUT THE AUTHOR

M. Warren Askins resides in the
Northeastern United States with his family.

Scan the following code to
check out his list of current works.

9 781734 120097